WOULD IT BE WRONG?

Hilary felt the air between them charged with sexual tension. When his hand accidentally brushed hers, or went to her waist to urge her around a car in the parking lot, she found it impossible to concentrate on what he was saying. His face was impassive and she thought, It's only me. "Home?" he asked, when they were in the car.

Her whole body felt alive to the static between them. She reminded herself that it wasn't between them, that it emanated from herself alone. Nothing had changed because of one stupid dance when she allowed her mind to drift off into a fairy tale of delight. Jonathan Marsh was still her boss, as impersonal as ever, and she would be grateful in the morning that the situation remained as it had been.

With her eyes closed, she felt rather than saw the car come to a halt. His hand gently grasped her shoulder. "Hilary? We're home."

Marsh's eyes were on her face, questioning again. His lips were slightly parted, as though he meant to speak, but he said nothing. Hilary could almost feel their pressure against her mouth. If she gave him the slightest sign, she knew he would kiss her. . .

FINDING MR. RIGHT

PAPER TIGER

ELIZABETH NEFF WALKER

⬥ AVON
PUBLISHERS OF BARD, CAMELOT, DISCUS AND FLARE BOOKS

For Paul, with love

PAPER TIGER is an original publication of Avon Books. This work has never before appeared in book form.

AVON BOOKS
A division of
The Hearst Corporation
959 Eighth Avenue
New York, New York 10019

Copyright © 1983 by Mr. Right Enterprises
Published by arrangement with Mr. Right Enterprises
Library of Congress Catalog Card Number: 82-90515
ISBN: 0-380-81620-2

First Avon Printing, February, 1983

AVON TRADEMARK REG. U. S. PAT. OFF. AND IN OTHER COUNTRIES, MARCA REGISTRADA, HECHO EN U. S. A.

Printed in the U. S. A.

WFH 10 9 8 7 6 5 4 3 2 1

Chapter One

"I'M SORRY, HILARY," he said, standing with his hands in the pockets of his blue jeans. Two suitcases and a box containing records and books were ranged on either side of the door she had just entered. He shrugged, unable to meet her eyes. "I can't handle it."

Hilary glanced beyond him to the living room, which looked neater than usual without the stacks of records leaning against the bookshelves, without his sweaters tossed on the sectional sofa, without his books on the coffee table. She removed the lightweight jacket of her khaki suit and laid it across the briefcase she had set down when she came through the door. "What is it you can't handle, Jack?"

"I can't handle you and your causes. Look, you know I agree with you about women's rights. I wholly support equality of the sexes, but your damn column . . ." He ran a hand through his shaggy brown hair before allowing both arms to hang loosely at his sides. "Every day you have to point out some new and outrageous inequity. It's your job. But my job is programming computers, and I work with a bunch of people who give me flak every day about what you write. They make jokes about it, Hilary, and they ridicule me for living with you."

The room felt stuffy. He hadn't bothered to turn on the air conditioner, she realized, because he hadn't thought he would be there that long. "I didn't think their kidding bothered you, Jack. You've never hesitated to tell me when you didn't agree with me. Why can't you tell them?"

He shook his head. "You wouldn't understand. I work

1

with these people. I'm up for a promotion, an important one, Hilary. I've told you about it. If they don't respect me, I'm not going to get it."

"And they don't respect you because you live with a woman who writes feminist columns in a local newspaper?" she asked, turning toward the kitchen, wondering whether he would even bother to follow her.

Jack came as far as the doorway but refused the glass of white wine she offered. When she poured herself a glass, he said, "It's not just the newspaper columns, Hilary. It's the national magazine articles, the speeches you give to women's groups. They assume I'm under your thumb, a henpecked boyfriend."

Carrying the glass of wine carefully, she walked into the living room and flipped on the air conditioner before seating herself on the sofa. He did not join her but stood uneasily just inside the room, as though he were ready to leave at any moment.

"We've worked hard to arrange an equal relationship," she pointed out. "Doesn't that give you some ammunition?"

"I haven't your way with words, and I don't like having to defend myself."

"Then don't, Jack. Our relationship is really none of their business, is it?"

"If they make it their business, I have to contend with their mockery. And I'm tired of it, Hilary." He made a vague gesture toward the suitcases. "We've reached the point of diminishing returns. What we have together isn't enough to counterbalance the negative feedback. You're not here half the time; you're preoccupied with your work. I'm tired of doing my share of housework. I hate housework! I don't care if it's fair, Hilary; it's the pits! I don't like living in *your* apartment and sharing the rent and the phone bills and the utility bills."

The phone rang, and they looked at each other. Jack answered it and looked questioningly at her before saying into the receiver, "She isn't here right now. May I take a message?" With his free hand he felt along the ledge for the pen that should have been there before giving an exasperated snort. "Hold on a second." He covered the receiver and said, "It's long distance from New York. Why don't you take it?"

If she did, Hilary felt certain he'd leave while she talked, and she didn't want to waste the only opportunity she was going to get to find out why he was leaving. From her purse she dug out a pen and notepad, which she silently handed him. He frantically scribbled down a message which was obviously delivered far too fast, balancing the pad on his knee and grimacing steadily. When he hung up, he handed her the paper, which she set on the coffee table without reading.

"You didn't want to live in your apartment, Jack. We discussed it before you moved in here."

"I know we did. That was my mistake. The whole thing has been my mistake."

She raised startled eyes to his. "In what way?"

"Thinking that I could handle it." He finally came to sit down beside her, not too close but on the same section of the sofa. "I'm not blaming you for a thing, Hilary. Honestly. You know I'm fond of you. When we first met, I knew there was no one like you. I was impressed with your devotion to your work, to your feminist causes, to living a really full life. It was you who didn't want to get married. I would have grabbed you up in a snap."

"It's a good thing you didn't," she interrupted in a neutral tone.

He winced. "Yes, it is. You were right even about that."

"No, I wasn't. Not marrying you wasn't an indication that I thought you would change or not be able to handle it, as you put it. I never doubted that you could handle it. The thought never crossed my mind." It was true, she thought, amazed. When she first met him, this shaggy, intelligent man, she had thought: He believes in women's rights as strongly as I do. He's one of the few men I've met who will be able to cope with my career. Everything pointed to his involvement, his real conviction. Jack had appeared to her as almost a miracle, the one man in all of San Jose who cared so little for the opinions of his chauvinist colleagues that he introduced her to them not only by name but by specific occupation.

His horn-rimmed glasses had settled far down on his nose, endearingly close to falling off. Hilary had to resist the temptation to push them back up since he apparently was unaware of their precarious position, so intent was he on making her understand.

"I don't feel any different about you now from then, Hilary." He spoke softly, almost sadly. Those gentle hands, which had caressed her innumerable times, which had brought untold pleasure, gripped his knees through the faded blue jeans. "And I don't feel any less committed to women's rights. I simply find that I haven't a skin thick enough to protect me from the gibes. Yesterday I found a cartoon on my desk. It was a feminist cartoon, where the man was patting the woman on the head as he took away the *Wall Street Journal* and saying, 'When I want your opinion, I'll tell you what it is.' Only my name was printed across the woman's face, and yours was above the man's head."

"But that's childish, Jack. Why should something like that bother you?"

"It bothers me because it's symptomatic of the way I'm regarded at work, as your lover and mouthpiece." He held up a hand to halt her angry outburst. "I know, I know. I should ignore the stupid idiots. But it's my career, Hilary. I want that promotion. I need it for my self-esteem. And if the only way to get it is to leave you, I'm sorry. Not sorry for you, really, but for myself. Sorry that I'm not strong enough, or things aren't different enough, that none of this mattered."

Hilary leaned wearily back against the cushions, slipping her feet out of her shoes. "And what are they going to say when you tell them you've walked out? Aren't they going to think that's a little cowardly? Or are you going to waltz in there, grinning from ear to ear, protesting that you've finally seen the light? A reborn chauvinist."

His brows lowered in two shaggy dashes over his eyes. "I

4

don't intend to compromise my principles. I feel strongly about this, and I plan to work quietly for equality in the company. But, Hilary, any move I make with you at my back is seen as something different. I'm regarded as being under your influence. You're so goddamn visible!"

The air conditioner was beginning to have some effect on the room, and Hilary could feel her perspiration-soaked blouse chilling against her skin. Discouraged, she pushed back the glossy brown hair and attempted a smile. "Not that visible apparently. I haven't changed the world yet."

"You know you won't change the world. You've made inroads, good, solid ones. And I hope you'll continue to do it. I'll be following your career." He rose and held a hand down to help her up. When she stood beside him, he said, "I'll miss you—us."

"I'll miss you, too." She stood on tiptoe to kiss him softly on the lips. "Not just because of how I feel about you, either, but because you were the end of the road, the only man I've met in the last half dozen years who seemed to understand, who seemed impervious to the slanders of the ignorant. For you, I might even have done the dishes."

The light tone she attempted did not quite come off, but he went along with her anyhow. "For you, I even did the vacuuming." He smiled, but it was not the warm smile he had shared with her in those early months. "It wasn't the housework, Hilary. You know that."

"Yes."

"I would never have thought of asking you to give up your work on the newspaper."

"No."

"I'll call you sometime, if that's okay."

She shrugged. "If you feel like it. I'll want to know if you get the promotion."

"I've left my address and phone number in the bedroom. Just in case you need me."

With an effort she swallowed down the current need. "Thanks. I'll be all right."

"I know you will, or I wouldn't leave," he said, very hearty now as he picked up the box of records and books.

When she held the door for him, he set the box in the hall and returned to grab each of the suitcases by a handle. Only then, burdened by the heavy luggage, hands occupied, did he kiss her. "Good-bye, Hilary. Take care."

"I will. You, too."

The door closed with finality, but she stood for some time staring at it, feeling slightly numb. Unable to concentrate on any one thought, she wandered from room to room, opening the medicine chest to see the empty shelves where he had kept his shaving cream and razor, peering blankly into the drawer of the bedside table where he had kept his spare pair of glasses. He had forgotten nothing. Hilary couldn't find so much as a shoestring that belonged to him in the whole apartment.

This wasn't the first time it had happened, but usually some stupid little thing was left behind: a receipt for a business luncheon, an old sweat shirt in the laundry. But it was different this time: She hadn't expected it. This time she had found a man who could cope with her career. He was different from the others. They shared so many things in common. And because of it, she had allowed herself to love him a little more deeply than the others.

At thirty-two she was more skeptical, more suspicious, than at twenty-one. Yet even just out of college she had not expected to find someone so completely in tune with her own beliefs and interests as Jack had been. Hilary had let her guard down considerably. Who wouldn't with a shaggy bear of a man who knew from the start what you did and approved? Somehow it was crushing to find that even when he approved, even when he felt a strong emotional tie, it wasn't enough.

Her own record collection was meager, but she fingered her way through it until she found a suitably heartening selection, Dvorak's *New World* Symphony, to put on the stereo. Having turned the volume considerably louder than usual, she wandered into the kitchen with her half-finished glass of wine and stood uncertainly in front of the refrigerator. She had intended to make spaghetti, but the meal no longer appealed. Nothing did. Eventually she opened the refrigerator and withdrew the remains of the Brie they had served two nights before at a dinner party for two of Jack's co-workers and their wives.

In the microwave it took only a few seconds to warm the cheese to room temperature, and she sat at the kitchen table, in his seat, spreading it on the remains of the crackers. The dinner party, she had thought, had been quite successful. The women had perhaps been a little cautious with her at first. Fearing that some quote of theirs would appear in her column? But she had promised Jack—when was it, six months ago?—that she would never do that. Actually it was her habit to use only chance remarks she overheard from strangers, usually as the idea which inspired the columns. For that purpose she frequently wandered through downtown San Jose and the shopping centers around the city, looking for inspiration. The dinner party, all the dinner parties, might have provided ideas, but if they had, she found some other vehicle to introduce them into her writing.

Jack's colleagues had been curious about her, had sounded her out on her feminist stands, had argued on a friendly level. Nothing rancorous in the evening. Jack hadn't been tense the way she had seen some of her previous male acquaintances react when their associates were thrown into proximity with her. As though I were some sort of pariah, Hilary thought indignantly. As though I had some disease they might inadvertently catch by speaking with me. And the warnings ahead of time. "Now don't get on your hobbyhorse with Mr. Trumbull. Talk to him about real estate or something. And not about whether women are discriminated against by lenders!" Jack hadn't done that. He had never done it. Hilary munched thoughtfully on her third cracker. Probably he had wanted to do it.

If he was able to move out and leave an address, then he'd found an apartment, and probably not just today. Jack must have been planning to move before the dinner party, Hilary realized. But he'd wanted to have it. Why? To get rid of a social obligation before he lost his hostess? That was not in keeping with the man she knew. Much more likely he wanted to show his colleagues that she was a presentable woman, an intelligent woman, even a reasonably domestic woman—with the gourmet meal and the tastefully furnished apartment. Look, fellas, she doesn't sacrifice male egos on her feminist altar. Sort of a parting shot, a last-ditch effort to prove the equality of their relationship, that he was no more her henpecked lover than she was his mistreated mistress.

Against the music from the stereo the doorbell sounded weak and uncertain. Hilary refused to allow herself even the passing thought that it would be Jack returning. If it were, it would be for something he had forgotten that she had failed to unearth. There was no reversing a decision such as he had made. It was as irrevocable as a five-year-old divorce.

Her visitor was a neatly uniformed flight attendant who lived directly above her and who now carried her traveling bag—either coming or going. The woman was in her late thirties, with short blond hair and skillfully made-up blue eyes, petite and attractive.

"I could hear your stereo from the moment I walked in the door, Hilary," she complained, smiling. "I'm in from a two-day trip and intend to sleep for the next twelve hours, so if you don't mind . . ."

"I'll turn it down." Wanting some human contact, Hilary asked, "Would you like to come in for a glass of wine?"

"Sure. I never pass up a glass of wine before bed." Mary Lou Meyer negligently tossed her traveling bag in the corner inside the apartment and kicked her shoes in its general direction. "I'm getting too old for this game, you know. More and more I think about retiring."

"What would you do?" Hilary took a wineglass from the shelf and filled it from the bottle she'd left sitting on the counter.

Mary Lou grimaced. "Become a full-time mistress, I suppose. Or a wife. Wayne is making noises about leaving his wife again. Ugh! Can you imagine being married to that playboy?"

"I've never met him, remember?"

"Well, he's all right for a good time, but God knows he'd make a hell of a husband. Look what he's doing to his wife."

"It's never bothered you before," Hilary reminded her as she took a seat on the sofa.

"It doesn't bother me now." Mary Lou stretched her legs out on the other side of the sectional sofa and took a sip of her wine. "Lovely. Look, I don't know his wife, and I don't feel responsible for her. He's a pilot, and he makes a bundle. If he wants to spend some of it on me, who am I to object? I wouldn't marry him, though."

"Why not?"

"Because we'd be bored with each other in a month. It's the excitement of the affair that turns him on. I'm not his first, and I won't be his last."

"Then maybe you should tell him not to think of getting a divorce. It could wreck a lot of people's lives. He has children, doesn't he?"

"Three or four. I don't remember. But they're teenagers. I'm not responsible for them either."

"Who are you responsible for?" Hilary asked, exasperated.

"Myself. Only me." Mary Lou twirled the wineglass between slender fingers. "He's not going to get a divorce. Wayne is so dumb he thinks I expect him to say it, that's all. You should hear the rosy castles he builds in the air. He'll come and live in my apartment; he pays for it after all. And I'll be there to bring him his slippers when he gets back from a flight to Dallas, with a bottle of wine and a sheer black negligee. Shit. The man's crazy."

"He's the type of man you always pick."

Mary Lou pursed her lips, her head cocked to one side. "Do I pick them? I always thought they picked me. Oh, you have no idea how many of them I turn down. The businessmen on trips, who want me to go off to Hawaii with them for a weekend, the doctors who promise to set me up in a palatial suite on Russian Hill. I never pay any attention to the ones who want me to quit my job. My job is my security."

"It's also your source of sugar daddies," Hilary remarked dryly.

Mary Lou laughed. "That, too, of course. But none of them lasts. The job lasts."

Abruptly Hilary changed the subject. "Jack left today. Permanently."

"Left? That great teddy bear who adored you? Why?"

"He said he couldn't handle it—my columns and articles and the kidding he takes at work."

"Hey, I'm sorry." Mary Lou reached across and squeezed Hilary's wrist. "I thought he was in for the long stretch."

"So did I."

"If anyone had the guts to stand by you, I was sure he had." Mary Lou set her glass on the coffee table and waved one beringed hand in erratic circles. "What the hell's the matter with men? Does someone whisper in their ears at birth that they can have everything, that there won't be any hard times? They're ready to jump ship the minute some problem comes up that can't be solved by midnight."

Hilary's shoulders lifted slightly. "Jack has his career to think of. He can wield more influence with more power. I don't think it's exactly that he put his career before me. It's more that he was disturbed that he hadn't the detachment and indifference to ignore the gibes. They got to him, and he considered that a fatal flaw."

"It is—for anyone attached to you." Mary Lou drained her wineglass and rose.

"Yes, I suppose it is." A forlorn note had crept into Hilary's voice, and she tried to dispel it with a grin. "Living alone again will give me more time to work at least. I have two articles coming due that I haven't even started yet. Do they ever think about how they interfere with *our* careers?"

Chapter Two

THE OFFICES of the *South Bay Reporter* were in the deteriorating older section of San Jose, the fastest-growing city in the United States. The whole South Bay was expanding steadily, expensively, because of the infusion of life given by "Silicon Valley," turning out computer chips like popcorn. San Jose hadn't been ready for the burst in population, and crumbling parts of the city vied with the newer, sleeker areas for trade and housing. The *South Bay Reporter* had a five-story building filled with eager souls intent on putting out a daily morning paper which had to compete for an eclectic audience with the rest of the Bay Area newspapers. Hilary often suspected that her column, with its controversial subject matter, was a drawing card for the *Reporter* because whether people loved or hated her views, surveys taken by the newspaper showed that, after the comic strips, it was the most likely section of the paper to be read. She was adequately paid for her efforts and was given a great deal of freedom in the column's content, but because of possible libel suits, hers was the only feature which had to be submitted to the executive editor for approval before going to press.

The day after Jack left, Hilary arrived at the paper a little late, having spent a restless, lonely night pondering the vagaries of men and her own increasingly solitary position. She was determined not to let her feeling of depression creep into the day's column and collected her stack of mail with a smile from the receptionist, who warned, as usual, "Don't worry about the hate mail, Ms. Campbell. We all love your column."

People spoke to her as she made her way through a sea of desks with their display terminals. She greeted them all by name, but her preoccupation was evident, and no one attempted to draw her into a conversation. The office she shared with the paper's financial columnist was large and well appointed, if a little sterile in appearance. On the walls of her side she had hung several colorful prints, but the rest of the room was barren of even the smallest artifacts. Harry Stevens (Hairy Harry to the staff) had no photographs, no personal mementos, no disorderly clutter on his desk. Invariably he filed anything which arrived, usually after reading it, and banged away on an old typewriter he had received as a college graduation present. He and Hilary were old friends.

"You look as if your cat just got run over," he remarked as she entered and tossed her briefcase on the room's one comfortable chair.

"Jack moved out yesterday." There was no sense trying to keep it a secret, she realized, when she spent eight hours a day with people trained to dig up the most closely guarded secret.

"Tough break. I liked him." Harry had not liked all of Hilary's friends, in fact, had not liked most of them. "Now maybe you'll let Carol introduce you to that flaky brother of hers she's so eager to foist on you."

Hilary laughed. "Not a chance. I'm going to become a nun."

"Well, this one's some sort of monk, so you should get along really well." Harry grinned his sympathy and lit a cigarette, absently offering the pack to her before putting it away.

"No, thanks—to either. I'm going to quit smoking and give up men." To prove her stubborn determination, she seated herself at her desk, toying for at least a minute with a pen before withdrawing her own pack of cigarettes and lighting one.

"You could always write a column about domestic bliss," Harry suggested, "throwing in a few glamorous recipes and descriptions of cocktail gowns. They'd be beating down the doors to get at you." He judiciously studied her tall, elegant figure, the masses of brown hair, and the rueful hazel eyes. More the trim businesswoman look than the model, he decided but definitely nothing there to repel even the pickiest male. "It's the column that puts them off."

"I know, and it's just one more reason for writing it, isn't it, Harry?"

"Carol thinks you're slitting your own throat."

Hilary chuckled, a deep, warm bubble of mirth. "Carol should talk. Bringing up three children, keeping a difficult husband in line, going to law school when her children started school, and now practicing law with Legal Services."

"What's difficult about me?" he demanded.

"You're obsessed with tidiness, Harry. Look at your desk. You haven't a paper out of place. What do you do at home with three teenagers and a working wife?"

Harry snorted. "That's why I'm so neat here—because everything is chaos at home." He put up a hand to ward off her verbal attack. "I help! I pick things up. I've trained the kids to pick up after themselves at least once a week. We're your ideal, liberated family."

"Well, tell Carol thanks, but no thanks. I have two articles due within the next month, and I don't need a monk distracting me."

"Which reminds me," he said. "Marsh wants to see you."

Unlike Harry, whose nickname related directly to his rather hirsute body, the executive editor's derived from the opposite of his amorous propensities. Jonathan Marsh, called the Monk only when he was nowhere within hearing, led a well-publicized social life both because of his position on the newspaper and because he seemed to prefer variety. His secretary was known to have had a rather noisy clash with him over the number of phone messages she took relating to his private life, the content of which she studiously refused to divulge to even the most ardent of her interrogators.

"What have I done now?" Hilary demanded. "He reads every one of the columns before it gets printed. No one would dare feed it into the computer without that bold JM in the upper right-hand corner."

Harry turned to his typewriter, saying, "He probably wants to congratulate you on what a fine job you're doing."

"Very funny," Hilary snapped, but she couldn't resist laughing. "I'll see the day."

"You probably will," he returned, morose. "No one gets excited about the financial news."

The executive editor's office was on the top floor of the *Reporter* building, an enormous corner room entirely furnished in comfortable, elegant antiques. His secretary had an office half the size of Hilary's, with more customary furniture, and owing to Hilary's daily pilgrimage to the top floor, the two women had developed a shorthand regarding her column. If Hilary's column were totally inoffensive for the day, she would say, "He'll just need a look." On the other hand, if she had doubts of his approval, she would say, "I'd better see him." In either case she had spent more than her share of time in the reception area, frequently perusing the magazines there for some idea that would inspire a column.

Perhaps a third of her columns required an actual meeting with him, in which he was usually very businesslike, if not brusque. Mr. Marsh was a busy man, as Hilary and his secretary frequently quipped, and she had never, even when he was at his most disparaging about what she had written, remained closeted with him for more than ten minutes.

"Harry told me I've had a summons," she announced to Susan, the secretary, who had worked in the position for the entire time Hilary had been writing her column.

"Yes, but he's with someone. Let's see, sports. I'd say three more minutes." They both glanced at the clock on the wall and waited in silence to see how accurate Susan's estimate would be. Three and a half minutes later a harassed young man exited, wiping his brow with an enormous handkerchief.

Hilary looked questioningly at the secretary. "One of those days?"

"It's not one of his best," Susan admitted, "but I've seen him a lot worse." She punched a button and announced Hilary's arrival. "You can go on in."

Both the room and its occupant were well enough known to Hilary that she did not pay particular attention to either. The handsome Georgian desk and its equally handsome possessor ordinarily signified a mild professional confrontation. Marsh always rose when she entered, nodded her to a moderately comfortable Sheraton chair, and resumed his seat. He was a few inches taller than she, but not quite six feet, with thick black hair, eyes so penetratingly dark as to appear black, and a square, determined jaw. When he frowned, a solitary line creased his entire brow, two deep grooves formed between his nose and the corners of his mouth, and his lips thinned to a disapproving slash. He was frowning when Hilary entered.

"Ms. Campbell, I don't wish to take time from your work, so I'll be brief. You know that your column has the support of the editorial office. I may not agree with everything you have to say, but in general the way in which you say it is effective, and it is without doubt a popular column in the *Reporter*."

Hilary nodded her thanks. "But—"

"Not 'but,' Ms. Campbell. The word I would have chosen is 'and.' " He picked up an engagement calendar from his desk and began to tick off dates. "On the thirteenth, the nineteenth, the twenty-seventh, and the thirty-first I found it necessary to represent the *Reporter* at various social and civic functions. Actually"—he glanced up at her, and the frown relaxed somewhat—"I attended others, but it was on the thirteenth that I began counting. Now, to be precise, I had five queries on the thirteenth, four on the nineteenth, six on the twenty-seventh, and eight on the thirty-first."

"What kinds of queries?"

After snapping the book shut, he shoved it aside and leaned back in his chair with one hand lying on the armrest and the other casually flung across his thigh. "Queries about your column, of course. Did you think I would bring you here to discuss something else?"

His impatience was nothing new to her. "Yes, Mr. Marsh, but what sorts of queries? Did people want to know why you published it? Did they want my home address so they could bomb my building? Did they want to know where my ideas came from? Did they ask about me personally or how I happened to write the column?"

"All those, save for your home address. No one indicated any desire to bomb your building." His eyes narrowed slightly. "Do people threaten you, Ms. Campbell?"

"Not precisely. I keep the best ones on my bulletin board." She grinned at him.

"The best what?"

"The best of the hate mail. Harry thinks it's perverse of me, but I give points for the degree of rage (though I have to ignore grammar), and each week I display the most worthy on my bulletin board."

Marsh leaned toward the desk, frowning again. "I think you would be wise to let the legal department have a look at any irrational correspondence, Ms. Campbell. There are disturbed people wandering the streets of every city."

"Now what could the legal department do?" she asked, impatient in turn. "Most of my correspondents don't bother with return addresses, and as I said earlier, these are not precisely threats. Violent disagreement, yes, but no suggestion of bodily harm. I was joking about someone's wanting to bomb my building."

"Has anyone else read your mail?"

"I show some of them to Harry Stevens, who shares an office with me." Hilary met his eyes steadily. "It's my mail, Mr. Marsh. I'm perfectly capable of judging whether there is any danger to me or, perhaps I should say, as capable as someone in the legal department. My column is designed to be provocative, to be controversial. There's nothing unusual in my eliciting angry responses. Some people tend to get annoyed when they think they're being ridiculed."

The frown had descended in full force on his brow, but he made an attempt to alleviate its effect by sitting back in his chair, very much at ease. "Would you mind showing me some of your mail, Ms. Campbell? Just so that I have an idea of what we're discussing? I admit I never considered that you might be subjected to unsavory letters from disgruntled readers, though I should have." A vaguely propitiating smile appeared briefly on his otherwise impassive face.

"I'll photocopy a few and send them up to you. They'll be the worst, a selection of the last month or so from my bulletin board." She sat a little straighter in her chair before remarking offhandedly, "I do get my share of positive response as well, you know."

"I'm sure you do." Marsh dismissed the subject with a wave of his hand. "I had another purpose in mind when I summoned you. Up to this point I have asked you to attend very few civic functions to represent the paper, in keeping with our policy that an employee is first and foremost a writer, an investigator, a researcher, et cetera. But I've come to the conclusion over the last month that your appearance at some of these functions would be a decided advantage. I would not be pestered by questions I can't answer, my time absorbed by curiosity seekers rather than productive business contacts. In short, Ms. Campbell, you could defend yourself, and I could get on with my job."

"I see," Hilary said, trying to rapidly calculate the consequences of such a step.

"Since this would be an infringement on your time and energies, we would, of course, make a commensurate increase in your salary. Considering the nature of your column," he remarked dryly, "I think you would probably find a great deal of usable material at these functions, though I would caution you to employ it circumspectly."

Hilary smiled sweetly. "I'm always the soul of discretion, Mr. Marsh. How would I know which functions you wished me to attend?"

"My secretary draws up a list of them weekly. I would have her send a copy to you with my indication of which I preferred you to attend. Probably that would be one a week, occasionally two, and sometimes none. I presume you'll have no difficulty finding a suitable escort."

With Jack gone, it was not necessarily a reasonable assumption, Hilary thought. She would be forced to find someone, doubtless different men, continually. Her wardrobe would have to be considerably expanded, and her free time would diminish. Many of the functions would fall on weekends, preventing her from getting out of town for a break. Not that the plan didn't have its merits. Hilary was sure she would find grist for her newspaper mill, something for which she was always on the lookout.

"How much are we talking in terms of a raise?" There was no use pussyfooting with Marsh.

He hesitated for only a moment. "Three thousand."

Hilary was sure he'd had a smaller figure in mind and had increased it because of her bluntness and apparent indecision. It was not the sort of raise one refused for the expense of a few dresses and the inconvenience of finding an escort once a week. "When would I start?"

"Immediately." He pulled the engagement calendar toward him and read off the evening's function, a benefit for the local performing arts center.

"I'm not sure I'm free this evening." Her mind scanned her various male acquaintances for someone she might induce to accompany her on the spur of the moment. There were objections or problems with everyone she could think of, and she knew Marsh expected an answer on the spot. "Would it be necessary for me to have a date this time?" When he eyed her speculatively, she shrugged and decided to be honest with him. "My friend moved out last night. I'm out of touch with everyone else right now. With the short notice, I don't have time to write a column and phone every man I know, looking for someone to take me. How about if we start next week?"

His eyes were darkly unreadable as he tapped a long finger against the engagement calendar. "Where do you live?"

"Willow Glen."

"All right. Miss Winslow and I will pick you up at seven. Please be ready on time."

"What if I can find someone?"

"Don't bother. Write your column, and worry about what you're going to wear."

Hilary suspected that he was teasing, but she had little experience of his humor and couldn't tell if the gleam in his eyes was mirthful or sardonic. Certainly the unsmiling lips gave no indication. She uncrossed her legs and rose. "All right. I presume my raise is effective today as well."

"Certainly. I'll have Susan notify the accounting department."

"Thank you."

As usual, he escorted her to the door. "Don't forget to send me copies of your hate mail, Ms. Campbell."

"I won't."

In her office Harry looked up from pounding at his typewriter. "Well, did you get a raise?" he asked, grinning.

"Yes," Hilary admitted.

"Son of a bitch!" Harry swung around in his swivel chair to face her. "How come?"

"He felt sorry for me, what with Jack moving out and all."

"Damn it, be serious. Out of the blue, he just gave you a raise?"

"Not exactly." Hilary dropped onto her chair, feeling suddenly enervated. "He wants me to be more visible. I'm to represent the *Reporter* at various civic functions and answer everybody's questions about my column. Marsh was fed up with being asked about it when he has more important things to do."

"I'll be. Congratulations." Accompanying his question with a rueful grin, he asked, "Will this make your salary bigger than mine?"

"Don't be ridiculous! It just means he'll finally be paying me what he should be."

"Good." Harry swung back to his typewriter. "I don't want to start being jealous of you."

"They put us in an office together," Hilary told his back, "because you were older, more experienced and made so much more than I did that I would be humbled into behaving myself."

"They didn't either," he retorted, never pausing in his typing. "They put us together because I was the only one who wasn't intimidated by you."

Chapter Three

SINCE THE WEATHER continued blisteringly hot, Hilary chose a navy silk shirtdress with an oblong floral silk scarf and wore her long brown hair loose against her shoulders. It was an outfit she'd bought for her sister's wedding five years previously, but she had been sparing in its usage, saving it for only her most important social occasions. In the year she'd spent with Jack she had probably not worn it more than twice, some indication, she decided, of her avoidance of dressy entertainments.

Dressing alone was depressing. Hilary was used to Jack's teasing her as she attached her earrings and used a shoehorn to put on her narrow but comfortable leather pumps. To drown out the silence, she wandered into the living room and put a record on the stereo, softly this time, though she thought it unlikely Mary Lou was in bed—unless her pilot lover had arrived. For comfort she sipped at a glass of wine and mentally reviewed the celebrities she had previously met, whose names were bound to elude her when she needed them. She was reminding herself that she herself was supposed to be some sort of celebrity on these occasions when the doorbell rang. It was five to seven.

On her way to the door she slipped the wineglass onto the kitchen counter, not sure if her employer would approve of her fortifying herself for the evening. Even on a day when she attended a highly alcoholic entertainment, she never allowed herself more than two glasses of wine, as much for the sake of her calorie intake as for sobriety.

But Marsh was unlikely to know that. Jack had known it very well.

Hilary answered the door with a light shawl already about her shoulders. There was no need to antagonize Marsh by seeming unprepared, even if he was a little early. He stood casually with his car keys in his hands, prompting Hilary to wonder if he was afraid his date would drive off with his car.

With a practiced glance he took in her outfit and nodded his approval. "Ready?"

"Yes."

"Do you have your keys?"

"What kind of question is that?" she asked, annoyed. "I'm not ten."

"I've found it expedient to ask. How old are you?"

"Thirty-two, though I can't see that it's relevant. Should I know how old you are?"

He smiled for the first time. "Almost thirty-nine, and I'm sure it's totally irrelevant. I keep telling myself it's irrelevant." He watched as she double-locked the door behind them. "I hope you won't mind, but I brought my cousin as your escort."

Dropping her keys back into her purse, she shrugged. "So long as he's 'suitable,' I daresay I can tolerate him for an evening, but in future I'll provide my own dates if you don't mind."

"Not in the least. I expect it of you. Running an escort service has never been my idea of stimulating employment."

They were approaching the front door, and Hilary paused to stare at him. "I didn't ask you to provide me with a date, Mr. Marsh. If it was necessary, you should have told me so, and I'd have managed."

"You'll be more comfortable this way, Ms. Campbell. Actually my cousin is in town for only a few days, staying with his parents, and it worked out very well to match up the two loose ends."

Hilary wasn't at all sure she liked being considered a loose end, but she said nothing. As they approached the car, a man who bore a faint resemblance to Marsh climbed out and came forward to greet her. He was introduced as Tim Marsh, and she, somewhat to her surprise, as Hilary Campbell. She had rather expected Marsh to identify her as Ms. Campbell, since he apparently took a subtle satisfaction in the liberated formality of the designation.

"Jon gave me your morning's column to read on the way over," Tim explained, handing her into the car. "The name sounded familiar, but I only realized when I was reading it that you wrote an article my wife pointed out to me in one of her magazines. I could tell by the sting at the end. You lull your reader into a false sense of security and then zap him with a hard truth just when he thinks he's home free."

" 'She,' usually," Hilary said with a laugh. For the first time she noticed the woman in the front seat. "Kitty! I never thought about your being Miss Winslow. I didn't know you'd taken back your maiden name."

"A regular family gathering," Marsh murmured.

"At least a year ago," Kitty confessed, reaching over the seat to press Hilary's hand. "I'm sorry we've lost touch. I went back to Ohio for a few months to sort things out. Might as well have stayed here, for all the good it did."

"I don't know," Hilary replied, "you look great. Are you still living in Los Gatos?"

"Same place. Promise me you'll come to see me this weekend, or next if you're busy."

After casting a rueful glance at his cousin, Marsh disposed himself behind the wheel but made no attempt to interrupt the dialogue between the two women, which continued for several minutes before they returned their attention to their respective escorts. Hilary learned that Tim Marsh was married, had two children, owned a thriving printing business in Stockton, and was visiting his parents because a great-uncle had died.

"No need to condole with me," he assured her. "I've hardly seen the old fellow in the last five years because he's been in a nursing home and didn't recognize anyone. He was ninety-two and a crusty old fellow before I left home. My wife hadn't even met him, so we didn't think it necessary for her to come down." Realizing he had held the limelight far too long, he asked, "How long have you worked for the *Reporter*?"

"Eight years, five of them on the column. I worked on a paper at home, in Klamath Falls, before I came to San Francisco. When I couldn't find anything in the city, I came on down to San Jose."

"How did you get the column? Was Jon executive editor then?"

"Yes, Mr. Marsh had had the position for a year or so. The *Reporter* had been running a column for a few years, but its author decided to take a job in Washington, so I applied for the slot with some samples of my ideas, purposely outrageous to gain his interest. For a few weeks he ran a spectrum of different types of columns and eventually told me I had the job." She looked to see if her employer was well occupied before whispering, "He preferred the gossip column, but reader response was in my favor."

"Apparently it still is." Tim put his arm along the back of the seat, not touching her. "Jon said you have a devoted readership, and my wife will be delighted to hear I've met you. Do you go to many of these functions?"

"Starting today, it's part of my job. Mr. Marsh is tired of defending me and expects me to cover for myself."

Kitty's head swung abruptly back toward Hilary. "Did he say that?"

"Yes, I did," Marsh answered her, "but not quite in the way Ms. Campbell has phrased it. People are interested in finding out about her column, and I feel she's the best person to answer them. The repeated distractions are an unnecessary nuisance."

Because he was driving, Hilary felt no deterrent to raising her brows humorously at Kitty, but when she caught Marsh's eye in the rearview mirror, she hastily turned to address his cousin and avoided the subject of her column for the duration of the ride.

Despite Marsh's accounting earlier in the day of how frequently he was asked about her column, Hilary was surprised by how many people approached her with questions. Not all of them were pleasant, but most were in no way abusive. One elderly gentleman, who was introduced by Marsh as Harold Franklin, scowled at her through thick bifocals and said, "You don't look like a women's liberation advocate."

"What do they look like?" Hilary asked.

"They don't wear makeup and they dress sloppily," he said.

"Have you met a lot of them?"

"I haven't met any, but I've seen pictures of them. You folks don't seem to understand how important it is for a woman to stay at home and rear her children."

"Not every woman has children, Mr. Franklin, and those who do have a very difficult decision to make as to whether they should stay at home with them or not. Sometimes they work from financial necessity; sometimes, solely from a desire to further their careers. In either case I promise you very few women make the decision lightly."

The old man shook his head throughout her answer. "If a woman has children, she should stay at home. Period."

"For how long?"

"Until they're grown. A mother should always be available to her children."

Hilary smiled to take the sting from her words. "It sounds like an eighteen-year jail sentence, Mr. Franklin. I'm sure few men would be willing to switch places with such a woman."

"Nonsense," he snapped. "Men have always had the harder lot, going out to work to support their families, and you don't hear them bellyaching about it. All we're getting is a lot of whining from women whose lives have constantly been improving with every sort of laborsaving device. Women have more leisure time than they've ever had before."

"Perhaps that's why they want to use it more productively, Mr. Franklin. They want to use their minds and their skills instead of lolling about the house popping bon-bons in their mouths. It would be a great pity for a woman to waste her education, wouldn't it?"

With a snort, he turned from her, growling, "You don't know what you're talking about."

Hilary met Marsh's dark eyes for a moment but could not tell whether he was displeased with her antagonizing the old man. It seemed possible that after this initial epi-sode Marsh would decide he preferred to answer the ques-tions himself. Actually Hilary realized that she wouldn't greatly care if that were the case. The contact was stimu-lating but exhausting. Sometimes it was wholly disheart-ening to her, as was the situation with the next person who engaged her in conversation.

This was a well-groomed woman of perhaps forty-five, who smiled incessantly while she talked. "My dear, I'm afraid you have no idea how your column affects women like me. You're young and have boundless energy. And you've never been married, have you?"

"No."

"I thought not. You can tell," she said, nodding and smiling to herself. "No children, of course, or you wouldn't think it was all so easy. You can't really understand the responsibility. I have five, you know. The youngest is ten. And my husband's in the army. We've been transferred all over the country, and abroad as well. We lived in Germany for some time. I went where he asked me to go."

Hilary watched the woman take a gulp of her drink. "That can be a difficult life."

"Oh, no, I didn't mind. That was my job, to go where he went and to bring up his children. That was my part of the bargain. I made a nice home for him and provided emo-tional support to the children, and he gave me financial se-curity. You don't understand. I've put in my time, and he owes me a comfortable life. But he reads your column, and it's given him the idea that I haven't done anything, that I should be out working at a career, doing something excit-ing and bringing in money myself."

"He can't expect to change the rules in the middle of the game," Hilary said gently. "I hope I haven't given the impression that a woman who stays at home isn't a working-woman, a woman with responsibilities. My point has always been that women should have the same choices available to them as men. A father should be able to stay at home with the children; a mother should be able to go out to work."

The woman took another gulp of her drink. "That's unrealistic, Miss Campbell. What father would want to stay at home with his children rather than go out to support his family?"

"I grant you there may not be many, but it should be an option. Sometimes in families where the woman has the ability to make more money, she is the one who goes out into the marketplace."

"That must be a very small percentage of families." The woman continued to smile as she said, "The feminists are making life very difficult for those of us who wish to live the kinds of lives our parents lived: the traditional life of the husband going out to work and the wife staying at home to take care of the home and the family. You're giving the impression that women should be able to do everything, have everything. In order to do that, she has to make innumerable compromises, has to juggle every facet of her life, while her husband continues to lead the kind of life he's always led."

Hilary could feel Marsh's gaze on her. "Men have to adjust to the changes as well as women. They have to take responsibility for their share of the housework and the child care so that their wives can lead more productive lives." But she was remembering Jack's comments on the housework. Even Jack, liberated, gentle Jack. "Many women won't choose to make any change at all in their roles, but the change must be available to those who want it."

After finishing off her drink, the woman said, "It was easier before the feminist movement. You've raised expectations too high, have placed too many demands on women, have made our traditional role look small and unimportant."

"That isn't the purpose of the movement, I assure you. What you need to do is point out to your husband what it would mean to him if you did go out and get a job. He would be expected to share in the housework and the child care, and his dinner wouldn't be ready when he came home from work, and you would be as tired as he from your daily efforts. He probably doesn't want that kind of change any more than you do, or wouldn't if he considered the consequences."

"I can't talk the way you write, Miss Campbell. My thoughts aren't so organized, and I fumble when I try to explain to him."

"I'll write a column about it," Hilary promised. "Cut it out, and keep it in your drawer for the times you need ammunition. Most of all, don't let any man intimidate you. It's habit with them. If you know that for you personally what you're doing is right, don't let anyone undermine your confidence. The most important message I try to get across is that women must learn to be responsible for themselves. That doesn't mean they have to have careers; it means they have to have enough respect for themselves that they don't relinquish their rights as individuals. We are trained to be dependent when it is independence that is really admired. It's an attitude, not a situation. You can be an individual in a marriage just as easily as you can be a nonentity on your own. All the feminist movement asks of you is that you believe in yourself."

Uncomprehending, the woman nodded, and smiled, and moved away.

A man of her own age, who had been standing close by and obviously listening to this conversation, introduced himself to Hilary. "I'm Bob Taylor, and a great fan of your column, Ms. Campbell. I couldn't help overhearing what you said just now. Do you really think that's all there is to the feminist movement—a woman's belief in herself?"

There was a suppressed excitement in his voice with

which Hilary was familiar. To her it meant either that he was interested in her as a woman or that he was planning to bait her under the guise of being a supporter. She thought it more likely the latter but determined to keep an open mind. "I think it's the cornerstone, Mr. Taylor. In order to achieve an equal status with men, women have to have the same confidence in their intrinsic worth as men do. No one questions a man's value as a human being."

"Come now," he said with an engaging smile. "It is women who produce each new generation. It's they who bring up the sons and daughters. Surely a woman doesn't purposely rear her daughters to believe they aren't worth anything."

Definitely a baiter, Hilary decided, and wondered if she had the energy left to stave off his attack. Writing the column was easy compared to this, and she caught Marsh's decidedly amused eyes on her. Wishing he would go away and leave her to counter in peace, she twirled her empty wineglass for a moment's reflection, aware that Bob Taylor was ready to pounce on any answer.

Finally she said, "I can see you're really interested in the dynamics of the problem, Mr. Taylor. And I won't do you the injustice of trying to cover the topic in a few moments' discussion at a party. In my office at the *Reporter* I have a bibliography which would clarify any number of matters for you on women's rights and the various facets of feminism. Why don't you call me there to give me your address and I'll mail you a copy of the list?" And just to clinch this act of aggression, she smiled provocatively at him.

Behind her there was a snort of mirth, but she didn't turn to see from whom it came. Mr. Taylor, dissatisfied but dismissed, agreed and melted off into the crowd.

Hilary found Kitty at her side, amused. "I take it you're used to that sort of thing," Kitty remarked.

"It happens all the time because of the column. I'm used to it, yes, but I don't like it. I've come to expect certain reactions, definite patterns in how people regard me. There's no separating myself from the column, even in very personal relationships." They moved away from their escorts toward a table of hors d'oeuvres. "Even Jack couldn't handle it. Did you meet him?"

"I'm not sure," Kitty admitted. "Was he the cuddly one?"

Hilary laughed. "Yes, he was the cuddly one. Very lovable and very concerned with the women's movement. He moved out last night."

"I'm sorry."

"So am I." Hilary helped herself to a bacon-wrapped date. "I was really fond of him."

"Was?" Kitty's perfectly arched brows rose questioningly. "Can you shut it off that easily, Hilary?"

Remembering Kitty's traumatic divorce, Hilary made a gesture of impotence. "I can't do anything about it. I miss him. Maybe I don't have the capacity to love that other women have. There have been several men in my life. Some of them have dropped me; some of them I've dropped. Some of them I've thought I loved; some of them have said they loved me. But none of them is around now. It doesn't say much for my enduring devotion."

"At least you've never let a man define your life." Kitty watched as her wineglass was refilled and smiled her thanks. She had a charming smile, wholesome, sincere. Hilary could remember when her face had looked haggard, when the green eyes had continually pooled with tears and the chestnut hair had been allowed to straggle out of a faded headband. Not so very long ago, yet now Kitty glowed with health, her complexion restored to its normal color instead of the deathly paleness, her hair well groomed and her eyes once more alive. No more housedresses and bathrobes. She had survived.

"I've never let anyone else define my life," Hilary agreed, "which is probably only to say that I'm selfish. I gave a lot to Jack, and I got a lot from him. It seemed a really workable partnership. Fooled again."

Kitty nodded. "Come over Saturday for lunch. I'm up, and that's what you need right now. I haven't forgotten what you did for me. Bring your tennis racket, and we'll work it out of your system."

"Sounds good to me. Unless, of course, Mr. Taylor of the feminist interest should decide that he needs to spend the whole of the weekend consulting with me on the growth of his consciousness." And she laughed.

"Much better," Kitty said approvingly. "I'll make you crepes."

Before they left, Marsh cornered Hilary on her way to the rest room. "I read the letters you sent up, and I think you're right. None of them is threatening. Vitriolic, scathing, vulgar, but not threatening. You might consider having Harry read all of them as they come in for a second opinion. If either of you sees any problem, hand it over to the legal department immediately."

"I can't ask Harry to read them. It's not part of his job. And I don't want to, Mr. Marsh. He'd only worry that some nut was lurking out there with serious intent."

"Don't you worry about it?"

Hilary lifted her shoulders carelessly. "Not often. I'm not important enough for someone to get excited about. I carry a shriek alarm and stay out of dark alleys, just like most of the women I know."

People were beginning to leave in a steady stream, and Marsh watched them thoughtfully, nodding to acquaintances. "Do you think you can handle evenings like this?"

"Don't you think I can?" Hilary countered.

"I'm sure you can. What I should have asked is: Do you want to?" A very faint smile curved his lips.

Hilary turned her attention to the departing crowd of elegant people. "Frankly I'm not sure. May I give it a month's trial?"

"If that's the way you'd like to do it." Marsh studied her face for a moment before continuing. "Did any of them upset you?"

"Not really. I've heard all the questions before, made all the answers other times. It's so immediate, being face-to-face. When I write the column, I imagine that I'm having some effect. In person I see that it isn't so, that I haven't influenced anyone to my point of view. Only . . . every once in a while, very seldom, I seem to say the right thing, the thing that will make a small change in someone's life. It didn't happen tonight, but it might some other night. What bothers me is that I'm likely to see the same people, or people like them, at any of the gatherings you want me to attend. You're hitting only the upper crust."

"This is where the power is, Ms. Campbell. These are the people who run the businesses, who advertise in the *Reporter*. These are the community leaders who influence the lives of South Bay residents." He motioned to Kitty across the room to join him. "Are you ready to go?"

"Yes, whenever you are."

In the car she regretted that she hadn't bothered to use the rest room, but it was a relatively short drive. A four-way conversation ranged over the people and the evening's benefit, which Kitty broke by demanding, "Hilary's impressive when she stands up to people, isn't she?"

Though the remark was directed more to Tim than to his cousin, it was Marsh who answered first. "Yes, she's impressive. A little strident, perhaps, but that's precisely what people expect."

"Strident? Me?" Hilary sat forward on the rear seat and glared into the rearview mirror, though she couldn't tell if he was observing her. "I prefer to consider myself forceful. You don't win any points by cooing in their ears, Mr. Marsh. I don't believe in sugarcoating the painful facts. Take someone like the army wife. She's an alcoholic, two to one. And why? Because she's been reared to believe she has no worth. She desperately wants to believe that being a wife and mother is enough, but her husband undermines her confidence even in that, though you can be sure it's just what he really wants her to be. She can't win."

"No, no," Tim protested. "I met him. He was okay."

"He may have been okay to you," Hilary said, "but he's not okay to his wife. She's probably spent twenty years building up his ego, and he puts hers through the shredder every day."

"You're speculating, Ms. Campbell," Marsh interrupted. "You didn't meet him at all, and in the short time you spent with her you couldn't possibly have learned enough of the situation to comment on it."

Hilary gnawed at her lip for a moment. "Of course I'm speculating. I beg your pardon. But I've known women like her; I've talked with them. I've even talked with their husbands, who range from indifferent to condescending about their wives. Oh, they may even love the 'little woman,' but they have about the same respect for her as for the family dog!"

In the front seat Kitty laughed and stretched out a hand to tap Marsh's thigh. "She's right, you know. I've met men like that myself."

"And I've met women who have the loyalty of a snail," Marsh muttered, covering her hand with his to show, Hilary assumed, that his comment had nothing to do with their relationship. "Every case has to be judged on its merits, as Ms. Campbell should know from the days when she was a reporter. Generalizations are worthless. It is always the specifics which are vital and fascinating."

An awkward silence followed his rebuke. Hilary broke it as soon as she could think of some comment to make. "Maybe I'll take up fiction. I could write a series of fairy tales with happy endings. He was a generous, liberated husband and she was a considerate, industrious wife and they lived happily ever after. I won't mention that he steals candy from babies and she passes bad checks."

The car was halted in front of her apartment building, and her escort moved to open his door, but Marsh said, "I'll see her up, Tim.

"My whole point," Marsh said as he waited for her to unlock the front door, "was that we don't need fairy tales, Ms. Campbell. Any misguided assumption makes a story, or a column, worthless. You have made a career of discouraging men and women from adopting just that kind of attitude. Every day you ask them to question their unconscious suppositions about male and female roles. You don't want to lose credibility by doing precisely the opposite."

As he followed her into the building, she said, "I can make it safely to my apartment."

Ignoring the remark, he continued to walk beside her. "What if I were to say, 'Women like to exaggerate to make an interesting story'? You'd write a whole column on the effrontery of such a statement by a male. It's a generalization I've heard men make, and you just supported it by doing precisely that."

"We were *talking*, for God's sake. And you may remember when I began the whole discussion that I said 'someone *like* the army wife.' I wasn't formulating an exposé for my column."

"I should hope not." Marsh quickly put a hand behind her back when she stumbled on the dimly lit stairs. "But because of your position on the paper, because of the necessary integrity of your column, you have to be more careful of what you say in public."

"Public! I hardly consider my executive editor's car a public place. Did you have any objection to what I said at the benefit?"

"None. I thought you handled yourself extremely well." When she scowled at him, he said, "I didn't mean that to sound condescending, Ms. Campbell. You were given a fair amount of provocation, and you didn't lose your temper or resort to too much sarcasm. It was necessary for me to satisfy myself on that point. You could hardly expect me to dump you on the public if you were going to detract from the paper's image." He held his hand out for her door key, but she inserted it herself.

"I always try to live up to the paper's image."

"You see, sarcasm comes quite naturally to you. You employ it with good effect in your column, but it could be offensive at a civic function. If you can turn your column out in less than a whole working day, I won't object to your coming in late after an evening such as this."

"You're too kind," Hilary murmured. But she knew he

was teasing this time, by the sardonic gleam in his eyes. "Good night, Mr. Marsh."

Hilary closed the door behind her with a sigh. Nothing like a good scold to top an exhausting evening, she decided as she wended her way toward her bedroom. And no one at home to discuss its merits or lack of them. Marsh was always the proper editor: praising where he could and criticizing where he couldn't. Hilary could think of no occasion on which he had treated her with other than a distant businesslike politeness. Exactly as it should be, she reminded herself as she brushed her teeth. Nothing but problems could arise from a more personal interest on either side. You don't mix business with pleasure when you're a professional career woman . . . especially when one of your friends is dating your boss. Hilary was too tired to mourn the empty pillow beside hers as she crawled into bed and instantly fell asleep.

Chapter Four

"**W**HAT'S HE LIKE to work for?" Kitty asked as she passed the mushroom sauce to Hilary. "He was a little hard on you the other evening."

"Ah, but he does it for my own good." Hilary grinned. "Marsh expects us all to be as professional about our jobs as he is. The legend at the paper is that he was a hell of a reporter. A real go-getter. A twelve-hour-a-day golden boy. No one ever seems to have minded his rapid advancement. I guess everyone thought he deserved it. He's not difficult to work for, so long as you're giving a hundred percent of your capabilities. He's all business. I don't think I've ever heard him laugh. This was something new for me—going to a benefit where I represented the paper. Or maybe you know that."

"He said it was a new part of your job when he picked me up. Later he said you were giving it a trial run."

Hilary finished a bite of mushroom crepe before answering. "I impulsively took on the additional burden because it carried additional wages. I'm not so sure I want to do it forever, after Wednesday night. It may become very old very fast. The salary increase is nice, though, and Marsh is apparently accosted all the time by people who want to know about the column."

"Yes, I'd noticed that."

"Do you go out with him regularly?" Surely not an unnatural question for her to ask, Hilary thought.

Kitty helped herself to more asparagus. "A couple of times a month. Some neighbors introduced him to me at a dinner party, oh, three or four months ago, I guess. Miriam is an executive with a department store that advertises in the paper. And I think her husband plays tennis with him sometimes. Jon doesn't talk about himself much. I gather he's divorced."

"Yes. Two years ago, from the scuttlebutt. I don't think I ever met his wife. For a newspaper office there was very little information floating around."

"Coffee?" Kitty rose and unplugged the pot. When Hilary nodded, she poured a cup and placed it on the table. "I'm not surprised about the lack of information. I don't think I've ever met a man who's more guarded in talking about himself."

"Do you like him?"

"Sure. I wouldn't go out with him if I didn't like him. But I'd like him a whole lot better if he weren't so uncommunicative. Not that he isn't pleasant. He can talk about almost anything that comes up and be knowledgeable about it. I suppose that comes from being a newspaperman for so long."

"He probably reads half a dozen papers a day. Any intelligent man is bound to pick up something."

Kitty hesitated in raising her cup, puzzled by Hilary's tone. "Don't you like him?"

"I respect him as a professional in the business. I don't know him well enough to know whether I like him or not. You get mixed feelings about someone who's in a position to pass judgment on your work. I adore him when he drops some little nugget of praise, and I resent him when he finds fault with my work. I find him attractive but coolly withdrawn. At work everyone calls him the Monk."

Her eyes crinkling with amusement, Kitty said, "Terribly inappropriate. You don't have to warn me about his women, Hilary. Miriam gave me the word right from the start. I don't think I'm in any danger of getting too involved. But then we always think that, don't we?"

"Every time."

"Are you missing your friend—what was his name?"

"Jack. Yes, it's empty at home. He hasn't even called."

"That's probably better. A good, clean break. No shilly-shallying back and forth. I can't live without you, I can't live with you. It's a rotten way to exist."

Though Hilary had not met Kitty before the final "I can't live with you," she knew her friend was speaking from experience. "Luckily you've found you can live without *him*."

The effort to smile went slightly astray. "It's not as much fun—yet—as the good days. It's infinitely better than the bad ones. I like my job at the employment agency. What you told that woman the other night—about believing in yourself—well, it's coming, slowly but surely. I'm glad we met when we did, though I admit thinking at the time that you didn't understand, couldn't understand because you hadn't been there."

"That's why I put you in touch with the group. I knew there were plenty of women in it who had been there. Do you still go?"

"Sometimes. Not as often as before, but I've stayed friends with a couple of them, and we see each other for lunches and things."

Hilary rested an elbow on the table and propped her head against her hand, suddenly struck by an idea. "Would you tell me about some of them, Kitty? I mean, from what you've heard them say, do you think the breakdowns in their marriages were jointly caused? I don't want you to think about your own situation now. I want you to think about them and the impression you've gotten. Were they at fault? Will they admit it? Are they aware of it? Sometimes you can read between the lines and tell more than they say."

"The way you did the other night when Jon jumped on you for it?" Kitty teased.

"You know what I mean. Marsh was trying to curb my flights of fancy, not because he thought I'd do that in a column, but because he thinks I'm too one-sided in my feminist view of life. Well, here's your chance to give him some support. Tell me where it is the women have gone wrong. In our own situations you and I can't see where we've erred, but it's possible—just barely—that we have. What do you see in these other women's lives that you would have done differently?"

A slow smile gathered on Kitty's lips. "What an opportunity to be catty! But I do know what you mean. We all come in there full of anger, expecting every other woman to see how we've been wronged, and when the story unfolds . . . oh, sometimes it's so obvious that the speaker herself made half the mistakes. Let me tell you about Betty—"

"Hold on. I want to get my notebook."

And instead of an afternoon of tennis, Hilary and Kitty found themselves on the patio, talking, probing, speculating for four hours. At five Kitty glanced at her watch and groaned. "I have to be ready in an hour. God, that was fun. Is that what you get to do for a living?"

Hilary sniffed. "I work hard for a living. This is just the beginning. Now I have to make a whole week's worth of columns out of it, ones that Marsh won't have a fit over. Are you going out with him tonight?"

"Hell, no. I've had my treat for the week. This one is sweet and a lot more open than Jon. But he's a mortician."

"Terrific. One of these days, if I can arrange it, I'll introduce you to Jack. He's sweet, and very open, and a computer programmer. You'd adore him."

Kitty pressed her hand. "One of these days, when you don't mind anymore, I'd like to meet him."

Hilary spent the remainder of the weekend working, not on a series of columns for the coming week, but on the magazine articles she had under contract. The fact that she had uninterrupted time did not give her as much pleasure as she would have thought. Twice she nearly called to Jack, as though he were in the next room, to ask him to put on a pot of coffee. Each time she set to work with renewed energy, eager to prove to herself that this spare time was a blessing in disguise.

But it wasn't easy to convince herself, when she missed Jack's coming in and dropping a kiss on the top of her head or reaching around to fondle her breasts. Sometimes they had wound up in bed; sometimes they had simply laughed, with a promise of "later." Even more than the sex, Hilary missed the companionship. She wanted to try out her ideas on him, wanted him there to tell her about his week at work. And they would have done something together—played tennis, gone to a movie, had dinner out. Even one of their rare arguments would have been preferable to the heavy silence of her apartment.

In the back of her mind she kept the idea for the series of columns, so that when she went to work Monday morning, she had more or less decided how to present them. Of course, it was necessary to protect any woman's identity, so she had to invent a totally different context from the one in which she had learned of their problems. And the quip she had made about fairy tales the previous week seemed an ideal vehicle for unfolding their stories: "Once upon a time." Hilary was not unaccustomed occasionally to using women themselves as examples of their own mistakes, but doing a whole series was a novelty for her, and slightly unnerving. It would be harder to put the sting at the end of each column, knowing she was attacking her own sex.

Her office was empty when she entered. A neat note typed on Harry's unmistakable typewriter lay in the center of her cluttered desk:

> I'll be out on an interview until after lunch. Carol wants me to invite you to dinner Saturday to meet her brother. Why don't you call and tell her you're going to Paris for a month?
>
> Harry

There was the usual stack of mail, which Hilary divided into several piles: those which contained praise, those which contained abuse, and those which gave her ideas for further columns. Together with the mail was a list from Marsh's secretary noting the functions he would be attending for the rest of the month and his own notations of those he wished her to attend. Four were given priority, and they served to remind her that she should have spent the weekend trying to get in touch with some "suitable" escorts. A hell of a time for Jack to leave her, she decided, and his leaving didn't make her very enthusiastic about renewing friendships with men she'd lost track of over the last year.

From her attaché case she withdrew the notebook she had used at Kitty's to jot down ideas as well as notes. After she had read through them and made some additional notes, she drew her typewriter table up to a right angle with her desk and inserted the rough sheets that served the newspaper for copy paper. Hilary paused for only a few thoughtful minutes before deciding on the first sentences, and then her fingers flew over the keys in an attempt to get the words down as fast as they came to her. This was a draft and would be corrected before she submitted it to Marsh, but the essence of her statement would be there when she finally withdrew the sheets. The ending, the sting, usually took another period of reflection and more rewrites than any other portion of the column. It had to have a succinct punch that would make a reader reflect after finishing her column, rather than go on to the next item without a pause. If possible, it should have a longer-lasting effect, but Hilary didn't expect miracles.

Just as she was finishing the first column, her phone rang. Glad that the interruption hadn't come two minutes sooner, she answered with real cheerfulness, which quickly faded when she recognized her mother's voice. "Is something the matter? Is Dad okay?"

"You father's fine."

Hilary knew this to be a relative statement. Her father suffered from Parkinson's disease and was seldom really "fine." She pushed the papers out of her reach and said, "You've never called me at work before. Something's wrong."

"Yes." She could hear her mother's sigh. "It's your sister, Hilary. She's had a nervous breakdown and was taken to the psychiatric ward of the hospital this morning."

"Oh, my God. Poor Janet. What happened, Mom?"

"Bill left her a few weeks ago. She didn't want me to tell you. She kept insisting that it was only a temporary arrangement."

"But it's not?" Hilary twisted the phone cord around her fingers.

"No. We've all seen it coming, Hilary. Janet was the only one who wouldn't believe it. I tried to talk to her, but she wouldn't listen to me. She's been acting irrationally, and I've been keeping an eye on her. Because there was no answer when I called early this morning, I went over. She hadn't gotten out of bed. The baby was crying, and Jason was begging her to get up and fix him breakfast." Mrs. Campbell's voice broke, and it was a moment before she continued. "Her doctor came and said she should be in the hospital. We took her there and notified Bill, but he says he won't have anything to do with her."

"What about the children? Will he take the children?"

"No." Her voice was heavy with tears. "He won't have anything to do with them. I've brought them home with me, but your father in his condition . . ."

"I know. Let me think." Hilary had already used half of her vacation time for the year, with a further trip planned in the winter for skiing. But the very least she could do was fly to Klamath Falls as soon as possible. The very most . . . It made her breath catch. Did her landlord allow children? The baby, Lisa, was only six months old. Bill's parents were dead, and she didn't even know if he had brothers and sisters. Perhaps when she was there . . . "Look, Mom, I'll have to get things straightened out at work before I can leave, so don't expect me until tomorrow. Can you manage until then?"

"Of course."

"Does the doctor think Janet will have to be in the hospital long?"

Mrs. Campbell's voice was little more than a whisper. "He couldn't say. Janet's . . . suffering from severe depression. She'd have to be a whole lot better to be responsible for a baby and a four-year-old."

"I'll take the earliest flight I can get tomorrow. Don't bother to meet me at the airport. If I have a problem getting away . . ." Hilary didn't even want to consider the possibility. "Well, I just won't. These things happen, and they'll have to accept it." But she didn't feel at all certain Marsh would. He was in the business of running a daily paper, and he expected his columnists to perform faithfully come rain or family crisis. "I'll see you tomorrow, Mom. Give my love to Dad and . . . and everyone."

Her digital desk clock flipped to eleven as she hung up. Immediately she lifted the receiver again and dialed Marsh's secretary. "Is he free, Susan? I have to see him for a few minutes."

"Hmm. His calendar's booked full until noon, and he has a twelve-thirty luncheon appointment. Is it an emergency?"

"Yes. Definitely."

"Okay. Come up a few minutes before twelve, and I'll try to scoot you in before he leaves for lunch."

"Thanks. I'll be there."

What would happen if he wouldn't let her go? Would she have to quit? There was her contract, of course, but she would be breaking it. Hilary's eye fell on the first of the series of columns, and she abruptly turned to whirl another sheet of paper in the typewriter. If she could get the whole series finished before she left . . .

Susan grimaced when Hilary presented herself just before noon. "He's running late already. I told him you had to see him, and he told me you could wait until this afternoon at your usual time. But I said you couldn't wait." And she eyed Hilary questioningly.

"That's right. I have to see him as soon as possible."

"Cartwright just went in ten minutes ago. God, Mr. Marsh hates running late. You won't need long, will you?"

"I hope not."

They sat in silence for almost fifteen minutes before Mr. Cartwright exited. He was closely followed by Marsh, who was shrugging into a lightweight suit coat. The editor didn't notice Hilary until she rose to stand directly in his path to the elevator.

"Oh, hell, I'd forgotten," he growled. "Can't this wait until our usual time, Ms. Campbell?"

"No, it can't."

"All right, but make it fast."

He held the door for her and followed her into the room, where he proceeded to stand by his desk instead of sitting down. Hilary spread the two columns she had finished on the desk beside him.

"I've written two of a series of my next five columns. I can have the other three finished by tomorrow morning. There's an emergency at home. I really have to go."

"What kind of emergency? Has someone died? Is someone dying?"

"My sister has had a nervous breakdown. She's in the hospital."

"I'm sorry to hear it," he said with a respectable show of concern, "but in such cases I don't believe outsiders can be of much help at first. You could call her on the phone when she's well enough, but I see no need to rush off. Where is home?"

"Klamath Falls. And it's not Janet who's the immediate problem. She has two children." Hilary was trying to tell him everything as quickly as possible since he stood tapping his fingers against the copy sheets she had set down. "Her husband has left her and won't take responsibility for them. My mother would, of course, and she lives there, but my father has Parkinson's disease, and . . . well, it's impossible."

One brow lowered with disastrous effect. Hilary had never seen him look more incredulously critical. He picked up the papers and said, "You can't seriously mean to take on your sister's children. Have you lost your mind?"

"I don't see any alternative unless I can convince her husband to take them. I'll try that first, but my mother sounded absolutely despondent about it, and if anyone could convince him of his duties, she could. *Something* has to be done about them. I can manage if I have to."

Marsh snorted. "Nonsense. What the hell do you know about taking care of children? Have you considered what it would mean to take them on when you live in an apartment and work full time?"

"Of course I've considered it!" Hilary snapped. "Other women do it. I'm sure I'm no less competent than most. If it can be done, I can do it."

"They aren't even your own children." He was speaking more calmly now, urging the reasonableness of his argument. "A woman will withstand a great deal of hardship for her own children, Ms. Campbell. But even the ones who dearly adore their children and want to work have a very difficult time. It's exhausting. You can't have thought of half the problems. You may not be allowed to have them in your apartment building. You would have to find day care for them while you worked and sitters for them in the evenings. And they will likely be emotionally upset by being rejected by their father and, to their minds, abandoned by their mother. They need a more stable environment than you can give them."

"What do you suggest, Mr. Marsh?"

"A foster home, in Klamath Falls. They'd be near your parents and near their mother."

"But I'm family. They're my responsibility, in a fashion. There would be some advantage to their being in the area, I grant you, but who can be sure that it would be an appropriate foster home? And in Klamath Falls I can't imagine there are that many foster homes available." Hilary paused for breath and pointed to the two articles he held. "Anyhow, that will have to be taken care of when I'm at home. It's not a matter that can be decided from such a distance. I want to go home. In fact, I am going home. The only thing you have to decide is whether you give me permission to do it or whether you fire me. I'm sure I can be back in a week, one way or another. With five columns in hand, I'll be covered for that time."

"I assume you've forgotten the civic function you were to attend this week."

"Oh, for God's sake! Yes, I'd forgotten it. Take back my raise and forget the whole thing. Or fire me. Do what you want, but I *have* to go. Can't you see that?"

His mouth pursed, but he didn't speak. Instead, he started to scan the first column. Though he was a fast reader, nothing escaped his attention. He took a pen from his breast pocket and made a mark on the copy before continuing to the second column.

"You typed these in a hurry."

"Yes," Hilary agreed, trying to remain patient. "My mother called at eleven. I had finished the first column. I daresay you find the second much more carelessly written."

"It's not bad." He glanced at his watch, and a pained expression settled on his face. "I'm running fifteen minutes late."

"I'm very sorry. As catastrophes go, I would say it ranks right after having your sister committed to a psychiatric ward."

Except for a cold gleam in his eyes, he ignored her sarcasm. "Be sure all five columns are in my office before you leave. Give your Oregon number to my secretary in case I have to reach you there about any of the ones I haven't read. And, Ms. Campbell, take copies with you so you'll know what I'm talking about."

"Yes, sir. I'm sure I'll be back by next Monday."

Marsh was already walking toward the door. "Being back and being prepared to give the newspaper the necessary amount of your concentration and energy are hardly the same thing, Ms. Campbell. I urge you not to be so quixotic as to bring the children back with you. The *Reporter* does not provide child care."

"It should," Hilary retorted. "Maybe I should write a column about it."

"You'd be wasting your time."

Their last remarks were passed in front of Susan, who looked somewhat startled. Hilary didn't notice, but Marsh, always a keen observer, said, "Not her own children, Susan; her sister's. Call the restaurant, please, and leave a message that I'll be a few minutes late."

The elevator doors opened almost immediately, and Hilary suspected that Susan had punched the button every few minutes to keep the elevator available for her impatient employer. Marsh said nothing until they reached the first floor.

"I'll expect the columns you have finished this afternoon as usual."

"Of course."

"I hope you're able to settle matters satisfactorily."

"Thank you." And she watched him stride across the lobby without a backward glance.

Chapter Five

THERE WAS ONLY one airline that flew from the Bay Area to Klamath Falls, and it had only two flights a day, 8:50 in the morning or 5:35 in the evening. Catching an 8:50 flight from San Francisco International made it necessary for Hilary to rise at the break of dawn to finish packing, drive her columns to the *Reporter* office, and then continue northward on the Bayshore to one of the cheaper long-term parking establishments that bussed people to the airport. On the hour and a half flight she tried to organize her thoughts about her sister and the children, firmly thrusting the series of columns from her mind. She knew they could have been better even without Marsh's firm-jawed acceptance of the third before she had left work the previous day.

But she had been unable to clear her mind sufficiently to give them her whole attention. Worry about her sister, concern for the children, fear that her father's condition would be exacerbated by the whole situation plagued her continually. Nor could she fight a feeling of outrage at her brother-in-law for his callous rejection of his family. Worst of all, perhaps, was her sense of disloyalty about writing a series of columns about women's errors in handling their lives when her sister lay at that moment in a psychiatric ward hundreds of miles from where she sat, typing feverishly simply to rid herself of a week's work in fifteen hours.

From the Klamath Falls airport Hilary took a taxi to her parents' house on Pacific Terrace, in an area of lovely older houses. The usual nostalgia she felt on returning to her hometown was absent this time, her mind absorbed in the alarming possibilities before her. Maybe Marsh was right. Maybe she should look into the foster home care available. After all, what did she have to offer the children but nine hours a day of even less interested care in San Jose? And Lisa was only six months old, not an age at which it was easy to find the proper baby-sitting care surely. Hilary had seen her niece only once, on a weekend trip to Klamath Falls in the spring. Certainly she must seem almost as much a stranger to both the children as any foster parents would be.

The money she refused to think about at all. The expense of housing and feeding them would be minimal, and if the day care were expensive, she would manage. Her parents would help if necessary, and she had a healthy savings account to draw on. As the taxi sped through town, she caught a glimpse of the building she had jointly purchased with her parents. California real estate was too rich for her blood, but she trusted her father's business sense and allotted a portion of her monthly salary to him for handling. Unable to practice law any longer, he enjoyed the activity of overseeing her investments as well as his and his wife's own. And probably, Hilary realized, he would be able to advise them on Janet's legal position with regard to her husband and on her husband's financial responsibilities.

Even before she climbed out of the taxi, her parents were there ready to welcome her, with her nephew, Jason, yelping and skipping along ahead of them.

"Hilary! Hilary! Did you know my mom's sick? We're staying with Grandma. She makes cookies for me," he yelled in his child's excited voice, running to cling to her skirt with sticky fingers.

"Yes, Grandma told me, Jason. Are you helping take care of Lisa?"

"I give her one of those awful biscuits sometimes. She gets them all wet and yucky."

Hilary laughed. "But she likes them, doesn't she?"

"I don't know why. They taste terrible." He made a disgusted face and tried to lift her suitcase, which he couldn't budge.

Her parents hugged her, and her father attempted to take the suitcase, but she shook her head. "I'm a liberated woman, Dad. We do for ourselves."

She was led immediately to her old bedroom, unchanged except for new curtains in the eight years she'd been living away from home. It had never reflected her youthful interests to the extent of posters and yearbooks, pictures and stuffed animals. The room was done in earthy browns, rusts, and beiges, with flashes of red and yellow in the cushions of the window seat where she had spent hours reading and daydreaming that she would become the most famous newspaperwoman of her age. Well, she hadn't done so badly so far. And there was time. Hilary did not give more than a cursory glance to the room before leaving her suitcase there and following her mother back to the living room.

Lisa was gurgling and playing with a rattle in a playpen in a corner of the room. Jason was beating a tattoo on the top bar of the playpen to gain her attention, while Mr. Campbell looked on with assumed complacency. When he caught Hilary's eyes on him, he smiled ruefully. "I'd forgotten a child's noise level."

"I don't think I've ever known it," she admitted. "How's Janet?"

"Pretty much the same as when your mother called you. We saw her today, and she hasn't improved. She feels terribly depressed, unhappy, inadequate . . ." He waved an expressive, though trembling, hand.

Unable to speak, she nodded. Jason had abandoned the playpen to claim Hilary's attention instead. She allowed him to show her his toy cars, set up in a row for an imaginary race. They didn't move fast enough on the carpet, so she took him out onto the back patio and built a ramp with a cookie sheet. "See which one will go the farthest," she suggested. And when he became engrossed enough in the game, she made her way back to the living room, where

Lisa had begun to cry. Mrs. Campbell was trying to distract her with a new toy.

"I'll hold her on my lap for a while." The minute she did so, Hilary knew it was a mistake. She could feel the moisture working its way into her white linen skirt. "Would you hand me an extra diaper or something?" she asked her mother.

"They don't use regular diapers these days." Her mother sighed. "It's all these paper things. I'll change her; you'd better go rinse out your skirt right away."

Not a propitious beginning, Hilary thought as she stood at the bathroom sink immersing the skirt in cold water. Did she even know how to use the new paper diapers? She couldn't remember any time she'd done it. And worse, she didn't even know at what age children were trained to use the toilet. Would Jason be toilet-trained? It seemed to her that she'd heard little boys were difficult to train and that they had very poor aim when they were trained. Hilary changed into blue jeans and a casual shirt. Obviously she should have brought more rough clothes than she had. No wonder the women she knew with small children didn't dress in good clothes.

Her father had spread out a batch of papers on the dining room table when she returned. "I thought you might like to take a quick look at these before we forget about them in the bustle. Your mother's putting Lisa down for a nap, but Jason's likely to wander in at any moment."

It was painful for Hilary to watch his unsteady hands draw forward each sheet in turn, and she concentrated on the information he conveyed to her. When he was finished, he returned the sheets to a folder, saying, "You're building a healthy estate. I don't want you to strap yourself, though. You should always have enough money in your money market account for emergencies and trips and such. If some months you don't feel it wise to send money to be invested, I hope you won't feel obliged to."

"I won't." Hilary ran a hand slowly along the polished mahogany surface of the table. "My friend Jack moved out last week, so I won't have anyone sharing apartment expenses. If it makes things more difficult, I'll cut back."

Mr. Campbell patted her shoulder awkwardly. "I'm sorry to hear that. I liked the young man."

"So did I."

"Your mother and I thought perhaps you might even marry him."

"Sometimes I thought I would, too." Hilary flashed a brief smile. "I guess it's a good thing I didn't. Tell me about Janet and Bill."

Her father pushed his chair back from the table but remained seated, his eyes troubled. "They've been having a hard time for more than a year now, fighting constantly, even when they came here. Janet refused to see how bad things had gotten. Ever since the baby was born, she's been a little irrational. One day she would be compulsive about caring for the children, and the next she'd practically ignore them. Bill hadn't wanted another child at all and accused her of having had it to spite him. Your mother and I think she did it to hold the marriage together."

The story sounded so similar to one of the columns she'd just written that Hilary swallowed painfully. "Where's Bill living now?"

"In their house. He refuses to discuss matters and says he won't take responsibility for the children."

"Who does he think is going to?"

"He doesn't seem to care, Hilary. I don't understand it." He looked tired and confused, his eyes meeting hers almost as though he were begging her to explain it all to him.

"I can understand, maybe, about the baby, but what about Jason? Doesn't he at least want to see Jason?"

"No, he's decided that Janet had Jason without consulting him either."

"It sounds as if he should be in the psychiatric ward *with* her," Hilary said with a snort. But her father's expression made her control her more pungent remarks on the subject. There was no use making a bad situation worse. Hilary had always believed her brother-in-law immature and wondered at her sister's choice, but it was too late to voice such hindsight thoughts. "Well, perhaps he'll come to see that Jason needs him, especially now. In any case, it's too much for you and Mom to have the children. I'm prepared to take them back to San Jose with me. It's not the ideal solution for them, but it may be all that's available. With luck Janet won't be in the hospital too long. My editor, Mr. Marsh, suggested a foster home, which would at least keep them in the area."

Mr. Campbell put a weary and shaking hand to his eyes. "Your mother called an agency yesterday. You'll have to ask her what they said, but they weren't very promising."

"I'm not sure I'd want to do it that way anyhow," Hilary announced. "Janet is my sister, and I feel we should be the ones to see to Jason and Lisa. Or Bill should. But if his attitude is as rotten as you say, it would be worse than anything to force them on him. They'd be better off with the sitters I'd have to find for them in California."

"If it were only for a few days . . ." Her father grimaced. "But it won't be. There's no use fooling ourselves. It seems terribly unfair to lay the burden on you, Hilary. We don't see any other options. If my health were better . . ."

"I can manage, Dad. Don't worry about me."

Jason came bounding into the dining room, demanding lunch, and Hilary rose, laying a hand on her father's arm. "It will be all right, Dad."

In the kitchen she followed Jason's directions in slathering peanut butter and honey on slices of white bread and cutting them on the diagonal.

"Did Grandma tell you you might come home with me for a while, Jason? To California?"

"Why? Why can't I stay here?"

"Because Grandpa isn't well enough to have children in the house all the time. He has a nervous disorder, so it's necessary that he have quiet around him."

Jason regarded her with his most serious expression. "We could be quiet."

"Not quiet enough, I'm afraid. Lisa is too young to know not to cry; it's her only way of telling us when she needs something. And we don't want you to have to be quiet, Jason. You should be able to run and play and make some noise."

"Would I be able to do that at your house?"

"Well, I live in an apartment, and you couldn't be really noisy, but we'd go to the park, and I'd find you a play group during the day when I work."

Apparently this didn't sound particularly appealing to Jason. "Why can't I stay with Daddy?"

"Your daddy has to work during the day, too, and he doesn't know how to take care of children very well." Hilary wasn't satisfied with the answer, but she couldn't think of any other excuse under his beseeching eyes.

"Do you?"

"Do I what?"

"Know how to take care of kids."

"No," Hilary admitted, "but I'm going to learn. Grandma will teach me about Lisa, and you'll teach me about you, the way you did with the sandwich. Do you know how to use a toilet?"

"Sure."

She smiled at him and tousled his hair. "I'm glad. One set of diapers seems quite enough to me."

"I can button my shirt, too, but I can't tie my shoes."

"Maybe you'll learn while you're with me."

"Maybe," he said, skeptical. "Do you make cookies?"

Hilary couldn't remember the last time she had. She bought the specially wrapped kind at the supermarket. Her time was limited. "I will," she promised, "if it works out that you come home with me."

"Would there be kids to play with?"

"We'd find some for you. In the play group and in the neighborhood." Hilary felt tired just thinking of all the demands that would be made on her time. But he looked so sad and bewildered, sitting there with his elbows on the table. When did you teach them table manners? "I think you'd enjoy it, and when you came back home, you'd be able to tell your friends you'd lived in California for a while."

"When would I come back home?" he asked, more hopeful.

"As soon as your mother is well enough to take care of you again. No one knows, Jason, but I think it will be a few months."

"Is that very long?"

With a child's sense of time it must seem forever, Hilary thought. "Well, it doesn't seem very long to me. If we're all lucky, I think you'll be home before Christmas."

Jason made a face. "Mom said Christmas was a long way off still."

"About five and a half months."

"Would I see Daddy before I left?"

"I certainly hope so." There, that wasn't a lie. Surely Bill could be induced to take leave of his children.

"When would we go?"

"*If* you come with me, it will be in a few days. Probably by the weekend, so we can get settled in before I have to go back to work."

"What do you do?"

Hilary spent the rest of his lunchtime trying to explain about her work on the paper. Everything she said raised a question. Every answer she could not be sure he understood. When he lost interest, as happened rather quickly, and finished his sandwich and milk, which he seemed to inhale, she took him outside to play.

During the afternoon she had a crash course in baby care from her mother. If Mrs. Campbell found it strange that Hilary didn't know how to diaper a baby or how or what to feed it, she didn't say so. "We'll get you a copy of Spock," she said, "or whatever women use these days. One of the problems is that new mothers worry about every little thing. It's almost inevitable. Lisa's a fairly easy baby. She doesn't cry much, and she's been healthy as a horse so far. Jason is healthy but rambunctious. Janet hasn't exercised much control over him recently, so he's gotten even wilder. But I suppose all grandmothers think that. The best thing you can do is use your common sense, and don't panic. Children are amazingly resilient."

"They're going to have to be," Hilary complained good-naturedly. "I don't even own a jar of peanut butter. And ecologically I don't approve of paper diapers."

Her mother was amused. "There are a lot of principles that get compromised in child rearing, my dear. Do you have a washer and dryer in your building?"

"No. I take my laundry to a place near work."

"You may want to find something closer. You'll be astonished at the increase in dirty clothes with two children around. And it won't be only theirs."

Late in the afternoon, when her mother was starting to prepare dinner, Hilary made her first attempt to diaper Lisa alone. She had a soiled diaper in her hand when her mother called her to the phone. Since no one else knew she was at home, she knew it must be the paper, and she tried frantically to hold the wriggling baby while she dropped the diaper in a pail beside the changing table. She carried the cooing infant with her to the upstairs phone, straddling the baby across her hip.

"Hello?"

"Ms. Campbell? Jonathan Marsh. Can you hear me?"

"Of course. The long-distance connections in Oregon are every bit as good as they are in California, Mr. Marsh."

"What's that noise?"

"That's my niece. I was changing her diaper when you called and she's . . . oh, hell! May I call you back?" Hilary could feel the stream of warm moisture traveling down her pants leg.

"I'll only take a moment of your time. I want the second half of your fourth column rewritten. There are assumptions in it which aren't justified by the first half. I'm sure you'll see what they are when you read it over at your leisure. Call Susan tomorrow morning with the changes." There was a pause, and then he demanded, "Do you mean to tell me your sister's children are *babies*?"

"One of them is six months old. The other's four."

"Then I would sincerely question your sanity in returning with them, Ms. Campbell. I thought we were talking of rational beings, say, eight or ten. You can't possibly carry on a career such as yours with an infant to care for. For God's sake, neither of them would even be in school!"

"I'm well aware of that; I always have been. They'll have to be in child care situations during the day, of course. Lots of children are."

"Have you considered my suggestion of a foster home for them?"

Hilary was feeling very uncomfortable with wet pants, and the baby had taken to clutching at her hair in a very painful manner. "Uh, I really can't talk right now. My mother looked into foster homes, and there's nothing available right now. I still intend to approach their father. Really, I appreciate your concern, Mr. Marsh, but I may have no choice."

"Find one," he commanded, and the phone went dead.

Hilary looked at it in exasperation for only a moment before slamming it in the cradle and stalking back to the child's room, muttering to Lisa as she went, "What does he expect? Am I supposed to conjure up a mother for you and Jason from thin air? I *know* I'm not the ideal person to have charge of you, and I *know* it's going to make my life hectic as hell, but I can't very well abandon you, can I?"

Lisa cooed and twisted a lock of Hilary's long brown hair more tightly about her tiny fingers.

"And if you want us to get along well," Hilary continued, "you'll have to stop pulling my hair. It hurts. I don't particularly like your peeing on me either. Where is your sense of decorum? I'm your aunt. Nieces should not pee on their aunts. I presume Spock will have it in his book. Did you know there was another Spock? He had pointed ears and flew around in a spaceship on 'Star Trek.' Someday you'll see him on television." And she proceeded to enlighten her niece on the marvels of space travel as she awkwardly encased the little body in a diaper.

Despite her father's warning about Janet's condition, Hilary was secretly convinced she could be of some help to her sister. After all, she was close to Janet's age and had some understanding of the strains in her sister's marriage, having discussed similar problems with many women over the last few years. And she'd had her own problems—not at all the same, perhaps, but she had been subject to feelings of rejection, which she'd had to cope with to get on with her life.

Hilary felt that if she could just sit down and talk with Janet, her close friend from their shared childhood, she would be able to ease her sister's suffering. She was willing to offer her understanding, her sympathy, the strength of the special bond that held them together. Wouldn't that be the kind of thing most likely to bring Janet out of her horrible depression?

The psychiatric ward at the hospital was fairly new and not at all the depraved jungle one pictured from movies and books. Hilary talked with Janet's doctor, who tried to moderate her expectations.

"We want her family's help," he explained, "but you have to understand she's not ready to accept a rounded picture of herself yet. She's consumed with guilt and fear and loathing for herself. In her condition she can't see an end to it; everything looks unrelievedly black. Given time, that will change, but it does take time. Don't be discouraged by her negativity. Try to encourage her."

Janet's face was a little pale, but her hair had been brushed, though probably not by herself. She was crying when Hilary entered the room, but there was no accompanying sound and no facial contortion to give additional evidence of the pain she suffered.

"Hi, Janet," she said cheerfully, seating herself after a brief hug that brought little response from her sister. "How are you feeling today?"

The tears continued to flow, but Janet mumbled, "Okay."

"The kids are fine. Mom's taking good care of them, and I'm going to take them back to San Jose with me probably. I'll have Jason send you drawings, and when you're better, you can talk to them on the phone." There was no response from her sister, so she said, "We all love you, Janet. We're here for you to lean on. Don't be too proud to do it. We want to help you."

"I don't deserve to be helped," her sister whispered. "I'm not any good, Hilary."

"Of course you are," Hilary said stoutly. "You're just too unhappy right now to realize it. Things have been difficult for you recently, but they'll get better."

"No, they won't. Bill won't come back. I'm a terrible mother."

"You're a wonderful mother! How can you say that? Jason and Lisa are terrific kids. They miss you, you know, but we're keeping them busy. When you're better, you'll take care of them again."

"I can't ever take care of them. I can't get up in the morning. I can't cook meals. I can't remember what I'm supposed to be doing. All I do is cry."

Hilary bit her lip and reached across to press her sister's hand. "That will change. You'll sort things out. You have to give yourself time."

"It's hopeless. Everything's hopeless." Tears coursed more quickly down her pale cheeks. "I wish I'd never been born."

With an effort Hilary concealed the shock she felt. "Nonsense. You're going to be fine. Think of all the things you've done, Janet: all the meals you've cooked, all the dishes you've washed, all the games you've played with the kids. You'll do it again. I know you will."

"No. I can't. I can't do it anymore. I used to be able to do it, but not now."

"Soon," Hilary promised, fighting to make her voice enthusiastic.

"They might have died," Janet cried.

"Who? The children? Don't be silly. Mom always checks in with you. Janet, you can't blame yourself for things you couldn't control. You were too unhappy to carry on. Now you're going to get help."

"It won't do any good. Nothing will do any good."

Firmly Hilary insisted, "Yes, it will."

"I'm no good," Janet said again.

"You are good." Hilary wanted to cry but forced a smile. "Remember how you used to come to my rescue when we were little, when everyone was being mean to me? Remember how you lent me your very best dress when I spilled coffee on mine?"

Janet said nothing, turning her head away to stare listlessly out the window.

"Can I bring you anything?"

Janet shook her head.

"I'll come back tomorrow."

"If you like."

"Just get well soon. Jason and Lisa need you, love. They know you're a good mother. They want you home with them."

"I can't take care of them anymore." She sounded utterly defeated, but the tears had momentarily ceased.

"You will be able to, in a little while." Hilary rose to go and hugged her again. "You *are* going to feel better, Janet. Try to believe that."

"I can't. I wish I could, but I can't. I'm sorry. Don't hate me."

"I don't hate you. I love you, and I want you to get better. Let us help you get better."

Janet shrugged. "You shouldn't waste your time on me. I'm not worth it."

"Oh, Janet." But Hilary could say nothing further. Tears stung at her eyes, and she didn't want her sister to see them. In the hallway she drew a shaking breath, shook her head unhappily, and walked purposefully from the ward.

Though she went every day, there was no change in Janet's frame of mind. Their conversations were duplicates of the initial one, with Janet clinging almost desperately to her presumed inadequacy. Hilary tried not to let Janet's pessimism envelop her, tried to talk of happier times and interesting subjects, but her sister remained withdrawn and unresponsive to the hope that was held out to her. Few times in her life had Hilary felt so helpless. To counteract this disappointment, she turned her attention to Bill.

Her brother-in-law wouldn't take her calls at his office, and there was no answer at his house. Hilary suspected he was there and not answering, so on Thursday she followed the simple expedient of awaiting him at the house, to which her parents had a key.

When he entered, he had his sleeves rolled up and his suit jacket slung over his shoulder. He looked hot and irritable. For a moment he didn't notice Hilary, sitting in the corner of the living room. Then he scowled and said, "Can't you leave me alone? I thought I'd made it clear I didn't want to talk to you."

"Terribly clear, Bill, but we have several matters to discuss, and I have to get back to San Jose very soon."

He shoved a hand through his blond hair, automatically putting it in order. Even with someone he didn't want to see, he could not allow himself to look disheveled. His vanity was the first thing Hilary had recognized in him. He had the physique of a football player—tall, muscular—and the kind of looks which had made him a college idol. The years since his graduation had not affected his appearance, nor had they earned him any appreciable maturity. He was locked in the rosy glow of adulation he had received then and, for all Hilary knew, was still receiving. His intelligence was passable, but nothing to brag about, and his selfishness was not wholly disguised by his boyish charm, a quality he seldom bothered any longer to exhibit to the Campbells.

"Do you want a drink?" he asked, heading for the kitchen.

"A glass of white wine if you have it."

"I don't."

"Nothing then."

Hilary waited in the living room for him to return with a tall, cool drink. He had rolled his cuffs down and buttoned them. "Now, look, Hilary," he began immediately, "your sister's crazy. She didn't just get crazy on Monday, when they took her to the hospital. She's been acting like some kind of madwoman for months: obsessively jealous, careless of her appearance, neglecting the kids. It's not my fault if I don't love her anymore; she brought it on herself. She couldn't talk about anything interesting; she wanted to have long discussions about our 'relationship.' If I stopped for a drink on the way home, she made life hell for me, but when I came straight home, all she could talk about was whether Lisa had eaten her food and why Jason wasn't behaving. I got fed up with it. She didn't want to go anywhere or do anything. She was making me a prisoner in my own house."

"Did she ever try to get help? Did you ever suggest a psychiatrist?" Hilary asked.

"Are you kidding?" Bill threw her a disgusted look and took a long sip of his drink. "She wouldn't listen to anyone. Your parents tried to talk to her, and all she would say was, 'There's nothing wrong.' I can't tell you how many times I heard her say that. Nothing wrong, hell. She's a mess. She can't cope with anything. You should have seen what this house looked like on Monday. I had to have someone come in and clean it."

"You poor dear," Hilary snapped. "I feel wretchedly sorry for you. Watching your wife headed for a nervous breakdown, and all you can do is complain that the house is dirty. I suppose all your friends clap you on the back and congratulate you on getting out before you really had to exert some effort on your wife's behalf. But let's leave Janet aside. For her sake, I'm glad you left. Not because it brought on this crisis, but because now she'll have to learn to build her life without you. What I want to discuss is the children."

"I won't have anything to do with them," he insisted. "Did you know she went right ahead and got pregnant with Lisa when I specifically told her I didn't want any more children? Can you beat that!"

"Yes, I think you're doing exceptionally well at beating it, Bill. Those children need you right now. Jason in particular. He's frightened by his mother's illness, and he doesn't understand why you're not with him. You know Mom would help you take care of them, but she can't have them living at home because of Dad. She'd help you find day care for them or sit with them in the evenings when you want to go out. Anything. But they're your children; they're your responsibility until Janet is well enough to take care of them again. No one's going to slap you on the back for abandoning your children, Bill."

"Hey, Hilary, I'm not trying to make points." He bent his serious, sincere gaze on her. "I'm in no position to take care of them. What do I know about bringing up kids? And everyone knows babies are the most demanding. I'm not into changing diapers and spooning goo. It's your sister's fault we have Lisa at all. I didn't want any more kids. Actually I didn't want any to start with, but all our friends were having kids, and I let Janet browbeat me into it. What good would I be to Jason? He can't play ball with me; he can't even sit still. All he does is ask questions and make a mess of everything he touches. I can't live like that, and I'm not going to."

"Who do you think is going to take care of them?"

"I don't know, and I don't care. Someone will. There are agencies to handle that sort of thing."

Hilary rose and began to pace the living room from the mantel to the archway into the hall. It was an attractive room, well furnished in good taste, but with the signs of wear that children have a habit of inflicting on any place they live. There were scratches on the coffee table legs where Jason had probably banged his Big Wheel, and stains on the sofa where one of them had spilled food or drink. Near the door to the patio was an area of worn carpet which a potted plant only partially covered.

"You wouldn't mind seeing them in a foster home then?" Hilary asked at last.

"It would probably be the best place for them. People who do those things like kids."

"Unfortunately there aren't any openings right now." She was beginning to get a headache. "I can't leave them with my parents. Dad is already worse from the strain of having them around. If you won't keep them, I'll have to take them with me to San Jose."

"Fine." He smiled for the first time, a triumphant grin that set her nerves on edge. "I'm sure they'll love being with you. And you'll love having them."

"I'm not in a particularly good position to take them," she said, her voice cold. "My job is full-time and demanding. I live in an apartment where they won't have much space. I'll have to find day care for them. In fact, I'll take them only on two conditions."

Wary now, he attempted to appear at ease by taking another long sip of his drink. "What are they?"

"First, I'll expect you to send a monthly check for child support. You can arrive at a figure with my father. If you don't do it voluntarily, he'll take you to court on it."

"I doubt if he can, with Janet in the hospital."

"Trust me, he'll find a way."

"Okay, okay. I intended to contribute to their support, even though I never wanted Lisa."

Hilary breathed a little more easily. "The other condition is that you keep in touch with them. I expect you to see Jason before we leave, and I expect you to call him at least once a week while he's away. You don't seem to understand how your rejection of him and Lisa can affect their emotional development. This is a difficult time for them, and I don't want you making it any more difficult by being a full-blown bastard."

"I don't want to keep in touch with them."

"I don't care whether you want to or not, Bill. You're going to. Or I won't take them."

"You're bluffing. You'll take them."

Resting her hands on the back of the sofa on which he sat, so that he had to twist his neck to see her, she met his insolent gaze with furious eyes. "Try me. If you don't come over to see Jason this evening, you can expect me to bring both of the children to your office tomorrow morning and dump them on you. Do you think I wouldn't? What in the hell do you think I have to lose? You should be slavering with gratitude that someone is willing to shoulder your responsibilities for you. I'll be perfectly happy to explain to your secretary exactly why I'm there, and to your boss as well. In fact, I'd be happy to write a paper about your conduct in the matter and have it photocopied and distributed to every man and woman in your office. On paper I'm very good with words, Bill." She smiled at his pale face. "Afterward you can sue me. That should be a lot of fun for you, too."

He shifted uneasily on the sofa. "Your parents wouldn't like it."

"No, they wouldn't, but I'm a big girl, and I do what I have to."

"You'd probably be fired from your job."

"Not as fast as you would, and I could get another one."

His drink was empty, something he discovered when he convulsively lifted it to his lips. "You're blackmailing me."

"What's a little blackmail among family members, Bill? Maybe you should go to the police and tell them about it: your sister-in-law is threatening to expose your callous disregard of your children if you don't do something about it. Do you really want to make a fool of yourself?"

The hostile silence lasted for several minutes. Finally he said, "If you really think it's that important to the kids that I keep in touch with them, I will. You're wrong, though. They don't care about me at all."

"Of course they care about you. What do children know?" Hilary slumped onto a leather chair. "I'm sorry. That was unnecessary. You're their father, and I want them to know that you care enough about them to keep in touch. I don't want you to hurt them. Please come by this evening. Jason's been asking about you."

She smoothed down her skirt as she rose, remembering the sticky fingers that had clutched it and the wetness from the baby's diapers. "Obviously I haven't the first notion of what it's like to be a parent, Bill. The one thing I do know is that you can't just chuck it when you're tired of it."

At the door she paused to see if he had anything further to say, but he was staring straight ahead, and she let herself out without saying good-bye. Instead of going straight home, she drove around the town, memories mingling with esoteric speculations on how relationships went wrong between men and women. At the post office she had mailed her first résumés, at the Klamath County Museum she had done research for her first articles. Her first boyfriend had lived on Shelley Street, and her best friend on Portland Street. Those contemporaries who had stayed in Klamath Falls suffered most of the same problems that the ones who had moved away suffered because the problems arose from the people, not the location. There were divorces, and suicides, and affairs, and drinking problems, and failures at work for both groups.

Life was quieter in Klamath Falls. Quieter—or duller, Hilary wasn't sure which. By the time she pulled into the driveway in Pacific Terrace she felt exhausted, discouraged. She wasn't going to change the world one iota, and it seemed absurd that she'd ever believed she could. Degenerating to threats against her brother-in-law, recognizing her sister's helpless dependence on the man in her life were all so familiar and seemed so unchangeable. She didn't need to hear, when she walked in the house, that Marsh had called.

Chapter Six

"I'M GLAD I missed his call." Hilary breathed with whole-hearted relief. "In the morning I may feel more like talking to him."

"He wanted you to call back tonight," her mother said, holding out a slip of paper. "This was the number. He said you could reach him there after seven."

Hilary groaned. "Did he say what it was about?"

"No, just that you were to call. Did you talk to Bill?"

Pushing aside her concern about the call, Hilary tried to concentrate on the current family crisis. "Bill will send child support for the kids, and he'll keep in touch with them. He and Dad can arrange the details. If he keeps his word, he'll be over tonight. I hope he has enough sense to come before Jason's bedtime."

"I'm sure he will, dear. It's a good thing you went. I don't think your father or I could have talked him into both concessions."

"I didn't talk him into them. I threatened him." Her mother's face registered instant concern, and Hilary shook her head. "He's not exactly a doting father, but he had intended to come up with some child support. As for the other, maybe he thinks it's best just to walk out of everyone's life at once. I managed to convince him it wasn't. God, I was a shrew. I can't quite decide whether it's better to be soft and feminine and persuasive with someone like him or hard and cold and demanding. I'm sure he likes the feminine touch best, but he listens to authority. Do I have a minute to freshen up before dinner?"

"Sure. Take your time."

Hilary knew her mother's worried eyes followed her as she left the kitchen, not because Mrs. Campbell disliked a late dinner, but because she feared her elder daughter was becoming hardened. Were women supposed to act as she had? When they were given no choice, Hilary decided, and maybe whenever they wanted to. Who was the arbiter of how a woman should behave anyhow? Certainly Hilary didn't give that right to any man.

After dinner she sat at the table with her parents and Jason, nursing a cup of coffee as long as it would last. Finally Mrs. Campbell asked, "Don't you think you'd better call Mr. Marsh, dear? It's after seven, and you don't want to be interrupted by our visitor."

"I'll help you with the dishes first."

"But, Hilary, he may be planning to go out later. If you want to catch him, I think you should call soon."

Who says I want to catch him? Hilary thought. He can't possibly have anything good to say to me, and he's bound to ask what's been decided about the children. "Well," she said, rising, "I won't be long, so don't start the dishes without me."

Marsh answered his own phone.

"Mr. Marsh? Hilary Campbell. I had a message to call you."

"You should have called collect."

"Yes, I should have. I didn't think of it. Is there some problem?"

"You'll have to decide that," he said, and she could hear him shuffling papers in the background. "Apparently you authorized Harry Stevens to open your office mail while you were away, in case some emergency arose. I myself don't consider this an emergency, nor did Harry, but we thought you might want to know about it. You've been receiving an unprecedented amount of mail since the new series of columns began to appear. It's mostly from women, and it's mostly unfavorable. They seem to feel you've betrayed the cause."

"Have my columns been printed as I wrote them?"

"Certainly. You know we have an unwritten agreement

that they won't be changed without your specific permission."

"Then I don't see that it does me any good to hear about the response. I knew it might be negative. There isn't much I can do from here."

"Friday's column will have to go in as it is, of course, but if you wished to dictate a new column to Susan tomorrow, it could replace Monday's. You might think about it. You don't want to alienate your readers."

Hilary tapped the phone table with a finger, trying to assess the possibilities. "No, the columns were necessary. Men aren't the only ones making life hard for women. Some women are doing it to themselves, and it was my job to point that out to them. Am I getting favorable letters from men?"

"A few. Not as many as I would have expected. Harry said to tell you he has the perfect one for your bulletin board, something about your 'finally seeing the light.' So you want to let Monday's column stand?"

"Yes. I'll assess the damage when I return."

"Do you know when that will be?"

"Saturday probably." Hilary could hear the front doorbell ring, and she wanted to be with Jason when his father came. "I have to go now. I'll be at work on Monday."

"Then you're not bringing the children."

"I'm bringing the children, but I'll be at work on Monday."

"Have you considered that you're unlikely to be able to find care for them over a weekend?"

"Somehow I'll do it. It's vacation time. If I have to, I'll have a high school student stay with them for a day or two while I make other arrangements." She could hear her nephew's squeals of delight at seeing his father and said determinedly into the phone, "Good-bye, Mr. Marsh."

"Have you found out whether your landlord will allow children?" he asked.

"It's not relevant," she muttered. "They'll be only visiting me."

"For two months? Three? More? I'm sure he'll consider

that living there. It seems to me I saw a sign in front of your building that announced 'adult living.' Your neighbors aren't going to be any happier than your landlord."

"Mr. Marsh, I'll handle it. You're kind to be so concerned with my living arrangements, but I assure you everything will work out, and I *will* be at work on Monday. I'm convinced that's the only factor that truly interests you. If I have time, I'll even write Tuesday's column before I come to work so you can see it early in the day."

"If you have time," he emphasized. "I don't think you have any idea how time-consuming children are, Ms. Campbell. Especially young ones."

"Well, I'll learn." She forced herself to sound cheerful. "Now, I really must go. Bye."

"Good night, Ms. Campbell. And good luck."

Hilary didn't bother to answer the heavily sarcastic parting shot.

In the living room her nephew was asking his father when Bill was going to take him home. Bill threw Hilary an angry glance before answering.

"I can't take you home, Jason. Remember, I work during the day. There wouldn't be anyone to take care of you. Your aunt Hilary is going to take you down to live with her."

"But Hilary works," Jason protested, his lip quivering.

"Yes, but she can find someone to take care of you. And she'll be there in the evening. I sometimes have to work late, and I don't know how to cook." Bill disengaged the two small hands that clung to his arm, but rather than walk away from his son, he swung him up onto his shoulders, saying, "Let's walk outside for a while."

The Campbells watched in silence, relieved to see that Bill was not as immune to his son's needs as he wished them to believe. The man and boy walked down the street and back, talking and even occasionally laughing. Before reentering the house, Bill tousled his son's hair and hugged him. Through the screen door they heard him say, "I'll call you, Jason. Once a week, on Sunday evenings. Okay?"

"Okay. Won't you come to see me?"

"California's pretty far away. When you come back to Klamath Falls, I'll see you again."

"When will I come back?"

"When your mother is well enough to take care of you. No one knows how long that will be. A few months probably."

They came in, Jason smiling bravely and Bill looking exhausted. Hilary had Lisa on her lap freshly diapered, and Bill came to take the child. He gingerly raised the small, laughing girl in his arms as though she were breakable. Lisa grabbed a handful of his blond hair for security.

For a few minutes Bill didn't look directly at the child and seemed at a loss for something to say to her that didn't sound ridiculous to the adults surrounding him. Fortunately this didn't seem to bother Lisa, who snuggled against him, making gurgling noises and smiling happily.

"You going to take her for a walk, too?" Jason asked.

Startled, Bill nodded, thinking, perhaps, that it would be easier to carry out his fatherly responsibilities out of sight of the Campbells. Hilary told him Lisa liked the glider in the back, and he silently left through the sliding glass doors for the patio. Jason followed them, cheerfully telling his father about Lisa's antics, which ordinarily made him slightly jealous but now brought him sufficient attention in the telling that he actually began to relish her activities and even embellished them a little.

Mrs. Campbell sighed as she watched them. "I wish they didn't have to go so far away. If he could see them regularly he might understand how much they need him. Do you think he'll keep his promise to call every week?"

"If he doesn't, I'll remind him," Hilary said. "He's not going to want to hear about Janet, but I won't let him reject the kids if I can help it. I'll have Jason send drawings to him and to Janet, of course. When she's well enough to talk to them . . ."

"We'll look out for her," Mr. Campbell said, patting her hand on the sofa. "You're going to have more than enough to do with the children."

"They'll be a new experience for me. I'm constantly accused of not knowing what I'm talking about in my articles, so now I'll have a chance to learn." She gave her mother a conspiratorial wink. "At least a little."

"It won't be the same as having your own," Mrs. Campbell said. "In some ways it will be harder, because they aren't. On the other hand, you'll know that sometime soon the responsibility will be lifted from you, that it's not a permanent way of life. Mothers don't have that option."

"I've never even had a cat," Hilary said with a laugh. "My boss already thinks I'm crazy."

Mr. Campbell looked concerned. "It wouldn't be right of us to ask you to jeopardize your career for your sister, Hilary. If this is going to cause a strain in your working relationships . . ."

"Nonsense, Dad. Mr. Marsh has nothing to say about how I conduct my life so long as I turn out decent columns for him five days a week. He thinks everyone should be as dedicated to the newspaper as he is. We do our jobs, we do them professionally, and then we go off to lead our lives. We don't eat and sleep and drink printer's ink the way he does, and the paper doesn't suffer for it one bit."

"If it becomes too much . . ." Mrs. Campbell started to say.

"It won't. Thousands of women cope. I'm sure I can."

Bill returned with the two children, Lisa clasped more comfortably in his arms and Jason holding his hand. "I should go now," he announced. "Will you be coming over tomorrow to pack their things, Hilary?"

"In the morning." She accepted Lisa from him and smiled. "I'm glad you came. They loved seeing you. If everything goes smoothly, I'll be leaving Saturday morning. I've written my home number on my business card. They may be a bit unsettled at first, and I'm sure they'll be happy to hear from you Sunday night."

"What time do you go to bed?" Bill asked his son.

Jason wrinkled his little face in thought. "Eight?" he said hopefully.

"Seven-thirty," Hilary corrected.

"Okay, I'll call before then," Bill promised. After taking leave of the Campbells, he let Lisa grab his finger and gave Jason a thump on the shoulders. "Take care of yourself, old man."

And he was gone. Jason watched longingly as the car disappeared around the corner, then turned to Hilary. "Are we going on a plane?"

"Yep. Have you ever been on a plane?"

"No, I don't think so. Is it fun?"

"It's a real adventure," she assured him.

Hilary hadn't realized how much of an adventure it would be, with two small companions and an inordinate amount of luggage. In addition to the suitcases and boxes and the collapsible stroller, Hilary had the car seat. Her parents waved her off sympathetically, and Hilary's doubts about her ability to cope began to grow.

On the plane Jason never stopped talking, and the baby threw up, fortunately onto a cloth Hilary's mother had insisted she carry in a plastic bag in her purse. The flight attendants kindly relieved her of Jason after this episode and at San Francisco International assisted her off the plane with the unwieldy car seat. While awaiting her luggage, she momentarily lost sight of Jason as Lisa wriggled in the stroller. Forcing herself to be calm, she scanned the baggage area, missing two of their suitcases in the process. Jason was sitting on the counter of a car rental booth, happily chatting with the women who ran it. Within minutes Hilary stood surrounded by a small mountain of luggage, wondering if it all could possibly belong to them. The skycaps eyed her askance, but she finally flagged one down and told him she wanted a cab.

"You need a truck, lady," he said as he stacked the luggage on his cart.

The cabdriver was disappointed that it wasn't a fare all the way into the city. Hilary felt like telling him she needn't have spent the money for a cab at all, except that the thought of loading and unloading all that luggage onto the free bus was too daunting even to contemplate. Instead, she turned her attention to the children: Lisa had once again gotten hold of her hair, and Jason was pointing out the window asking what everything was. Once she had them all in her own car, she sat behind the wheel for a few minutes to recover her nerve and her strength. There was barely room for the three of them, since her minuscule car had almost no trunk, and suitcases were stacked on boxes on the floor and seats. In an hour, she promised herself, everything would look less chaotic.

But in an hour, although they were in her apartment, new problems arose to plague her. There were two bedrooms, but one of them she used as an office, which she left in a state of permanent untidiness, scattered with books, pamphlets, magazines, letters, her typewriter, and, more often than not, one or two empty coffee cups. The children would have to use the room, and there was a single bed for Jason, but she would have to purchase a crib that day for Lisa. There was no chest of drawers for their clothes. The closet, where they might have put some, along with their toys, was filled with her skiing paraphernalia. She gazed helplessly around her as Jason tugged at her skirt.

"Can we have lunch now?" he asked.

With a fatalistic shrug she led him and carried the baby to the kitchen. There was bread for sandwiches, but no peanut butter, and he wouldn't consider the cheese she set out. So before she even had a chance to get her thoughts straight, they were once again in the car headed for the store. That expedition led her to the realization that she would have to get a backpack for carrying the baby. It was impossible to carry a baby in one's arms while pushing a cart, and Hilary didn't trust Lisa's ability to sit well enough to put her in the front of the cart. She knew it would have been smart to stop on the way home at some store where she could purchase both a crib and a backpack, but she didn't have the energy.

After a hastily assembled and more hastily consumed lunch she put the baby down on a blanket for a nap and removed Jason's shoes so he could lie on the unmade bed. Later, she promised herself, she would make it for him, but he could manage for now. While they slept, she got on the phone and began to call friends who might have equipment she could borrow. Her calls elicited a backpack, but no crib, and half a dozen incredulous responses to her tale of bringing her niece and nephew to live with her. Hilary began to think she had underestimated the trials awaiting her or overestimated her friends' abilities. People did it. She knew people did it, and if they could do it, she saw no reason why she couldn't.

But shopping for the crib was alarming. The salesman told her she could take the box home and put it together in no time, but his expression of confidence did not quite reach his twitching lips.

"Is it so difficult?" she asked, skeptical now.

"Not at all. Every home has the tools you'll need to do it."

She didn't have any tools at all, except for a hammer and a screwdriver, and she wasn't at all sure where they were. In the end she decided to get a playpen instead, one that didn't have to be assembled and could be wheeled from room to room. It wasn't the ideal solution, but it was about as large a decision as she was capable of making at the time.

At home she dug toys out of the duffel bag and urged the children to play with them, but Jason informed her that Lisa stank, and Hilary was forced to change her diapers . . . using paper ones. Then she had to clear out the desk drawers so she had some place to put their clothes, and the closet so she could hang their coats and dump their toys. Her ski stuff she carefully wrapped in plastic and shoved under her double bed. Heaven knew if she would be skiing this winter.

For dinner she made spaghetti for Jason and herself and fed Lisa something that looked appalling from a jar. She knew mothers who gave their children, even the babies, only fresh foods they fixed themselves, nothing processed. How in the hell did they find the time? she wondered. Of course, they may have been the mothers who didn't work outside the home, but considering how her day had gone, that seemed to make little difference. Somehow she didn't manage to get the children to bed until eight, and if there hadn't been so much to do, she would have followed them immediately.

Their exhaustion didn't prevent them from awaking at six the next morning, long before Hilary ordinarily crept from bed. At first, when she heard Jason's voice and Lisa's squealing, she couldn't remember where she was. For a full thirty seconds Hilary wondered if she was merely dreaming, and then Jason slammed through her door with four-year-old energy and flung himself on her bed.

"What's for breakfast? What are we going to do today? Is there a park? Are there boys here to play with?"

She had a headache before she got out of bed.

It was the unfamiliarity of the routine, she decided, that was so fatiguing. In Klamath Falls her mother had been the one to rise early and change the baby and feed her, letting Hilary sleep in her old room. Trying desperately to plan ahead, Hilary calculated the time it would take on an ordinary (no longer) work morning to feed and dress her niece and nephew before she could possibly depart. Since she didn't know where she would be taking them or if she would have to have someone come in, it was impossible to be accurate, but it was depressing nonetheless. If she dressed first, she was likely to find her work outfit spotted with cereal and milk or smudged with greasy fingerprints. On the other hand, if she waited until last to dress, the children were likely to get restless and into things they shouldn't. Hilary made a mental note to buy those cabinet locks she had heard of that prevented kids from getting at cleaning products and other harmful substances.

Jason's repeated request to go to the park was the only thing she could think of to do with them. She did know where the park was because she had often played tennis there, paying not the least attention to the attached play-ground. But it seemed to her she might learn, from talking to other mothers, about day care and what children did, so she made preparations equivalent to a short trip to Carmel and pushed off with them.

Why hadn't anyone told her that four-year-olds walked so slowly? Or that pushing a stroller with a squirming baby was hazardous at best? And where did mothers change their baby's diapers in the park?

Sunday morning did not turn out to be a good time to meet other women with children. Hilary pictured the women at home with their husbands, getting ready for a day trip—where? The local mental institution was the only possibility that occurred to her. How did they stand the noise? Once there were half a dozen kids playing on the slide and swings, the noise level was agonizing. She'd never noticed it when she played tennis.

From the women who eventually drifted into the playground area, she was unable to get more than the names of three or four high school girls who might be willing (but were probably on vacation) to sit in her apartment while she made other arrangements. She was strictly admonished that she must check out play group facilities and the women in charge, because . . . and there followed horror stories of what had happened to Betty's little girl or Jean's small son. Hilary's head was spinning by the time they headed back for her apartment.

The rest of the day she spent calling everyone she knew, finding that most leads dwindled into nothing. Infant care was the hardest to find, she was assured. Play groups were possible for Jason, but she would have to check them out during the week. All the high school girls had mysteriously disappeared. Hilary started to panic. She *had* to get to work on Monday. Not that she so desperately desired to see her office again, but she would not allow Mr. Marsh to be proved right. This was, after all, a new and pressing situation for her, but she still felt sure she would be able to handle it when everything had shaken down.

Remembering the office, and Harry, reminded her that he had a teenage daughter. His wife, Carol, answered the phone. "Thank God you're home." Hilary sighed.

"That bad, huh?" Carol laughed. "I take it you have your niece and nephew with you. Harry's been predicting doom ever since you left for Oregon."

"Don't tell him he's right," Hilary begged. "I have every intention of coping, once I've figured out precisely what it is I have to cope with. Carol, I *have* to find someone to sit for the kids for a few days. Would your daughter be interested? I'll pay anything!"

"Anything? Then you've come to the right place. Lucy loves making money. Hold on, I'll ask her."

Hilary kept her fingers crossed. The murmur of voices reached her over the phone, and the longer she waited, the more alarmed she became. Lucy would have plans. Lucy wouldn't want to take care of an infant. Lucy was allergic to paper diapers.

After five minutes it was Harry who came back on the line. "Have a good trip?" he asked cheerfully.

"About what I expected. Not quite like spending the week in Puerto Vallarta."

"No, of course not." He was more serious now. "Lucy can sit for you Monday and Tuesday, but Wednesday and Thursday she has plans. Maybe you can make other arrangements by Wednesday."

"I hope so."

"Right. Well, what we were discussing is how we'll get her there, and it seemed most logical for me to drop her off on the way to work."

"But that's out of your way."

Harry grunted something that sounded like "humph" and said, "Hilary, you're not going to be able to pick her up, and bus service is rotten between here and there. For two days I can be inconvenienced . . . but you'll probably have to meet Carol's flaky brother."

A chuckle escaped her. "When do you suppose I'd have time to meet him?" she retorted. "I'm a working woman with two children now, Harry. Honestly I appreciate your help."

"You're new at it," he commiserated. "In time you'll get the knack. Marsh called you about the objections to your series, right?"

"Yes, and I told him to let it stand. I said only what I thought was necessary."

"People don't always want to hear the harsh truths. May I suggest a little softer tone this week to cool things off?"

"Sure. Jason, don't pull on that cord! Sorry, Harry. Yes, I'll be gentle this week. I feel like mush right now. Look, the baby's crying, and I'm going to have to take care of her. Is there anything else we should settle?"

"Nope. I'll bring Lucy by at eight-fifteen so you'll have a chance to fill her in before you leave."

"Thanks. I owe you."

He laughed. "Wait till you see what Lucy charges! She's trying to outearn her mother."

Hilary didn't even ask. She didn't care. The thought of leaving the children with someone and getting out of the apartment was so appealing that if she hadn't had to discover the source of Lisa's distress, she would have given a war whoop of joy.

Chapter Seven

DESPITE RISING at the crack of dawn (or so it seemed to Hilary), she did not make it to work by nine. Lucy had appeared when her father said she would, but it had taken Hilary longer than expected to explain where things were in the apartment, where the park was, who her doctor was, and the children's new routine. She was only ten minutes late arriving at the *Reporter*, but she had been determined to be on time. If she hadn't had to change her pantyhose at the last minute because Jason had clung to her in parting . . .

Unfortunately Mr. Marsh was standing in the lobby, talking to the sports editor, when she got there. She saw him glance at her and then at the clock high on the wall. His smile was rueful but not unkind.

"Not bad, Ms. Campbell. I congratulate you."

"Good morning, Mr. Marsh."

And she passed quickly by him so he didn't have an opportunity to ask if she had finished her Tuesday column already. She hadn't had a chance even to *think* about it.

In her office Harry surveyed her. "You don't look frazzled yet. Is Lucy going to be all right with the kids?"

"Oh, yes. She's a competent girl."

"Takes after her mother. I've stacked your mail in your in box."

There was a healthy quantity of it. Hilary read each letter carefully before consigning it to one of her piles. The response to her series was slightly worse than Marsh had led her to believe, and after she had finished her reading, she drew in a deep breath. "I think the letter from T. Moore should go on the bulletin board," she announced.

"Well," Harry replied, turning from his typewriter, "it was a toss-up between that and Annie Gunn, though I'm opposed to pseudonyms on the bulletin board, as you know."

"Maybe her name really is Annie Gunn. She gave a return address."

"The address is the state mental hospital, Hilary."

"Ah, I hadn't noticed." Hilary grinned at him. "Considering the heavy response, we'll break precedent and put both of them up."

"Good idea. What are you going to do about permanent arrangements for the kids?"

Hilary drew a list from her briefcase and laid it on the desk in front of her. "First, I'm going to call all these places and see if they have any openings. Then I'm going to visit as many as I can during my lunch hour and more after work. I told Lucy I might not be home until six, but I'll drive her home then. Is that okay?"

"If it was okay with her, it's okay with me."

Harry watched her work her way through the list, an enigmatic expression on his face. Her shoulders slumped after every discouraging call—no openings, wrong age group, or she didn't like the sound of the person in charge.

"Tell you what," he suggested after a while, "why don't you go to the paper morgue and see if you can find information on child care switchboards, that kind of thing?"

"You'd think I started on a newspaper yesterday," she said, scolding herself. "Thanks, Harry. I guess I'm not thinking clearly yet."

From her files she took what she called her "escape" material. These were biographies of admirable women she'd met in the Bay Area, and she wrote them up from time to time as examples of what could be accomplished by women with perseverance, ability, and/or resolution. For a change of pace they did very nicely; for a column they provided her with an escape from the exhausting search for something new and interesting to say on women and their role in society. Hilary made two or three phone calls to confirm her information on the woman from Cupertino before adjourning to the paper's morgue for child card information. To her relief, it at least gave her some leads.

Squeezing lunch in wasn't possible, so she brought a sandwich back with her and ate it at her desk while she made notes on a legal-size yellow tablet about the woman she was profiling, tying her in with the women in her area. It was one of the columns to which Marsh never objected, and when she handed it to his secretary, early, she said, "I'll just wait. There shouldn't be any problem."

When Susan came out, she motioned to Hilary. "He wants to see you."

Shrugging, she entered to find Marsh standing at the window overlooking the civic center. His hands were clasped behind his back, and the sun glinted on the wavy black hair. He turned to smile at her.

"There's nothing wrong with the column. I just wanted to talk with you for a minute." He waved her to a chair but didn't seat himself. "I should apologize for being so hard on you about your niece and nephew. They are none of my concern, of course, and I'm sure will cause you enough problems without my added burden. I realize you feel you did what you had to do. However, I must insist that the quality of your work be maintained whatever the odds against. I think you did well to choose today's column, but you won't be able to resort to profiles regularly."

"I know. Twice a month is all I've ever allowed myself."

He nodded. "A good rule. Any more would look like padding. Now, Ms. Campbell, I wished to discuss the matter of your attending civic functions. With the children you would have a more difficult time—finding baby-sitters, et cetera—but I'd like to urge you to continue. The one night you came did take the brunt of questions from me, and I appreciated it. You handled yourself well. Again, I don't mean that to sound pompous. I'm sure on any social occasion you handle yourself well, but we're speaking with regard to the newspaper."

"Of course," she returned, eyes laughing.

"What I thought might aid you in your decision, in addition to the question of the raise itself, was the matter of an escort. As things stand, the newspaper would save money if we simply went together to these functions, and it would save you the necessity of finding someone each week." He put up a hand to ward off her protest. "I'm not saying you would have the least difficulty getting someone to go, but the extra effort, on top of your housemother duties, simply seems foolish. It's a work-related project and may as well be handled professionally. Frequently the occasions are . . . shall we say, somewhat boring? Probably your men friends wouldn't thank you for dragging them along anyhow. I offer the solution as a perfectly businesslike compromise," he said, standing in front of her and looking her directly in the eyes. "You needn't fear anything personal is involved in the arrangement."

"It never crossed my mind," Hilary assured him with mock gravity. "I don't know what to say, Mr. Marsh. Right now I'm completely immersed in finding day care for the children and in just getting used to having them around. Eventually, of course, I'll have to find evening sitters for them, but it seems too much to accomplish right now. Harry's daughter is sitting for them today and tomorrow, but she lives too far away to use in the evenings even if she was available." Hilary played with the catch on her bracelet. "And it doesn't seem right, after leaving them all day, to go out in the evenings as well."

"We're speaking of only one night a week, Ms. Campbell. You can't seriously expect to be with them every evening. It would be suicidal not to have some pleasurable break."

"But as you just mentioned," Hilary said, "these are not particularly pleasurable occasions. The first one was emotionally draining. With having to find a sitter on top of that . . ."

Marsh had seated himself on the corner of his desk, the deeply etched frown well settled on his face. Rather than annoyed, however, he looked puzzled, and then thoughtful, and finally almost complacent. "If I were to bring you a reliable sitter and take her home at the end of the evening . . ."

"Really, Mr. Marsh, I couldn't ask that of you!" Hilary protested. "I'm not trying to be obstinate and put barriers in the way. All I want to do is be realistic and recognize my limitations."

"I have a neighbor in Los Gatos, an older woman, who likes to make a little pin money by baby-sitting. Actually I think it's more than pin money. She's a widow and having a little difficulty surviving on her fixed income. I hadn't thought of her until this minute, but if she would be willing to take on the job, would you be willing to have her?"

Since the offer was phrased that way, Hilary found it difficult to refuse. "Yes, of course, on your recommendation, but the sitter is only part of the problem, Mr. Marsh."

"Why not give it a try? The raise is surely nothing to throw away until you've at least seen how it would work out."

"What night are we talking about?"

"Friday. A reception given by the mayor."

By Friday Hilary fully expected to be in charge of her life again. They would have had almost a whole week to settle in. She rose. "Okay. What time?"

"I'll bring the sitter at seven, so you can have a few minutes to meet her and she has a chance to meet the children before you leave."

Hilary agreed, with unspoken misgivings. It wouldn't hurt to go once, just to see if they all could handle it—the kids, she herself, and Mr. Marsh, whom she had difficulty picturing in a car with a neighbor turned baby-sitter, conversing no doubt on the proper way to burp a baby. Before she left the office, she almost asked him how old the woman was but decided that if he'd called her reliable, there was no use questioning his judgment. She was becoming as nervously protective as the proverbial mother hen.

The days between Monday and Friday were a blur. Finding Jason a play group near the civic center had not proved terribly difficult, though time-consuming. Finding day care for Lisa had proved virtually impossible. When Lucy's promised two days ran out, Hilary had begged a day's care from a woman who generally took older children and continued the search. By Thursday she was desperate enough to start calling farther from the civic center and from her own apartment building. In the end she wound up agreeing to a motherly woman who lived five miles out of Hilary's way.

By the time she turned in Friday's column she felt as though she needed hospital care for exhaustion. Her column was a hodgepodge of nervous energy, rather than a blend of ideas, but Marsh said nothing except "I'll bring Mrs. Rainer at seven."

Hilary had intended to plead illness but, facing him, could not think how to raise the matter without seeming incompetent. Instead, she asked, "Is it formal?"

"Black tie."

He was observing her closely, so she nodded casually. "Fine. I'll see you then."

Oh, sure, fine, she thought as she rode down in the elevator. She hadn't remembered to ask him sooner or to check the list sitting in her office. Did she have something in decent condition to wear? By the time she picked up the two children and got them home and fed, she would just about have time to dress, so she'd better. It had been so long since she'd required a really formal dress that she began mentally to review her wardrobe with a sinking feeling. The two she could remember were old and out of fashion. Why hadn't she thought of it sooner?

Her intention had been to put her desk and files in order, as she always did on Friday afternoon, but she changed her mind. "I'm leaving now," she told Harry.

"Can't wait to see the kids, huh?" he said teasingly.

Hilary was mentally calculating whether it was logistically possible to shop with Jason (but not Lisa) or whether it would be better to pick him up afterward, even though it would make her even later because she would have to retrace her route.

"Harry, I don't know why Carol puts up with you," she grumbled, stuffing papers in her briefcase and tossing the cover over her typewriter. "I also don't know why people have children and certainly why any woman in her right mind would work when she does. I think I'm going crazy."

"You'll get used to it. The reason they work is to get away from the kids."

"Well, I suppose I can understand *that*." Hilary looked conscience-stricken. "Look, I don't mean I don't love them, you know. They're adorable, and I treasure them, but I'm too young to be a mother."

"At thirty-two? You're almost too old," he informed her succinctly. "And don't kid yourself that it's easier if they're your own. It's never easy. Right when you think you have things running smoothly, everything collapses. I remember the time Lucy had measles when Carol had started law school—"

"Not now, Harry," Hilary begged. "If I don't get out of here in five minutes, I'm not going to be ready in time."

He sighed deeply. "And this is the woman who owes me. Won't even stay to hear a little reminiscence about my wife's sacrifice and my own hard times. There's no such thing as friendship anymore."

"Monday," she promised, slinging her purse straps over her shoulder. "I'll listen to anything you want to tell me on Monday." And she sprinted from the office to the sound of his snort.

In the end she took Jason with her, and she wished she hadn't. He was curious and explored the shop minutely, alarming her by touching everything in sight. With no time to concentrate, she took the first decent dress, which turned out to be monumentally expensive, something she hadn't noticed when the salesgirl handed it to her. Of course, she hadn't noticed, what with calling Jason to heel every two minutes! There was nothing wrong with the dress except its price, so she cast her eyes heavenward and signed the charge card receipt. She decided that salespeople knew precisely how to extort the highest price from

customers: If you brought a child, you were ripe for pluck-
ing. Hilary vowed to remember in future.

More than anything she wanted to soak in a hot bath for
an hour, but there was no time to do more than shower,
and even that was hardly restorative what with Jason running in and out of the bathroom, telling her that Lisa was
crying. She wasn't sure she'd given them enough to eat or
enough attention since they got home. Her eyes constantly flew to the clock on her bedside table as the minutes
whizzed past in a whirl of Jason's complaining that he
couldn't find his pajamas and Lisa gurgling (and drooling)
on the bed, where Hilary placed her to keep an eye on her.
Shoes. Surely she had shoes that would go with the lemon
chiffon. Why hadn't she thought of that?

The doorbell buzzed decidedly at 7:17, and she was
forced to answer in her stocking feet. Marsh introduced the
gray-haired woman with him as Mrs. Rainer. The smiling
Englishwoman promptly offered her hand and said, "Don't
you look lovely? And what is this sturdy lad's name?"

Hilary remembered only then that she had left Lisa on
the big bed and scurried off, announcing, "That's Jason,
Mrs. Rainer. I'll be right back." Lisa was still safely in the
middle of the mattress, and Hilary grabbed her up in relief. How could she have forgotten that the baby could roll
right off onto the floor? When she returned to the living
room where the others had seated themselves, she said to
Marsh, "If you'd like a glass of wine while I show Mrs.
Rainer where things are, please help yourself. The kitchen
is that way." And she handed the baby to the older woman's extended arms, saying, "This is Lisa. I was about to
get her ready for the night. Would you like to see their bedroom?"

Mrs. Rainer followed, but not Jason, who still hadn't discovered his pajamas. Hilary found them tucked under his
pillow, where she had told him they were, and placed them
on the bed. "I've been improvising, Mrs. Rainer. Perhaps
Mr. Marsh told you these are my sister's children and I've
just brought them back from Oregon with me for a while.
The desk top serves as an adequate changing table. Jason

likes the night-light on when he goes to bed, which should be soon. He likes to have a story read to him." And she continued with instructions and information as Mrs. Rainer efficiently diapered the baby. "I don't know how late we'll be."

"It doesn't matter, dear. I'm a night owl myself, and I brought a book to read. You just finish dressing. I'll see to the children."

With a moment to herself Hilary found a suitable pair of shoes, not perfect but acceptable. When she returned to the living room, she found Jason on Marsh's elegantly clad lap, explaining in a rush of carelessly articulated words what sorts of things they did in his play group. Marsh was drinking wine from the baby's plastic cup.

"I do have wineglasses," Hilary muttered.

"Jason offered me this, and I find drinking chablis from a Humpty Dumpty cup a unique experience." His wide mouth twisted ruefully at one side.

The kitchen was not completely tidied after their meal, Hilary suddenly remembered. She had stacked the dishes and pots but had not had time to wash them. Really she shouldn't have sent him in there at all. "Come on, Jason. It's time to get into your pajamas. Mrs. Rainer will read you a story before you go to bed."

"Can't find my pajamas," he insisted, climbing off Marsh.

"I found them." And she clasped his little hand to lead him off.

When she returned, Marsh was standing at the mantel, looking at some framed photographs resting there. "My parents and my sister and her husband with Jason. Lisa wasn't born then," said Hilary.

His gaze went to her feet. "Are you ready then?"

Hilary flushed, wishing she'd had time to get a beautiful pair of shoes. "Yes. I'll take your . . . cup."

Marsh finished the last sip and handed it to her, while Mrs. Rainer brought the children to say good night. All things considered, Hilary would rather have curled up in a ball on her bed and gone to sleep.

They made their way in silence to the car, where he said, "I take it you've finally found day care for the two of them."

"Yes. Different places. Anyone who would have taken Lisa couldn't really provide Jason with enough activity to keep him content. He's an active child." Her hand went unconsciously to her bruised ankle, where he had accidentally smacked her with a push toy while she was fixing dinner.

"My wife had children about their ages when I married her."

The sentence hung on the air between them. Hilary didn't know how to respond. Kitty had said he revealed little about himself, and certainly he had never so much as mentioned his favorite sport to Hilary previously. She couldn't remember his even speaking of his family, except for his cousin Tim, whom she'd met. Feebly she offered, "They're good ages." She didn't look at him, but from the corner of her eye she saw his head turn briefly toward her before he returned his eyes to the traffic.

"They were fourteen and eleven when we divorced. I don't see them very often. Alice points out that they aren't my children."

Hilary was indignant. "They must almost think of you as their father, living with them for ten years from such tender ages! Surely *they* must want to see you."

"Oh, they come to visit once in a while or call me. They're teenagers, though, with busy lives of their own."

"What about their own father? Do they see him?"

"Less frequently, I believe. They have Alice's third husband in the house now. It's difficult to divide time among three father figures."

"Stepfamilies are a mess," Hilary agreed. "I don't know how kids survive the ins and outs of stepfathers and stepsiblings and stepmothers. Little children wouldn't even be able to keep them straight."

"And older children don't want to." He glanced at her. "Is your sister divorced?"

"Not yet, but I'm sure she will be."

"How's she doing?"

"No better. My mother said the doctors haven't really been able to get through to her yet. It's a severe depression."

"Is she suicidal?"

The question shocked Hilary somehow. Surely no woman with two adorable children would be suicidal. "I don't know," she said, her voice so low he could barely hear it. "No one said she was. She doesn't do anything but lie in bed."

"I didn't mean to alarm you." His tone was apologetic. "There will be several people at the reception tonight who've expressed a particular interest in meeting you." And he proceeded to enumerate who they were and what they did, easily keeping the conversation out of personal channels while they drove.

The evening went well. This time Marsh didn't stay so close to her side, but he managed to appear when she was temporarily not speaking with anyone. There were several references to her recent series of columns, mostly not complimentary. She was able, without rancor, to explain her position and let the matter drop, feeling no need to defend herself. The only problem was that she couldn't remember ever having been so fatigued in her life. Hilary felt as though she'd played tennis all morning and run a few races in the afternoon. Occasionally her mind wandered into a sort of dreamy netherland where all she absorbed was the flow of colors in the crowd around her. Two men showed an interest in her to which she could not respond. She didn't feel capable of assessing their merits, and she couldn't imagine finding the time to date them.

As soon as the first guests showed signs of departure, Marsh appeared to ask, "Ready to leave?"

"Yes, if you are." She stifled a yawn.

In the car they scarcely spoke as Hilary put her head back against the headrest and allowed herself to drift off, if not into sleep, at least someplace where she wasn't capable of carrying on a conversation. When the car stopped in front of her building, she started, trying to grasp the fragment of thought which had been nagging at her.

"Do you know how much she charges?" Hilary mumbled as she released her seat belt.

Where Marsh's thoughts were, she couldn't guess, because he stared at her for a moment before saying, "Oh, Mrs. Rainer. Don't worry about it. I'll pay her."

Her head came up sharply. "No, you won't. That's my responsibility."

"I told you I'd provide you with a baby-sitter. That included the cost."

"That was not my understanding," she said carefully, but he had already gotten out of the car to come around to her door. She repeated herself.

"Then you misunderstood," he informed her, laughing. "You know you're too tired to argue, Ms. Campbell. When we made the arrangement for a raise, it didn't include baby-sitting. I'll charge it to the paper. You can't go around buying dresses like that and paying for babysitters, too."

Hilary sleepily stared at him. "How did you know it was new?"

"Jason told me about your shopping expedition. Sounded like a lot of fun."

"If he enjoyed it, that made one of us," she retorted. "I forgot to look at the price tag."

"It was worth it."

With a grudging "Thank you," she unlocked the front door of the building, and he followed her up to her apartment.

Mrs. Rainer, comfortably ensconced on the sectional sofa reading her book, looked up to ask, "Did you have a nice evening?"

"Fine, thanks," Hilary said. "How were the kids?"

"Perfect angels." Mrs. Rainer slipped the book in her purse, and Marsh helped her on with her coat.

Hilary briefly looked away. "Mr. Marsh will pay you. Thanks so much for coming."

"My pleasure," she said with a cheerful wave. "I'll be happy to do it anytime."

Before he followed her out the door, Marsh said, "Good night, Ms. Campbell. You'll want to get a good night's sleep."

Hilary sighed. "You probably don't remember how early babies wake up."

The thick black brows rose in sympathetic acknowledgment. "I'd forgotten, but it's the weekend at least."

"Yes, it's the weekend." Trips to the park, to the store, hours spent amusing the two children. Surely they deserved her concentrated attention when they had passed the whole week with substitute care. But where was the time for the other articles she had due? And when did she get some time entirely for herself? She forced a smile as he nodded good night.

Chapter Eight

SIX O'CLOCK. Hilary tried to focus her bleary eyes on the clock. Yes, it was just five after the hour. She could hear Jason tearing around the apartment, being an airplane, and Lisa's hungry cries from the other room.

"Hush," she called through the open doorway. "You'll wake up everyone in the building." Her night's sleep did not seem to have restored her one bit, but she climbed out of bed and tossed a robe over her naked body.

There was something unsettling, she decided drowsily, about changing a baby's dirty diaper before breakfast. It put her off her share of the pancakes entirely. She sat nursing a cup of coffee for an hour while she pushed a truck aimlessly back and forth for Jason, saying, "Yes, it could be a dump truck if you want it to be," and "No, don't push it so close to Lisa. It scares her."

For another hour she read to them, bouncing the baby on her lap. By eight she was feeling desperate and turned on the television. Hadn't she once written a column about the dangers of using television as a baby-sitter? What the hell had she been talking about? It gave her another whole hour's respite, practically, during which she tried to figure out where best to put her typewriter for her at-home work. The distracting noise made it difficult to concentrate.

By nine they were restless again, and she did her small-trip organization to get them started toward the park. Who needed the exercise of tennis when one could lift a six-month-old baby in and out of a stroller or a car seat or a playpen? Or stoop one's aching shoulders to hold the hand of a four-year-old for a distance of about six blocks?

The park was already teeming with older, rougher children, she noted as she sat down on a bench. And Jason couldn't refuse a challenge from any one of them to do something highly dangerous. Hilary swung Lisa gently in the baby swing, trying to keep an eye on the daring little boy at the same time. Eventually he fell and scraped his arm, but he was soon up and going again. Just until lunchtime, Hilary promised herself. Then she would take them home and give them lunch and put them down for a nap. Naturally Lisa fell asleep in the stroller going back and wasn't interested in a nap after lunch.

To make matters worse, her landlord arrived at her door during the afternoon, complaining about the children. "You know they're not allowed," he said sternly.

"They're just visiting me," Hilary assured him.

"For how long?"

"Well, I don't know exactly. Their mother, my sister, is in the hospital." He looked unimpressed, and Hilary said desperately, "I'm sure it won't be very long."

"Look, Miss Campbell, it's a rule. The other tenants have complained about the noise. I had two calls this morning. They can stay here for a week. No more."

There was no pleading mercy against his uncompromising brown eyes. And she *had* signed a lease which made the situation perfectly clear. What was it Harry had said about things' collapsing when they were finally running smoothly? Not that everything seemed all that smooth, but things had gotten a little less chaotic.

She said helplessly, "Their mother won't be ready to take them back for a month or two. If they go, I have to go."

"Then go," he growled. "I'll let you break your lease, but I won't have the kids around here. They're disturbing the other tenants."

"Mr. Cramer, you always have vacancies in the building. You can't afford to have me leave. I'll try to keep the kids quieter. They've never lived in an apartment building before."

His face set stubbornly. "And they're not going to live in mine now. One week, Miss Campbell." He stalked off down the hall without waiting for her protest.

Discouraged, Hilary returned to the living room, where Jason had overturned a stool and Lisa had somehow managed to spill apple juice all over the playpen mat. In silence Hilary took the plastic-coated mat to the kitchen and washed it down. Even if she could find an apartment building that took children, she would have to keep them quiet; there would be nowhere for them to play outside. They were used to living in a house with a yard, Jason especially. Renting a small house would be the best answer, but it would take time to find one, and it would be expensive. Damn it, she didn't want to move, and she certainly didn't have the time to look for a place and pack cartons and all the other things that came with moving.

Her neighbor Mary Lou dropped in out of curiosity. "I thought I'd seen you with a couple of kids," she said.

"They're my sister's. Cramer has just kicked me out. I have a week to move."

"Rotten deal." Mary Lou watch Jason build a tower with blocks. "How long are you going to have them?"

"I don't know. A couple of months. My sister's had a breakdown, and her husband won't take them."

Mary Lou made a face. "Just like a man. Wayne would be horrified if his wife saddled him with theirs."

"Is he here? Visiting?"

"No, but he spent most of the week. In case you're wondering, I told him there was no way I was going to marry him."

Hilary studied the other woman's face for any sign of distress. "How did he take that?"

"He said I could pay for my own apartment and walked out." A smile lurked at the back of her eyes.

"Just like that? So you won't be seeing him anymore?"

"Nope. I've met someone I like better." Mary Lou's mouth broke into a wide grin. "He's a dentist and he's divorced, but he has no intention of remarrying and watching all his hard-earned money shelled out in alimony and a property settlement again. I think we're made for each other."

Hilary found herself shaking her head in perplexed astonishment. "Doesn't it ever bother you that you use them, Mary Lou?"

"Not a bit. Men have been using women since the beginning of time. I'm just taking my own small share of revenge. You see, they were onto a good thing, Hilary. Besides, they're usually too naïve to realize what I'm doing. They think they're still in charge. I get a big kick out of it."

"I should have used you in my recent series of columns," Hilary said, disgruntled.

Mary Lou cocked her head. "I read them. A little out of your usual line, but useful. Women do make mistakes, though I wouldn't say I properly belonged in that series. I know what I'm doing; I've chosen to do it. Those women you wrote about didn't know how destructive they were being."

"Aren't you being destructive? What's going to happen to you when you reach old age?"

"I'm going to marry an older-aged millionaire, I hope. Then he's going to die off, and I'm going to live in luxury for the rest of my life."

Hilary groaned. Mary Lou was seventy-five percent serious. "And what if one day you fall in love with some poor slob who can't even support you?"

"I don't think there's much chance." She tossed her hair back with a quick movement of her head. "Love is the trap, Hilary, and I'm pretty sure I'm immune to it. Take Roger, for instance. I met him when I was thirty, and boy, did I ever fall for him. But I'd met a lot of men, and it didn't take me more than a month to figure him out. He was tall, dark, and handsome, any woman's dream, but he was also immature, neurotic, and a user. After Roger, I knew I had nothing to fear. They all have their faults, and you only have to keep them in mind to protect yourself from making the big mistake."

"Women have faults, too," Hilary reminded her.

"Sure they do. But I don't have to worry about women. I only have to worry about men." Mary Lou smiled. "Which reminds me. Who was the fellow who arrived last night with the old English lady? I saw them in the hall outside your door, and she was telling him about her grandchildren."

"My boss. She's a neighbor of his, and she baby-sat for the kids."

Mary Lou's brows rose. "Going out with the boss now? You surprise me."

"It was newspaper business. Part of my job has become attending civic functions."

"With him?" Mary Lou laughed delightedly. "Nice job you have. I'll be happy to fill in some night if you can't go."

"He's a bit pompous and talks like a dictionary sometimes. Marsh is the executive editor of the paper and plunders my columns at will."

"Just so long as he doesn't plunder you," Mary Lou quipped. Then she became thoughtful. "He has sensuous lips, you know. Not the thick, greedy kind. His are the thin, bowed type, and in combination with that determined chin . . ." She shuddered with pleasure.

"For God's sake, Mary Lou, he's my boss!" But Hilary was well aware of his lips.

"That's unfortunate. I'm sure you'd never mix business and pleasure. Too bad. I'm betting he'd be great in bed."

"Well, you aren't going to find out through me. These dates are strictly business. And he goes out with one of my friends," Hilary added to clinch the matter.

"Pity." Mary Lou tapped a finger against the sofa arm. "You could ask her."

"Don't be absurd! I'm not interested." Not exactly a lie and not exactly the truth. Hilary admitted, to herself, some curiosity, which she would, of course, do nothing to satisfy.

"Suit yourself. What are you going to do about an apartment?"

Elizabeth Neff Walker

"I think I'll try to rent a small house. It would be better for the kids."

Mary Lou rose to leave. "That's the way it gets to be when you have kids, you know. You're always thinking about what's best for them. Me, I'd rather be selfish."

Hilary hadn't looked at it quite that way before. Surely having children was, in its way, just as selfish as not. She was beginning to feel, though, that having children was a much more time-consuming, energy-draining, responsibility-laden project than she had ever conceived. In her current state of exhaustion she couldn't imagine being able to manage both career and children with the proper amount of attention they required. She reminded herself, sternly, that her own situation was not typical, but she remembered that many facets of it were not untypical either. A lot of divorced women out in the world were called upon to do precisely what she was doing, if not so suddenly. Maybe just as suddenly in some ways—thrust from their home-maker roles into the business world to survive. Hilary was too pressed at the time to give the matter further thought, but she promised herself that she would—one day.

No houses were listed for rent in her area in the Sunday paper. None, that was, that she thought she could afford. The Willow Glen area, in which she had lived since she came to San Jose, was one of the nicest residential parts of the city to her mind. Most of the houses were owner-occupied, with a scattering of rentals coming up infrequently. As she set the paper aside, she remembered the rental house that *Reporter* people passed back and forth among themselves. Damn! She didn't want to have to pester Harry again with her problems, but he was the only one she could think of who might know about its current status.

Reluctantly she dialed his number, cautioning Jason not to hit his sister with the pillow, even if it *was* soft. "Harry? It's Hilary again. I'm sorry to keep bothering you at home. I've been given a week's notice to get out of here with the kids."

98

"I wondered if that wouldn't be a problem," he said. "Do you want me to tell you that story about Lucy having the measles now?"

"I've always been led to believe that men who wrote columns on finance were warmhearted and generous," she retorted. "Tell me your story if you must, but I want to know who's in the *Reporter* rental right now. Any chance that it's empty?"

"The last I heard Davis was moving out and Norton wanted it, but that was a month ago. Hold on a minute. I'll get you Davis's number, and you can check with him." In a few minutes he returned to read her a number. "He'll probably know who has it, or if it's empty, even if he's moved out. Now, Hilary, I know this is going to disappoint you, but we're in the middle of brunch, and that measles story is going to have to wait until tomorrow."

"Thanks, Harry. Give my love to Carol."

"She doesn't need it," he grumbled. "She has mine. What more could a woman ask?"

"Not a thing. See you tomorrow."

Bill Davis was a reporter in the city room. The number Hilary called had been disconnected, but she was given a new number, which she scribbled down with Jason tugging at her arm. Before she could call the new number, she had to find him something to do and recover the toy Lisa had dropped and couldn't reach. The thought of moving with the two children started to take on nightmare proportions.

When she asked her question, Davis said, "Norton was supposed to move in this weekend, but something strange happened." He sounded puzzled. "The property managers talked him into a different place at the last minute. Gave him a sales pitch about how convenient this apartment was, bigger and less expensive than the house. Talked about the laundry facilities in the building and not having to take care of the yard. And Norton bought it. So the house is empty."

Hilary didn't care why the house was empty; she was simply relieved that it was. "Will you give me the property managers' name and number? Is anyone at their office on Sundays?"

Because she had to wait until Monday to get in touch with them, Hilary spent the night worrying that someone else had already taken the house. By the time she arrived at her office she was practically wringing her hands with anxiety, or so Harry informed her. The secretary at Lindgren-Hansen, the property managers, said that yes, it was available and started to ask her questions. The information that Hilary worked for the *Reporter* seemed to please her, but she was alarmed about the children. "I don't think any of our rentals take children," she said dubiously. "Hold on a moment."

The secretary sounded surprised when she returned. "Mr. Hansen says it's okay about the kids. You say you've seen the house. Did you want to go through it again?"

"I haven't seen it in a year or two. I suppose I should. And then, if I want to take it, can I come right back to your office and put a deposit on it?"

"Sure. Come get the key, and if you want it, you can leave a deposit and sign the lease when you return the key."

"How long is the lease?"

"Six months. But don't worry about that. We always have someone from the *Reporter* wanting it, and if you pass it on to someone qualified, there's no problem with breaking the lease."

The house was in need of paint, and it came furnished, but Hilary decided she needed to take it. Most of the furniture could be stored in the small attic if necessary, and she really didn't have enough furniture for the children. When the children left, she would have to decide whether to afford the extra $100 a month or pay the moving expense a second time and return to her old apartment building. She hated to give Mr. Cramer the satisfaction.

"I'll take it," she told the secretary as she handed over the key. "Can I move in Saturday?"

"Oh, sure, if you want."

"There is one thing." Hilary hated to look a gift horse in

the mouth, so to speak, but she had never seen as much laundry as the children made. "The house has a small service area, but no washer and dryer. Would the owner allow me to have laundry facilities installed? And maybe buy them from me, at a reasonable price, when I move out?"

The woman shrugged. "I'll have to find out. Mr. Hansen isn't in right now, and he always handles this one. May I call you later?"

"Of course. I'll take it in any case." Hilary drew out her checkbook and began to write out a check. "Does Mr. Hansen own the house?"

"No, we just manage it."

Hilary made it back to her office once again with sandwich in hand. Harry shook his head in disapproval. "You're going to wear yourself to the bone."

"I'm taking the house," she said, ignoring his remark. "Now all I have to do is spend the week packing and find movers on short notice. Surely any capable woman can handle that."

"I don't suppose you have time to meet Carol's brother," he said morosely. "She's invited him over for dinner Saturday."

"For your sake I'd do it, Harry, but that's the day I'll be moving. I'm sorry."

"Carol says this may be the best thing that ever happened to you."

Hilary chuckled. "What? Having the kids? Does she think it will convince me to settle down with a brood of my own?"

"No, she thinks it will open your eyes."

"She's right," Hilary admitted as she unwrapped the cold hot pastrami sandwich. "I couldn't comprehend the half of it before I actually had the experience. I'll listen a lot more carefully from now on."

"Terrific." He grinned his lopsided grin. "Marsh wants to see you."

"Oh, hell. He can wait until I finish my sandwich."

Probably because of what Mary Lou had said, Hilary was especially aware of Marsh's lips when she was admitted to his office. In repose they formed approximately the same uncompromising line as they did when he frowned. Only his smile tempted them up into something softer, more open and welcoming, and he wasn't smiling now. But then again, he wasn't frowning either.

"I've just had a call from Lindgren-Hansen," he said without preliminary, "and they tell me you want to install a washer and dryer and have me buy them when you move out."

Somehow he made it sound like an outrageous request. "You own the house?" she asked, staring.

"Yes. Is it still not common knowledge? Well, I'd rather it stayed that way if you don't mind. I find it hard to believe those bloodhounds in the newsroom weren't curious enough to check. It's been useful to have some accommodation for *Reporter* staff."

"But it's been floating around among us for years."

"I know." He looked up from a report on his desk that had momentarily distracted his attention. "It was the first house I bought. I lived there for a year and then turned it into a rental property when I moved to Los Gatos. Does it need paint, too?"

"Well, yes, now that you mention it. But that doesn't bother me. I won't have the time to paint it, and besides, Jason's hands aren't always terribly clean."

"I'll have it painted. When do you move in?"

"Saturday. Really, there's no need."

He frowned. "Ms. Campbell, I don't want to own slum property. I'm sure the inside can be done before Saturday, but the outside will have to be next week probably. Is white throughout satisfactory?"

"Yes." She tried not to look startled.

"About the washer and dryer, I suppose it would be wisest for me to invest in them myself. They'd make the place worth more."

"I can't pay much more," she said carefully.

His brows drew together. "You've agreed to take the rental at its current figure. I had no intention of upping it on you, Ms. Campbell. Unless you have some preference in laundry facilities, I'll have Lindgren-Hansen take care of it."

"That would be fine."

"What did you intend to do with the furniture that's there?"

"Some of it I'll use; some of it I'll store in the attic."

"All right. Any problems you have concerning the place you should direct to the managers. I don't ordinarily concern myself with it directly."

Hilary asked bluntly, "Why are you doing it now?"

"Because I don't want it to be an embarrassment to me." The thin line of his lips curved up ruefully. "Knowing your penchant for causes, I could imagine you tracking down the owner and telling him (or her, of course) that the place was in disreputable condition, unfit for human habitation. Did you have to move because of the children?"

"I was given a week's notice when my landlord found out. My building isn't even full. You would have thought he could tolerate them for a few months."

His shrug was indifferent. "Some people have a low tolerance for children. Remember, I'd prefer it not to be known that I own the house, Ms. Campbell. Did you bring your column with you?"

"No, it's not finished yet."

"Then I won't delay you further," he said dismissively as he rose.

"Thank you." Whether she was thanking him for his consideration or his paint or his washer and dryer, she didn't know. The all-purpose appreciation. His interest in the house was temporary, and his acknowledgment of her thanks was curt; he turned immediately back into his office after he'd escorted her to the door.

Chapter Nine

IN THE MIDST of packing that evening Hilary had a call from Jack. It was the first time she'd heard from him since he moved out, and her reaction to hearing his voice was a mixture of sadness and already achieved distance.

"How are you doing?" he asked.

"Okay, I guess. A lot has happened since I last talked with you. My sister's in the hospital with severe depression, and I have her two kids."

"In your apartment? Jason and Lisa, isn't it?"

"Yes." Hilary smiled to herself at his remembering their names. Lisa had been only a few weeks old when she and Jack visited Klamath Falls.

"I'm sorry to hear about your sister. Did Bill leave her or something?"

"Left her and intends to have nothing to do with her, or the kids for that matter." Hilary sighed and rubbed a weary hand across her face. "He does call them once a week, but he wouldn't keep them. And now my landlord has found out about them, and I have to move."

"Do you have a place to go? Can I help you find something?"

"It's nice of you to offer, but I'm taking the *Reporter* rental. Everything's arranged, and it will be better for the kids." She pulled herself up abruptly, realizing that they had talked only of her. "Jack, did you get the promotion?"

There was a slight pause before he answered, "Yes, but only after someone else turned it down."

Considering the circumstances, Hilary didn't know whether to congratulate him or not. She knew it must have been a blow to his already flagging self-esteem. "Well, I'm glad you have it now. You know you deserve it, and the extra money will come in handy."

"That reminds me," he said hurriedly. "I never found out what I owed on the phone and utilities. If you have a figure handy, I'll send you a check."

Hilary bit her lip. "That's not necessary, Jack. I paid the bills and didn't keep a record. You don't owe me anything."

The phrase seemed to stand out, though she hadn't emphasized it in any way. He cleared his throat. "What happened about the promotion was that they offered it to Mary Lane, but she didn't want the extra responsibility and hours, what with her little boy and all. She told them she had only so much psychic energy, and it was balanced precariously enough with the job she had. So they gave it to me."

A perpetual problem for working mothers, Hilary thought unhappily. She didn't blame Mary Lane for not taking the promotion, though a few short weeks before she might not have understood. She was pleased that management at Jack's firm had offered the position to a woman, yet she knew it must have made Jack even less satisfied with his own position on women's equality. All well and good to espouse it in the abstract, but when it came to not getting an expected promotion, to competing directly with a talented woman . . . "Do you like the different work, Jack?"

"Oh, sure. It means slightly longer hours and more demands, but it's what I wanted, I guess. It doesn't feel quite as good as I thought it would." A trace of bitterness lingered in his voice.

"Do you blame the initial disappointment on me?"

"Sometimes. I know it's not fair, Hilary, but you asked. I know I was better than Mary Lane at my old job. But they may have thought she'd be better in this new position than

I am. I don't know. Part of me is glad they offered it to a woman; the other part is hurt. It should have been mine from the first. Offering it to her took away some of its shine."

"I can understand that. I'm sorry, Jack. Put it behind you. You have the job now, and you'll make them realize nobody was better suited for it." If she hadn't liked him so well, she would have been tempted to add, "Be grateful Mary didn't want it."

His laugh was not particularly joyful. "They'd better. I'm putting in some extra time to make sure I stay on top of it."

"How's your new apartment?"

"Sufficient. Would you like me to help you move?"

Hilary wasn't sure whether to read more into his question than its surface meaning, but either way she declined. "No, thanks. I have movers coming." Lisa had begun to cry in the bedroom. "I have to take care of the baby, Jack. Thanks for calling. I'm glad you got the promotion."

"Well, I hope things settle down for you and your sister is better soon." He hesitated as though he wanted to say more but only added, "Take care of yourself, Hilary."

"You, too."

The next night she was unable to pack at all because it was her weekly excursion with Marsh, to a fund-raising dinner-dance this time. It had not been his first choice on the list for her attendance, but that had been Friday night, and she simply couldn't manage it with the move on Saturday. When she asked which other night he preferred, he'd picked the charity function. Once again he brought Mrs. Rainer to sit with the children, and she looked around at the packing boxes with interest. "You're moving, Miss Campbell?"

"Yes, on Saturday. Not far away, but a better place for Jason and Lisa." She had driven past that morning on her way to work and seen a painter's truck outside the house, but didn't mention it to Marsh. "I'm afraid the apartment is a bit of a mess."

"Don't worry about that," Mrs. Rainer protested. "I wondered if I might help by filling some of the boxes for you."

"Oh, no. Please don't." Hilary had come home the first time Mrs. Rainer sat to find that the dishes she'd left in the kitchen had been washed and put away, and it had made her feel guilty. "Just put the kids to bed, and enjoy your book. And if we're late, I hope you'll feel free to lie down on my bed."

"We'll probably be late," Marsh interjected.

Hilary gazed helplessly at the stacks of boxes. When she had so much packing to do, she really couldn't afford to waste a whole evening. The only really good news she'd received in weeks was an extension on her article for the magazine, which she hadn't even started yet.

"Why are you frowning?" Marsh asked as they walked down the stairs.

"Was I? Oh, I was just thinking about how much I have to do in the next few weeks. And I was wondering if I could use something a friend told me last night as a possible column."

"What did she tell you?"

"He. He told me that he'd lost out on getting a promotion to a woman at his office, and then she wouldn't take it because of her responsibilities at home. So he got it in the end. The situation is something I'd like to comment on, but I'm afraid Jack would recognize himself."

"Does that matter?" he asked as he opened the car door.

"Definitely. I try not to involve my friends in my column. Hmm." Without paying any attention, she slid onto the seat and gave a muffled squeal as something crunched beneath her. Shifting to see what it was, she yelped and glared up at him. "You left your sunglasses on the seat." Trying to avoid jabbing herself on the broken glass, she climbed stiffly back out of the car.

"Damn. I tossed them through the window after I helped Mrs. Rainer out." Instead of looking apologetic, however, he began to laugh when she glowered indignantly at him and brushed at the back of her skirt. The glasses had shattered under her, leaving slivers in the rough texture of her dress. "Hold still," he insisted, turning her around. "You're only managing to work them into the material. Let me."

"Don't bother!" Hilary begged. "I'll go in and change my dress. It's probably ruined anyhow."

"No, it's not, but it will be if you don't stop playing with them."

"I'm not playing with them! I'm trying to get them out."

"And doing a rotten job of it." Without waiting for her permission, he began to pick carefully at the slivers he could see, but on the dark material it was impossible to tell if he had them all and he ran his hand gently over her bottom to see if he could feel any others.

"For God's sake, Mr. Marsh!"

As she swung to face him, his eyes twinkled wickedly. "I promise you it was necessary, Ms. Campbell. They're hard to see on the dark background. You don't want to sit down and jab one into yourself, do you?"

Having no desire to act like an outraged virgin, Hilary grumbled, "I could have done it myself, but thank you . . . I suppose. I'll try to restrain myself from writing a column about sexual harassment in the line of duty."

"Please do." He continued to smile at her.

"You're making me feel ridiculous." What he was making her feel was slightly breathless, but she wasn't going to admit *that*.

"Forgive me." Marsh briefly touched her shoulder and then turned to the car, where he carefully removed the frames and any pieces of glass he could see.

Then, since she was watching him, he ran his hand over the car's seat, as he had hers, and muttered an oath. Hilary pressed her lips together to keep from laughing when he stood up with a bleeding finger. Her voice gurgled as she asked, "Shall I go in and get you a Band-Aid?"

"Don't bother." He sucked on the bleeding finger and shook his head. "Are we even now?"

"I think so. I feel much better."

"I'll bet you do." From the glove compartment he took a

large, flat travel guide, which he placed on the seat. "Better sit on that in case. I'll check the seat for more glass when I get home."

"You'll probably forget, and poor Kitty will be impaled the next time she gets in the car with you."

Marsh studied her thoughtfully for a moment but said nothing. His silence made Hilary feel slightly foolish once again, but she strove to ignore the discomfort and continued the interrupted conversation. "What I'll do about what Jack told me, I think, is make a note of it for my idea file and use it a few months from now. By then it won't be so immediate to him, and if I change the circumstances, I think I can get away with it."

"Do you have a large idea file?"

"I used to think it was." She stared out the window as the car pulled away from the curb. "I've been steadily depleting it recently."

"Do you mean you aren't getting any new ideas?"

Suddenly alert to his probing questions, Hilary answered more sharply than she meant to. "Of course I get new ideas. Sometimes I need to let them simmer for a while, though, in order to make a column of them. I'm still working on the best way to make use of something I heard at the reception last Friday."

"What was that?"

"I overheard two men talking. Apparently one's wife had just gone out and got a job. He said something like 'It's just for fun, you know. She doesn't make enough to mention. Probably just puts us in a higher bracket and every cent of it goes for taxes.' It made me madder than hell."

"Why?"

Hilary glared at him. "If you don't understand, you'll have to wait for my column to find out."

"I think it's wonderful how you always remember I'm your employer and never snap at me. You'd be surprised how many of my employees forget themselves."

Unchastened, she said, "I have no patience with stupid questions from intelligent people."

"Flattery will get you nowhere, Ms. Campbell. I'm

afraid the burden of your niece and nephew is making you a bit short-tempered. Have you heard of any improvement in your sister?"

"She's slightly less lethargic," my mother said. The doctors can get her to talk once in a while. Nothing much. It's going to take time." She glanced at him surreptitiously. "Does it matter how long I'm in the house?"

"Of course not, as long as you pay the rent."

"That won't be any problem. My brother-in-law sent a child support payment today. In fact, if you think I should pay a little additional, for the washer and dryer, I'm sure I can manage now."

"Were you in financial difficulty?"

"Not at all," she said stiffly. "I have myself on a budget so I can make investments through my father, and I save some in addition each month. The unusual expenses of flying to Oregon and getting things for the children and now the movers and the extra expense of the house rental simply made it a little tight this month. I'll rearrange my budget and have no problem at all."

"Don't forget you'll be seeing extra from your raise."

She mimicked her story of a few minutes previously by saying, "It will probably just put me in a higher bracket and all go for taxes. Maybe I shouldn't have taken it after all. Money made by women is, when all is said and done, not quite the same as money made by men, you know. It's frivolous, unearned. Women don't actually work, you see; it's just for fun with them. And of course, those who stay at home don't work at all."

Marsh was pulling into the parking lot and was momentarily distracted by taking his ticket. When he could pay attention to her again, he said, "Do these things eat at you all the time, Ms. Campbell? Are you forever on the lookout for some disparagement of women? Does every word have an innuendo?"

"It's my job to look for them, Mr. Marsh."

"But they affect you personally," he insisted. "An attack on any woman is an attack on you."

"If you mean I feel strongly about the issue, you're right.

The attitudes that denigrate one woman today could deny me my rights tomorrow. To you, to many men, it may be an irrelevancy that half of our species doesn't have equality with the other half. That's because you belong to the privileged half."

"Would you have preferred to be a man?" His gaze took in the luminous eyes, the soft fall of her shining hair, the light sheen of her lips, not with unkindness, but with curiosity.

"No, I like being a woman, but I prefer not being at a disadvantage. Look, I know it's difficult for men to understand what women want, especially when not all women want the same things. Some like the way things have always been, mostly because they haven't been faced with the difficult problem of supporting themselves. Occasionally I think that the desire to be protected, the need to nurture are inherent in women, that they go way back to our very beginnings. But that's not the way the world is today, and the most (or the least) we can ask for is equality. Fairness is how I think of it. That's what every group which is kept in an inferior position wants. It seems so little to ask, and it's so hard to get."

"But you personally don't seem to have been adversely affected by being a woman," he said, frowning. "How did you become so vocal for women's rights?"

Hilary shrugged. "I don't know. Just from seeing other women struggle, I suppose. Whatever diminishes my fellow woman diminishes me—or however it goes. I've been lucky. Most women find they have to do *better* than men, sometimes a whole lot better, to get ahead or sometimes just to stand still. I don't like the unfairness of it. Every instance offends my sense of rightness."

He came around to open the door for her. "Why do you let me do this?" he asked, puzzled.

"Because," she said, and laughed, "it would offend your dignity if I didn't. We both know I'm capable of opening a car door. You do it as a courtesy, and I let you as a courtesy. I try not to trample on men's feelings, Mr. Marsh, just as I expect them not to trample on mine."

They had started to walk toward the hotel when he surprised her by asking, "Would you mind if I call you Hilary? It's a little awkward addressing you as Ms. Campbell at these things."

"No, of course, I wouldn't mind." She smiled up at him. "Do I get to call you Jonathan?"

"Jon. No one but my mother calls me Jonathan, and then only when she's annoyed with me."

His hand came to her elbow to guide her through the crowded lobby. Some of the faces were becoming familiar to her now, and she spoke to half a dozen people as they made their way to the restaurant. The charity dinner-dance was an annual occasion, more lighthearted than one would have expected for so dire a disease, Hilary thought. But the object was to have a good time, once the contribution had been wrung from one's pocket.

The food was good, and the conversation at their table interesting. When the dancing started, however, she found that each of her partners was bent on discussing her column from his particular viewpoint. She tried to store up some of the more intriguing statements for future columns and wished she were able to carry a notebook in her hands as she danced. Only with Marsh did she have a respite, and she took advantage of it by saying very little. One of their dances together was a slow one, and she liked the way he held her, surely but not intimately. She had been forced with two other men to protest the enforced proximity, since they danced as though in the privacy of a bedroom, about to fall upon a bed with her. One of them was even half-ready. Hilary refused his invitation for a tryst.

Marsh hummed while he danced, and Hilary could feel the light breath on her hair. By the tightening of an arm he warned her of his intention to move her out of the way of another couple or to execute some more intricate dance step. It was the first time in ages that she'd danced to slow music. She'd forgotten how much fun it was. She also forgot, for the span of a few minutes, whom it was she was dancing with. Not in the sense that she didn't remember it was Jonathan Marsh, but she felt so comfortable, almost enchanted in his arms, that for a short span she was in another place, another time, in the loving embrace of a man with whom she had a relationship. There weren't all that many moments she could remember like this, where she gave herself up to the magic and forgot to question, to probe, to wonder if this would be another disappointment. The stirrings of sexual attraction coursed through her, but pleasantly, without urgency. In her trance there seemed no reason they shouldn't be satisfied later with this man who made her feel so warm and feminine, who shut off the flow of angry insights and made her feel at peace.

Unconsciously she had pressed a little closer to him, or he had drawn her more tightly within his arms, because when the music ended, she found herself awakening almost with a start to find herself carefully released from the presence of his body, tingling with the remembered, shadowy contact of his length. His eyes met hers, silently questioning, as she, embarrassed by her folly, relinquished all contact and moved away a step.

In a stifled voice she said, "You must have thought I'd fallen asleep, Mr. Marsh."

He didn't correct the use of his name. "Would you like to leave, Hilary?"

"No! Thank you, I'm fine. It was just having a break from being questioned about the column, you know. I'm always a little astonished people are so interested." One of the men who had proved a nuisance earlier was approaching her, and she forced a smile. "I'd like to avoid this one, though. Could we get a glass of wine?"

"Of course." He took her elbow and guided her toward the bar, but before they reached it, they were intercepted by an acquaintance of his. They stopped to talk, and Hilary, instead of having the wine, which would have been her third glass anyhow, soon found herself on the dance floor with Tony Parker. This was a fast song, and she felt some release from her tensions in the energetic movement. Her partner was amusing, kept her laughing while they danced, and insisted on another when the first ended. Before she left him, he asked her out, and she was tempted to accept, if only to shake the grip of that unnerving dance with Marsh. Regretfully she declined, suggesting with a laugh that if he were still interested in a few months, he might give her a call. "I've got my sister's kids living with me, and life looks too full and too complicated right now to add even one new element."

"Lunch?" he suggested. "You have to eat lunch."

Again she was tempted, but she shook her head. "I'd better not. But thank you."

As Hilary and Marsh walked to his car, he talked about the country's economic situation, the composition of the University of California regents, and a city proposal on sewage. Nothing could have been less romantic, yet Hilary felt the air between them charged with sexual tension. When his hand accidentally brushed hers or went to her waist to urge her around a car in the parking lot, she found it impossible to concentrate on what he was saying. His face was impassive, and she thought: It's only me. And it's only because I've been so tired recently and missing the physical contact with Jack.

"Home?" he asked when they were in the car.

Hilary almost said, "Where else?" but realized it might sound leading. "Yes, please."

The night was clear and reasonably warm. She opened her window a fraction so the air would help clear her head, cool her body, do whatever air was supposed to do. A feeling of suffocation, or perhaps panic, had seized her, and she ran her fingers nervously along the seat belt where it crossed her chest. The absurd thought that she might faint angered her, helping clear some of the confusion from her mind.

"Do they make a substantial amount from evenings like this?" she asked into the car's heavy silence.

"I believe so. The dinner-dance has a reputation for being an enjoyable time, and they can ask a high contribution."

"It was nice," she said, knowing her words to be inadequate.

"Yes."

The silence grew between them. Hilary's throat ached with the need to say something, but she couldn't think of a suitably impersonal topic. March concentrated on his driving. After a while Hilary closed her eyes, pretending she was dozing. Even if he knew she wasn't, it released her from the need to say something. Her senses were alive to the sounds of the car as it sped through the streets, to the smell of her own perfume, but mostly, keenly, to his presence inches from her. Her fingers could still sense his touch from that damned dance. And not just her fingers—her whole body felt alive to the static between them. She reminded herself that it wasn't between them, that it emanated from her alone. Nothing had changed because of one stupid dance when she allowed her mind to drift off into a fairy tale of delight. He was still her boss, as impersonal as ever, and she would be grateful in the morning that the situation remained as it had been.

With her eyes closed, she felt rather than saw the car come to a halt. His hand gently grasped her shoulder. "Hilary? We're home."

We're home. What a nice sound it had, she thought foolishly. Hilary opened her eyes and said, "Yes. I'm not asleep."

Marsh's eyes were on her face, questioning again. His narrow lips were slightly parted, as though he meant to speak, but he said nothing. Hilary could almost feel their pressure against her mouth. If she gave him the slightest sign, she knew he would kiss her, and if he kissed her, she wouldn't be satisfied to walk up the stairs and into her apartment, where Mrs. Rainer awaited them. Where would they go? All the way to Los Gatos? To the empty rental house? Did he have a key? There was a double bed there, perhaps the one he himself had used when he lived there so many years ago. Would it be just the once? Would that get it out of her system?

And then she thought of their working relationship and of Kitty, her friend. She hadn't talked to Kitty recently, but things might have progressed between her and Marsh. Kitty might be more involved than she let on. And even if she wasn't, there was the newspaper. One night's sexual pleasure was likely to distort her whole career. She needed distance between herself and Marsh in order to write the kinds of columns she wanted to write. They both were sexually sophisticated people, and one encounter might have passed without any recriminations were it not for their working together, were he not her boss and she a controversial writer.

Their attitudes toward each other would alter, maybe only fractionally, but that would be enough to set her off-balance, to give, if he chose to take it, an edge to him, a subtle weapon. Hilary knew that their attitudes toward a sexual liaison were all-important and that she didn't know him well enough to judge his response. For herself, it was a choice she could make and accept, not feeling used or user. But for him? It was too risky.

"Don't forget about the glass on the seat," she said.

Not by a flicker of his eyes or a twitch of any facial muscle did he acknowledge that a decision had been pondered and made. "I won't. I'll leave the book on the seat to remind myself."

When they let themselves into her apartment after a silent walk up the stairs, they found Mrs. Rainer busily packing books into boxes. "I couldn't resist," she admitted. "I hope you don't mind."

"No, of course not," Hilary said, "but you shouldn't have bothered."

"It was no bother, dear. You have the most interesting library."

Hilary, relieved for a moment, grinned at Marsh. "She means my feminist collection, I'll bet. Some of them have fascinating titles."

"It's a fascinating subject." He helped Mrs. Rainer on with her coat. At the door he said, "I'll see you tomorrow, Hilary."

"Yes, I think I'll write the column about a husband's opinion of his wife's frivolous job. You'll want to read it."

"I'm sure I will, and in any case, I'll have to, won't I?" There was an edge to his voice, but it didn't seem directed at her somehow. He touched her arm briefly, as though he needed the minimal contact. "Sleep well."

"You, too." For a second their eyes met and acknowledged that they might have slept together, but for the circumstances. Hilary closed and locked the door. It was the right decision. They both knew it, and they both, at least momentarily, regretted it.

Chapter Ten

FOR HILARY the next few weeks turned out to be something like a bad dream. The move was totally exhausting, and it seemed to have an adverse effect on the children. Jason started to have nightmares despite the care Hilary lavished on him. Lisa was teething, restless, and cranky. Their father called when he was supposed to, but Jason moped afterward. His continual questions about his mother, unanswerable questions, left Hilary's nerves tightened. There started to be discouraging reports about his behavior in the day care play group: he was becoming aggressive with the other children, disobedient and surly with the woman in charge.

At home he was more withdrawn and treated his sister with less consideration than before. Hilary romped with him in the yard each evening to exhaust him before bedtime. His appetite was almost as poor as his teething sister's. Hilary's evenings were absorbed by the attempts to entertain him and the baby. The magazine article was almost due, and she hadn't had the time to work on it. Eventually, in despair, she took it to the office, trying to sandwich it in with the work on her columns.

Marsh had become coolly impersonal both in his office and on their weekly dates. Because she could not bring herself to call him Jon, he reverted to the use of Ms. Campbell on most occasions, though once she was startled into attention on her daily trek to his floor when he snapped, "Hilary, you've got to pull yourself together! This is the third column in a row that has shown unmistakable signs of being written in haste, in addition to being dangerously close to deadline." He scribbled all over her copy, making changes in every paragraph—carelessly used words, sloppy grammar, questionable "facts." Then he insisted that she sit there and read it while he watched her.

"Are my changes acceptable?" he asked when she finished.

"Yes, they're fine."

"Do you understand why I think them necessary?"

She swallowed before answering, "Yes. I'll try to be more careful in future." When she made a move to rise, he waved her back into her chair.

"Is there something the matter?" he demanded. "Your views and mine don't always coincide, but I've never seen you come up with such weak ideas or word them so poorly."

Despite the fact that she knew he was right, she felt mutinous, trapped. She was not going to spill out all her worries about the children, dared not tell him about the magazine article. Pouring her energies into the article, she had little reserve, after her concern for her niece and nephew, to put into the columns. She knew it was unfair of her to pay so little attention to her major employment, but she had promised the article, and she *had* to deliver it. With the baby waking half a dozen times in the night, Hilary was getting no unbroken sleep. Every spare minute seemed destined to wash clothes or dishes, make meals, shop, tidy the house, dress or undress the children, change diapers—all the little domestic chores she had always thought so simple and unchallenging. They remained unchallenging in their repetitiousness; their simplicity was more than made up for by the energy and time they required.

"No, there's nothing the matter," she told him now, her face set stonily. "I haven't given my recent columns the proper concentration. I'll do better Monday."

But Monday the baby was sick. Lisa threw up the breakfast Hilary had painstakingly fed her just before it was time to take the children to their day care facilities. Hilary paced around the living room of the small house, trying to decide what to do. Why hadn't she made some contingency plan for a sick child? Harry's daughter was back in school and wouldn't be able to come. Hilary didn't know how to reach Mrs. Rainer, and she didn't think she dared take the baby in the car while she took Jason to his group. Lisa lay listless in her playpen, pale and miserable.

Cursing herself for being unable to make an intelligent decision, she picked up the phone and called in sick. She'd never done it before, and it made her *feel* almost physically sick. Then she called a friend to get the name of a pediatrician. Incredible that she hadn't done that before, merely leaving the name of her own doctor for the sitters. This doctor didn't make house calls and insisted that she bring the baby to his office. So in the end she was forced to put Lisa in the car seat with a worried Jason sitting next to her, and drive across town to his office.

His diagnosis was flu, and he warned her that Jason was likely to come down with it as well. Hilary just stared at him, trying to absorb his instructions, trying to figure out what was happening to her well-ordered life. On the way home she stopped to pick up the prescription he'd given her, and when she walked into the house, the phone was ringing.

If she'd thought for a moment, she probably wouldn't have answered it, but she was beyond reasonable thought. "Hello?"

"Where the hell have you been? I thought you were supposed to be sick." Marsh didn't bother with a greeting.

"I've been to the doctor," she answered truthfully.

"And what's the matter with you?"

"It's Lisa who's sick. She has the flu, and the doctor said Jason would probably get it."

"Hilary," he said, with an almost palpable attempt to be reasonable, "you're a columnist on the *South Bay Reporter*. When you're sick or call in sick, you have the responsibility of speaking to someone who can arrange for your job to be done. You're not like a reporter. A column is expected of you five days a week. You didn't even ask to speak to Harry, for God's sake. He might have handled the matter for you."

"I didn't think," she mumbled.

"You haven't been thinking for weeks, and I'm getting a little tired of it," His tone had hardened imperceptibly, but he hadn't raised his voice. "Here's what we're going to do. You're going to take the next two weeks off and straighten out your life. I would suggest that you return the children to their father or make some arrangement for them in Klamath Falls. While you're away, I'll have Lois Greer substitute on the column. Marcy tells me she's capable of it, a good solid writer, if without your flair."

"But—"

"Hilary, I'm not giving you any choice in the matter. Your work has deteriorated dangerously. Take the two weeks to pull yourself together. You have a career, and it's not meshing well with your expedition into motherhood. The last good column you turned in was the one we discussed the night of the dinner-dance." There was a pause before he continued. "Since then they've barely been adequate, and not even that the last few days."

She wanted to argue with him, but she had no grounds. Lisa was in her arms, and Jason at her feet, both restless and unhappy. Apparently she wasn't managing any of her jobs very well. With a sinking heart she said, "Very well, Mr. Marsh. I'll take two weeks off. I have only a week's vacation left, so one of them will have to be without pay. When I come back to work, I'm sure I'll have everything under control."

"I hope so." As though he thought that sounded too harsh, he added, "And I'm sure you will. Do you want to speak with Harry, have him bring you anything from your office?"

"I'll call him later. I have to get the baby to bed. Goodbye."

When she hung up, she stood staring at the phone for a moment, digesting what had just happened. It wasn't only the enforced vacation. Her job was threatened. After she had put Lisa to bed and sat Jason down with a picture book, she called their day care groups and said they wouldn't be there for two weeks. It seemed an eternity, yet not long enough to straighten out her complicated life. At least she could finish the magazine article. That was the sole benefit she could see in the whole setup. Big deal. It was probably as badly written as the columns, and she'd have to start all over again.

Mrs. Campbell answered when Hilary called briefly to explain her situation, the nightmares, the flu. "Bring them home," she urged, "as soon as Lisa's well enough to travel. They've been shuffled around too much and need to see their house and their father, even us. If Janet's well enough during the two weeks, we'll see if she can come home to visit them for a few hours. I'll see what the doctor says, and I'll look into foster care again, Hilary."

"I was coping all right until the nightmares and the teething," Hilary insisted. "If we can't work anything out, I can bring them back down here with me. I'll just have to be more organized, plan ahead for emergencies like this. Tell Bill I want to stay in their house with them. He can stay or leave as he pleases, but he'd better plan to spend a lot of time with them. I'm exhausted, Mom, and I'm not altogether sure I'm not coming down with the flu, too."

"When you're run-down, you're more susceptible," her mother agreed. "Let me know when you're coming, and we'll meet you at the airport."

In the end Hilary didn't even wait for Lisa to be better, fearing that by the time she was, Jason would be down with the bug. Instead, she called in a favor due her, having a friend drive her to the San Francisco airport that afternoon so she could take the evening flight to Klamath Falls. She didn't want to be in San Jose and read the substitute column; she didn't want any calls from the paper, especially from Marsh; she didn't want to have to cope with the children by herself.

Across the aisle from her on the plane was a man who vaguely reminded her of Jack—not so shaggy and not so cuddly-looking, but with the same aura of patient consideration. Jason started talking with him first, but soon Hilary found herself drawn into the conversation. George Meadows was a businessman from Klamath Falls who owned a sporting goods store. The area was ripe with outdoor activities, and it was apparently a thriving concern, though he didn't actually say so. Hilary admitted to writing a column in the *South Bay Reporter*, which impressed him.

"Local girl makes good, eh?" he said teasingly. "What does your husband do?"

"I'm not married." At his surprised look she laughed. "These are my sister's children. I've been taking care of them." And slowly he managed, through his evident interest, to get the whole story from her—right down to her problems on the paper.

"What you need," he told her, "is a good rest and some country air. Have your mother take care of the kids tomorrow, and I'll drive you up to Crater Lake."

"I think I may be coming down with the flu," she said uncertainly. The thought of a whole day spent dawdling almost made her mind boggle.

"Nonsense. All you need is a break."

Hilary liked his optimism. She liked his concern. "Let me see what I can manage, will you? If not tomorrow . . ."

"Any day," he prompted. "How can I reach you?" He carefully took down her sister's, and her parents', phone numbers. "I know your father."

"Do you?" Klamath Falls was not, after all, very large. "How?"

"He comes into the store, and we don't live far apart. I live on Eldorado."

"You're not married?"

"Would I ask you out if I were?"

Hilary laughed. "If you were from the Bay Area, you might. But I take it you aren't. Divorced?"

"Never married. I suppose that would make me suspect in the Bay Area." He grinned at her.

"Probably."

"How long will you be here?"

"Two weeks."

"Good. That will give us lots of time to do things together."

The insinuation was not sexual, yet it wasn't asexual either. He was smiling, friendly, and casually rather than aggressively masculine. Hilary returned his smile. "I'll have to check out your references."

"Are your parents meeting you? Or can I take you into town?"

"They're meeting me."

Before they parted at the airport, George asked again if he could call Hilary the next day. "Of course," she said. "If my parents tell me you're depraved, I can always hang up."

Mr. and Mrs. Campbell assured her, earnestly, that there wasn't a depraved bone in Meadows's body. He was a highly successful businessman, they told her, and an upright citizen. A sportsman and a gentleman. Polite, considerate, with a good sense of humor. His list of merits discouraged Hilary. She decided with regret that he wasn't likely to be the sort of man who would understand the things that were important to her.

She was deposited with the children at the Thomases' own house, where Bill greeted her halfheartedly. Jason clung to his father, talking incessantly, while Hilary put the baby to bed. The house had only three bedrooms, and Hilary chose the family room with its convertible sofa as her temporary home. Bill did not plan to leave, though when Hilary returned, she found him discussing the matter with her father.

"When Janet gets out of the hospital, I'm sure she'll want to stay with you for a while," Bill said. "When she's ready to come home and take care of the children, I'll move out."

The subject was a delicate one since the elder Campbells had lent the money for the down payment on the house. Hilary had no intention of involving herself in it; her father and mother were the ones most closely involved. Instead, she went into the kitchen to see if there was something to feed Jason. Her mother followed her, saying, "I thought we might eat out tonight. Just you and Ted and I. Jason isn't going to want to leave his father, and I think Lisa will sleep for some time."

"Sounds good to me," Hilary admitted as they worked to assemble a meal of soup and sandwich. "I haven't eaten out in weeks, except for a pickup hamburger on the way home from work with the kids."

"It's been a bit of a handful, hasn't it?" Mrs. Campbell asked.

"More than I'd expected. I wasn't able to give Jason and Lisa all they needed. Jason's nightmares—I just didn't know how to cope with them. There wasn't much I could do about Lisa's teething. Between the two of them I didn't get a whole night's sleep for weeks. I don't know. Maybe Janet, being their mother, could have coped with all of it better, but some things don't change no matter who's taking care of them." Hilary set the plate and bowl on the table, looking over at her mother. "Is it worth it, having kids?"

Betty Campbell didn't shrug off the question. "Your father and I think it is, but plenty of people don't. The responsibilities, the pressures, the disappointments, the pain, the expense. You have to set them against the positive aspects, and there *are* positive aspects. The rewards are perhaps less tangible than the deficits, but they exist. Mostly they're emotional: your pride in your children and your love for them, their love for you. Those are strong bonds. Men especially appreciate the feeling of continuity, I think, and women the dependency that fulfills their need to care for others. Children satisfy some basic human longings. You have to remember that your feelings for Jason and Lisa aren't the same as a parent's, Hilary. Where there's more involvement, there's more patience, more adaptability, more—oh, I don't know—resourcefulness maybe."

"Well, it's not a matter I have to worry about just yet," Hilary said, thankful. "Maybe I won't ever have to worry about it."

"The urge to have children becomes particularly strong in your mid- and late thirties, the biological clock running out and all that. It's more than a cliché really. I can't tell you how many women I've known who've suddenly had children then, even if they'd planned never to have any, or who have had more, years after the first batch."

"I know. I see it happen all the time, too. Shall we call Jason for dinner?"

Hilary's parents were adamant that she have a break from the children, so when George Meadows called the next morning at nine, she told him she could get away for the whole day. He arrived at ten in a red plaid Pendleton shirt and tan corduroy jeans, driving a four-wheel-drive vehicle which was loaded with sporting equipment: a sleeping bag, a backpack, boots, fishing equipment, a pair of binoculars, gloves, flashlights, the lot. Hilary raised her brows. "You come prepared."

"I always leave a bunch of stuff in the car so I can just take off when I feel like it. You get into business, and you miss the spontaneity of going fishing or boating on the spur of the moment. So when I see there's a good time at the store, a quiet time, I just pick up and take off." He tossed a down jacket off her seat and into the back, beaming at her with gray-green eyes. "The store's going to be real slow for the next two weeks."

"I'll bet." She laughed as she climbed in. She could tell he had tried to control the shock of light brown hair that insisted on falling forward across his brow because it was still damp. His mustache was neatly trimmed, shorter than on the previous day, and his shoes shone, the faint odor of shoe polish evident in the car. He thrust his tall, lanky frame behind the wheel, looking a little crowded, and turned on the ignition. The radio came on at the same time, a country station at low volume.

"Do you mind?" he asked. "I sort of like it as background when I'm driving, but it might bother you while we talk."

"No, it's fine. Have you lived in Klamath Falls long? I don't remember you from high school."

"I moved here from Eugene after I finished college."

"Did you go to the university there?"

"Yes, in business."

"I was in journalism."

Hilary enjoyed the simple, uncomplicated procedure of gathering and giving information on the drive to Crater Lake. At times George's openness and good nature, his boyish enthusiasm underpinned with a wide practical streak reminded her peculiarly of Jack.

"I love outdoor sports—hunting, fishing, boating, hiking—so it seemed a natural to go into a business that handled the equipment for them. It took me time to learn the ropes, but now I have a couple of small branch stores in the county. I was in San Francisco on a buying trip. I get down there once or twice a month." He glanced over to see if this had any effect.

"Do you like San Francisco?"

"Sure, there's a lot to do, but I don't know very many people there. I've never been to San Jose."

She grinned. "Most people avoid it if they can, and curse it if they can't. It has its good points, though downtown is crumbling and the rest of the city is growing so fast nobody seems able to keep track of it." Perhaps she should have issued an invitation for him to visit her there, but she decided it was too soon. There was plenty of time to make that decision.

At the national park they left the car to hike along the crater rim surrounded by multicolored cliffs and the tang of early autumn in the air. The summer season was past, and there weren't many people around as they followed the trail to the lake's edge. It was a glorious sight with Wizard Island and the cliffs and the clouds above reflected in the deep blue water. Hilary had long since decided that the restorative powers of nature were overrated, but she realized her life hadn't offered much room for purely outdoor activity in years. The closest she came was a week's skiing each winter, usually in company with friends at an overcrowded lodge where contemplation of nature was not the order of the day. She hadn't stood quietly by a lake with the scent of pine overwhelming her for ages.

Even the exercise felt good. It had been more than a month since Hilary had played a game of tennis. Striding along the spectacular trails, setting a brisk pace (which probably wasn't as fast as George usually went), she felt fresh and fit. How could she possibly have forgotten how *wholesome* it felt just to forget all the nagging worries and to drink in the splendors of nature? She giggled to herself at the triteness of the thought.

"What's so funny?" George asked.

"I am. You wouldn't believe how impossibly lyrical I'm becoming in my head about the glories of the outdoors. You'd think I'd been locked in a newspaper office for the last ten years."

"Maybe you have been." He stood beside her at the lake's edge, squinting his eyes against the sunlight. "People get compulsive about their work, especially in the cities. The pace is faster, the demands greater; you forget life isn't like that everywhere. If I don't get away from the store every three or four days, I go a little crazy."

"But the cities have compensations," she protested. "You can get out of them when you need the break, and when you don't, there are things to *do*. As I recall, Klamath Falls shuts down at sunset."

"Not altogether." He laughed and added, "You could look at it the other way around, Hilary. How often do the people in the cities actually visit museums, go to hear operas, symphonies? And what percentage of them? Most live in overcrowded conditions because the jobs are there. And of those who take advantage of the opportunities, my guess is that most do it infrequently. When was the last time you went to a museum or a concert?"

"Well, it's been a couple of months, but—"

"And every couple of months you could go to the city from the country and get exactly the same benefits." He sighed at her slight frown. "What happens is that you become a city snob, you know. You start to think there's something unsophisticated about people who don't live in cities with all the noise and crime and pollution. You use the cultural activities as an excuse, but you don't go to them all that often. People are leaving the city in droves now for the good life on the farm or whatever, but most of them won't make it. They're too accustomed to the convenience, to having their senses, if not their bodies, assaulted. What they tell their friends is that they miss the intellectual stimulation, but my guess is that they haven't the inner resources to keep themselves occupied. In the city you don't have to make any effort; there's a whole slew of entertainments to choose from. In the sticks you have to make your own good time."

"So you don't get bored here?" Hilary knew she'd asked the question defensively, but she felt, rightly or wrongly, under attack.

"Sure I get bored, sometimes. Not often. The things I like to do are here for the most part. When I go to San Francisco or Seattle or Los Angeles, I take advantage of the things I can get only in the city. And that's enough —for me."

Hilary seated herself on the ground and drew her knees up toward her chin. "But you have a lot in common with the people here. I mean, you like the outdoor life, the small-town life. People know you, they invite you to their parties, they speak to you in the street. You probably have the same values, the same political positions." She looked at him as he lowered himself to the ground beside her. "Generally the people in small towns don't understand the problems of disadvantaged groups because they've never been faced with those kinds of problems. They think everyone leads the good life they do, or could, and that there's just a lot of bellyaching going on."

"Are you trying to find out if I'm conservative?" he asked, his eyes amused.

"Yes," she admitted, disgruntled. "I suppose I am."

"Well, I'm a businessman, and I naturally like to look out for my own interests." At her resigned sigh, he grinned. "On the other hand, I lived in Chicago for a few years when I was growing up and saw a rougher side of life. I think you'd either call me a middle-of-the-roader or a freethinker. As you get older, and if you have property to protect, you become more cautious, but you also have more experience to draw on." He lay down on his back to watch the clouds move across the sky. "For what it's worth, I'm generally left of your father and right of Jane Fonda."

"And how do you feel about women?"

Startled, he switched his eyes to her intent face. "I like women just fine. I'm not gay, if that's what you mean."

"No, I'm talking about women's rights. Equality."

His lips twitched. "There's no excuse I can think of for women not to have equal rights. If we were drafting a constitution for our country today, we wouldn't very likely hold out for inequality on account of race, creed, age, or sex, would we? Habit doesn't hold any appeal for me, and that's the only excuse anyone gives, so far as I can see. Bad habit at that. But things have been moving too fast for a lot of people, and they're frightened. Entrenchment is the only way they can handle the change. It's sad but understandable."

"Maybe to you," Hilary said. "That's what I write about. My column, I mean. It's a feminist column."

"Really?" He sat up, interested. "That's all you write about?"

"Pretty much. The world from the feminist point of view. I write magazine articles, too."

"On the same subject." It wasn't a question. "Is there that much to say? It sounds rather limited to me."

Hilary pressed her lips together. "There's plenty to say. For centuries men have directed articles and columns to other men. My column is *by* a woman and *for* women."

"Don't men read it?"

"Of course they do! Just as women have always read the columns by men, and I hope they're just as subtly influenced as all those women were by the male point of view."

He didn't say anything but lay back down on the ground to gaze up again at the clouds. Hilary felt a little absurd, getting "strident," as Marsh would have called it, about women's rights while she sat on a beautiful autumn day overlooking a lush landscape with a perfectly innocent bystander who had already declared his partiality for women's rights. Eventually, when he didn't speak, she, too, lay down on the ground, directing her eyes toward the billowy clouds passing overhead.

"That one's an elephant," he said, pointing to the left. "See the trunk? And that one"—pointing in the other direction—"is a paper tiger, like you."

The formation he indicated did indeed bear some resemblance to a tiger, having wisps of cloud in stripes and looking as translucent as tissue paper. His voice was full of good-humored teasing, while his eyes softly questioned her ability to be the object of a joke. Hilary felt the faint tuggings of a smile.

"You're not the only one who thinks I take myself too seriously." She sighed.

"If you don't take yourself seriously, no one else is going to. On the other hand, if you want to prove your point, you're going to have to enjoy yourself. No one is going to want to buy feminism if it looks like a lot of drudgery, Hilary. You've got to make being an independent, liberated woman look like fun." His eyes crinkled with mirth. "It's only good advertising."

"Now that's just what I needed: the businessman's view of selling equality. I like your philosophy, George." ·

"Good. How about lunch?"

By the time he brought her back to Klamath Falls they had eaten and hiked and laughed and talked until she felt more relaxed than she had in months, maybe years. The fresh air, the exercise, the good company, the absolute absence of problems and responsibilities made her feel almost like a different person. The only question that stuck in her mind was when she would see him again.

"I'll call you," he told her as he left her at the house.

Hilary would have liked a firm date. Barring that, she would have liked to hear him add, "Or you call me." But she settled for waiting to see.

Chapter Eleven

THE BABY was better, and Jason showed no sign of coming down with the flu. Mrs. Campbell, determined that Bill bear his share of the child care while the children were in town, invited Hilary to come home with her, leaving Bill with dinner preparations in hand.

"It will do him a world of good," she insisted as they drove across town. "Let him see what it's like to feed them and bathe them and change diapers. Jason loves the attention, and he obviously needs it. It won't hurt Lisa either. Bill can call if a real emergency develops."

Hilary was impressed with her mother's determination in the matter. "Are you doing this so I can leave them here?"

"Partially. I'm afraid I stepped in too quickly last time. If Bill had been forced to take care of them, make arrangements for them, he might have accustomed himself to the idea. He could have gotten day care, just the way you did, I suppose, though it may be harder here. I don't think as many women with children go out to work. But I could have stepped in for emergencies like Lisa's illness, and I could have sat for them in the evenings when he wanted to go out. Let's see if this brings him around."

Hilary felt strangely mixed emotions on the subject: a sense of elation at the thought of being relieved of the time-consuming obligation, yet disappointment that she hadn't proved to her own satisfaction she could handle the situation of working and child care. And she would miss the children, for all the demands they made on her resources. Her mother was right, though. They really should force Bill into taking charge of his own family in Janet's absence. Relieving him of the necessity was only reinforcing his selfish attitude, undermining any developing sense of responsibility.

After dinner Hilary sat and talked with her parents, vaguely aware that she might be missing a call from George at the Thomases', but insistent with herself that she not leave early on that account. How many women had she chided for sitting at home waiting for a call? "If he wants to reach you, he'll try again." And she had seen through every excuse they used to stay safely at home, where the awaited phone call might or might not come. If he wants to reach me, Hilary thought, he'll manage.

And he did. He called her that evening at her parents' home, suggesting an expedition to the lava beds the next afternoon. "I have to work in the morning, but we could have lunch together in town before heading down there. Does that appeal to you, or would you rather go museum hopping?"

There was suppressed amusement in his voice, and Hilary retorted, "I have every intention of taking Jason to see the Favell Museum while I'm here."

"How about the day after tomorrow? I'll take all of you. And he'd enjoy the Collier State Park Logging Museum even more. We can see both of them."

"Can you spare all that time from work?"

"There's no use having a business if you can't delegate responsibility. I can make the time. How about tomorrow?"

"Sounds fine to me."

On Wednesday they went to the lava beds and explored the caves; on Thursday they took Jason with them so he could climb on the old logging equipment; on Friday they went alone to Rocky Point at the north end of Upper Klamath Lake where George had a boat docked. Every morning Hilary worked on her article and called or visited her recovering sister, and every afternoon she completely divorced her mind from her work and escaped to a carefree world where she had nothing to do but enjoy herself.

George was the most attentive, considerate man she had recently come across, she decided as they returned from the boating trip. So considerate that he hadn't yet done more than kiss her, a restraint almost wholly foreign to her experience of the past few years, one she wasn't sure she appreciated. A sexual attraction that she saw no reason not to consummate was growing between them, but he made no move. True, they had seen each other entirely during the daytime hours, returning to the house where her mother was taking care of the children. Did he think it would bother her to appear there after going to bed with him? She dismissed entirely the thought that he didn't want to make love with her; it was in his eyes, in his voice, in his hands, in his whole bearing toward her. Even as he pulled into Prescott Street, she could feel the crackling atmosphere in the car, with the country music for background and the tidy houses for setting.

His voice was husky when he asked, "How about a movie tonight, Hilary?"

She didn't need to ask what movie. It didn't make any difference. In fact, it wasn't what he was asking her at all. "Yes."

"Dinner? I could pick you up at seven."

"Would seven-thirty be all right? I'd like to have a good long soak." And I have to get to a drugstore, she thought suddenly. There had seemed not the least reason to bring her diaphragm with her. She hadn't even thought of it. It was a reasonably safe time of the month for her, but she never took chances. Very likely he had condoms. She didn't leave things to chance, though. For all she knew, the men in Klamath Falls expected every sexually active woman to be on birth control pills despite the reports of increased risk of heart disease. The responsibility for birth control since the advent of the pill seemed to have slipped irrevocably to the woman, even when it didn't make sense any longer for her to be using it.

"Seven-thirty it is," he agreed, giving her a long, seductive kiss before walking her to the house.

As soon as he had left, she turned to her mother and asked, "May I borrow your car for a few minutes?"

In San Jose Hilary didn't have the least hesitation buying birth control products, but in the smaller community of Klamath Falls, where she was known, or her parents were known, it was a little unnerving. She parked the car not far from the store and walked in like any eighteen-year-old on a similar expedition. If she had ever known where they kept what she was looking for, she didn't remember now, and she wandered about the aisles running her eyes over toothpaste and shampoo, acne medication and aspirin. She had no intention of asking anyone and ignored any other customers in the store. Her concentration and single-minded purpose were eventually rewarded when she found the contraceptive foam in a back corner. As she reached for it with a sigh of satisfaction, she felt her waist encircled in a tight hug. Startled and considerably annoyed, she swung around to face her molester.

George stood there with an enormous grin on his face and not one but two packs of condoms in his hand. Hilary tried hard not to laugh, but a choked gurgle rose from her throat, and for several minutes they had only partial success in restraining the waves of amusement that swept over them. At length she said, "Now I'm going to go pay for this, and I'm going to pretend I've never seen you before."

Following her to the counter, he played the part of an interested stranger, noting her purchase with a jaundiced eye. When the foam was in a paper bag and he laid his two packs of condoms on the counter, she turned to him and said, to the astonishment of the salesgirl, "Let's skip the movie."

"Okay by me. It isn't a very good one anyway." And he gave her a lecherous wink as she retreated from the store.

When George picked her up at her brother-in-law's, they took one look at each other and burst out laughing. Bill stood by with a frown, but Jason and the baby seemed to think it was wonderful fun, not understanding, but willing to join in the general camaraderie. George made a point of speaking with each of them before he and Hilary left.

"They're good kids," he remarked as he held the car door for her.

"Yes. Jason's nightmares have stopped since he's been home, and Lisa seems to be over the flu. Bill's looking a little worn-down, but actually he's doing a good job. I haven't broached the matter of leaving them with him when I go back to San Jose, but I'm beginning to think there's a chance he'll keep them."

"Don't talk about going back to San Jose," George protested. "You've only just gotten here."

Hilary was perfectly willing to forget San Jose for a while, to forget the daily pressure of the column, to forget the exhaustion she had experienced in taking care of the children, to forget Marsh's constant insistence on her best work, to forget Marsh himself. With George she felt pampered and taken care of, treasured in a way even Jack had never duplicated. She wasn't willing to look too closely at the developing relationship. How far can things go in two weeks? she asked herself contentedly as she settled onto her chair in the restaurant. This is a vacation for me and a break in George's Klamath Falls routine, something to be enjoyed for the moment by both of us with the realization that it ends soon.

"My secretary photocopied a couple of your articles from magazines for me. I found them in my office when I checked in there—after meeting you in the drugstore," he said as he picked up the menu. "They're good, Hilary. Very good. Is that the sort of thing you're working on now?"

"Yes, and I'm almost done with it. I should be able to get it off in the mail Monday and be well within my extended deadline."

He studied the menu briefly before laying it aside. "I had no idea you were talking about magazines of that quality. Forgive my underestimation, but I thought you were talking about obscure journals that had little circulation, ones that were so narrow in scope that no one had ever heard of them. Most of these are on every newsstand each month."

"Um-hum," she said absently as she decided on the prime rib. "You might as well aim for the top, I figure. It's a lot more fun getting rejection slips from the best than from the least."

"Do you get many rejections?"

"Not now. Usually I write on assignment these days. There's not the time to spend on it with my newspaper job, and when an idea works its way up from the column, I'll suggest it to some editor for consideration." She put aside her menu and studied his face quizzically. "You're impressed, aren't you?"

"Of course I'm impressed. I've never known any women who had articles published in national magazines, let alone ones who write columns for newspapers." His grin became rueful. "Well, I did know a woman who wrote a gardening column for a local paper once."

"You'd meet more if you lived in a big city," she said teasingly. "I'll have the prime rib."

They ate a leisurely meal, then dawdled over their coffee and liqueur. There was no rush. Letting the tension build between them only served to make the interlude more enjoyable. When George finally asked, "Ready?" Hilary nodded and retrieved her purse from her lap to stand beside him. As they started toward the door, they were hailed by some friends of George's, who invited them to join their party. "Sorry, we can't," he said, without a pause, squeezing her fingers as he waved good-bye to the other group.

"You'll meet them all tomorrow night, if you want to," he promised. "We're invited to a party at the Mortons."

"One of the women looked familiar, as though she might have been someone I went to school with. Susan something."

"Kieffer. At least that's her married name." He dismissed the subject with a negligent wave of his hand. "We're going to my house, aren't we?"

"I hope so."

His house was older than her parents', probably from the turn of the century or before, wooden, with gables on either side and a round turret at the left-hand corner. It was painted white, and Hilary thought immediately of how in San Francisco the Victorian details would have been emphasized in a contrasting color. A golden retriever met them at the door, deliriously happy to see George. The dog followed them into the living room, where Hilary was more than a little surprised to find the room furnished in antiques. If anything, she would have guessed that George's house would tend toward the masculine rustic or decorator modern from a former girl friend.

"My mother has an antiques store in Eugene," he explained. "I grew up with the stuff, and I like it for the main rooms, but not for my study or bedroom. It's not comfortable enough, and it's too formal. A couple of the other bedrooms are done in antiques. My mother and father never fail to bring something when they visit. I could start a store of my own."

Hilary followed him into the kitchen, which had been remodeled but retained an old-time flavor with its gleaming copper and braided rug, a collection of antique cooking utensils hung on the walls, and a potbellied stove separating the room from the breakfast area. He regarded her bemused expression with amusement. "Did you think it was going to be hokey?" he asked.

"No, not exactly, but I didn't expect it to be like this." Her eye was caught by a copper warming pan which she lifted from the wall to examine more closely. "Did your mother have a hand in the decorating?"

"Look who's being prejudiced. Do you think that I'm not capable of it or that good taste belongs only to people who live in cities?"

Her eyes met his, and she shook her head. "You didn't answer my question, George."

His laugh was a deep rumble. "Can't fool you, can I? Yes, she's an interior decorator, too, and oversaw the whole operation. But I did make the major decisions, say, if I wanted two ovens or one."

"Good for you." Hilary replaced the warming pan on its hook. "Do you feel comfortable with it?"

"Oh sure. I grew up in a house furnished this way. My real interest in my surroundings extends to the outdoors mainly. All I had to insist on was that it not be fussy. I let her go wild in one of the bedrooms to make up for it. What would you like to drink?"

"White wine, if you're going to have something. Otherwise, I'll pass."

While he poured them each a glass of wine, she wandered through the breakfast room into the dining room. It was furnished entirely in mahogany pieces: table, chairs, sideboard, and plate rail with blue and white Wedgwood plates. George followed her into the room to hand her a glass.

"Do you do much entertaining?" she asked.

"In spurts. Maybe a dinner party every other month and something during the Christmas season. It depends."

"On what?"

"Whether I feel like it, whether it's necessary, whether I can find a hostess. That sort of thing." He took a sip of his wine. "Do you want to see upstairs?"

The tour ended with his study and bedroom. The study was overflowing with papers in baskets, in open file drawers, on the rolltop desk, in the wastebasket, even stacked on the floor. "I'm not particularly neat here," he admitted, tossing a catalogue of outdoor clothing onto a different stack. "I was distracted last night; I've already been through that one. After I dropped you off yesterday, I intended to get a lot of work done, but I couldn't concentrate."

"Why not?" Hilary asked with mock concern.

"I kept thinking of that empty bed in there," he retorted, putting an arm about her shoulders and drawing her into the other room. A bureau, a bookshelf, a beige love seat, a bedside table, and a king-size bed were its only furnishings. He led her to the love seat. "We can talk in here as well as anywhere," he said cheerfully. "And it's closest to the bed."

His lips came down to meet hers even before they sank to the cushions. Hilary wrapped her arms around his waist, holding him for the first time. She could feel his hands taking the clips from her hair so it fell forward around her face. Their kisses were long and longing, tender and passionate. George drew slightly away to run his fingers over her face, tracing the line of her jaw, the high cheekbones, the narrow brow. "You're adorable," he murmured as his hands came down past her shoulders to cup her breasts. His thumbs rubbed rhythmically across the light wool fabric of her dress until the nipples beneath became firm. Then he reached behind her to unzip the dress. Hilary leaned forward so he could unfasten her bra as well and slide the dress to her waist, entirely disposing of the lacy confection she had worn especially for the occasion.

"Hey, you were supposed to notice how provocative it was," she protested, laughing, her breasts bare to his exploring fingers.

"I'll notice when I put it back on you."

Hilary, determined feminist that she was, didn't believe in being the only one partially nude. She unbuttoned his shirt as expertly as he had undone her dress and bra, and ran her hands over his chest, caressing with her fingertips. By the pattern of her movements she sought to instruct him in what pleased her, a simpler, more subtle method (and much more acceptable to men, she had found) than speaking her desires out loud. It didn't always work; it didn't work now. George was far too mesmerized by his desire to find any significance in her motions, and he wasn't doing half badly in raising her temperature, so she smiled and started to unbuckle his belt.

He regarded her with puzzled eyes. "Are we in a hurry?"

"Not that I know of. Aren't you used to aggressive females?" She continued what she was doing, unsnapping his pants and lowering the fly, while he watched her. "Sex is a mutual activity, George; the shared giving and receiving of pleasure." Bemused, he shifted so she could slide his boxer shorts down along with his pants. "I presume you like to be touched as much as I do."

"Yes," he said in a strangled voice. After a few minutes he slid her dress and panties down, rising to remove them entirely, along with his own clothes. "Do you want to use the foam or shall I use the rubber?"

"The foam, I think." She dug in her purse for the package. He watched, a mildly incredulous look on his face, as she shook the container and filled the tube. She grinned at him. "George, I'm absolutely shattering your delusions about proper female behavior, aren't I?"

"No, of course not," he muttered. "It's just . . . the first time . . . well, usually a woman tries to maintain a little mystery about everything."

"Yes, and the first time it's usually not as great for her as it is for him." She handed him the tube filled with contraceptive foam, smiling wickedly. "It's all yours, George."

"Oh, for God's sake," he said, laughing now. "On the bed, woman. I'm adept at working contraceptive devices into lovemaking. An old girl friend gave me an article on it once. I presume you didn't write it."

"Not that I recall."

Very conscious now of how he acted, he gave her bottom a gentle pat as she scrambled onto the king-size bed. Holding the tube carefully, as though it contained something precious, he climbed in after her and set it down on the bedside table. "Now where were we?" he demanded, reaching out to draw her close to him.

"We were about to have a wonderful time," she whispered as his hands returned to explore her body.

"I don't think I've ever met anyone quite like you," he grumbled as, at her urging, he rolled over with her resting on top of him. "Do you like it there?"

"It's better than being squashed to death," she said. "Don't you like me here?"

His voice softened. "I love it."

"I didn't mean to spoil anything, George."

"You didn't." He kissed her eyelids. "Better to set the record straight from the start. Otherwise, bad patterns get set. A woman I was very fond of years ago stormed out of here one night accusing me of acting the conquering hero.

I didn't know what she was talking about at the time. There's a mystique about women wanting strong, forceful men."

"In some ways it's true." Hilary sighed, snuggling against him. "But we're talking about character and self-confidence, not the use of physical superiority and the establishment of dominance. Oh, I don't know. Some women are as confused about it as men, but I swear that if a woman allows herself to be physically abused by a man, she's going to end up being a battered wife. I for one don't get my kicks from fear."

"But, Hilary, that's not what they're looking for. They're looking for protection."

"All very well if they can't protect themselves against something, but it degenerates into dependency: physical, emotional, financial. And it's a dependency every man can point to, whereas a man's dependency is much more subtle and less obvious."

"What dependency?" he asked, running his hands over the length of her body.

"Not just sexual," she insisted, serious. "Men depend on their wives for emotional support, for creature comforts, for all the physical chores they find so demeaning and think could easily be done by someone else. Women haven't learned to point out to them that the financial and physical protection they offer could be just as easily replaced. In fact, women tend to believe they couldn't be, which is why they tend not to rock the boat. But if they get thrown overboard, either they learn to swim or they find someone to rescue them."

Despite the intensity of her subject matter, she found that his hands were arousing her body again, and she lapsed into silence, shaking her head wryly at him. "Anything and everything gives way to pleasure, doesn't it?"

"It's only human nature, honey," he whispered huskily. "Male and female nature. To store up against the rougher times."

"There are always plenty of those." She sighed, momentarily forgetting them.

Chapter Twelve

"DO YOU THINK you could ever live in Klamath Falls again?" George asked her as they rested after a few games of tennis the next day.

Hilary wiped her brow and glanced over to where Jason and Lisa tumbled about the playground with their father. "I don't know. I haven't thought about it in years. When I left here, it wasn't a complete break because I knew I'd be back to see my parents and my sister. But to live here myself, I don't think so."

"You think you'd miss the city?"

"Not just the city itself. I have a whole life built up in San Jose. My friends are there; my job is there. I like the Bay Area, though San Jose leaves something to be desired." The sun was glaring down on them, and she squinted to study his face. "Maybe you could come visit me there next time you're down."

"I intend to." He ignored her lifted brows. "Do you have any particular men friends there?"

"Not at the moment. The kids have really kept me busy." Again her eyes turned toward the children and their father. "I'm beginning to think Bill intends to keep the children."

"Good for him. He should; they're his responsibility, not yours."

"Janet's coming home for a visit tomorrow. To my parents'. I'm to take the kids over. Everyone agreed that she wasn't ready to see Bill, and I don't think he wants to see her."

"So I'm not going to see you tomorrow?"

"Not during the day. Janet goes back to the hospital after dinner."

"The evening is mine," he insisted. "You'll need a break after all that trauma."

"Probably." It seemed too much bother to tell him she liked to be asked rather than told. After all, he was only trying to be considerate of the emotional strains the day would produce.

"How about another game?" he asked.

"You've got to be kidding! I'm out of shape, at least compared to you. May I buy you lunch?"

He agreed, but when the check came after their meal, he took it, insisting she could pay "another time."

After the party that evening they went to his house and made love, with less urgency now but with a growing intimacy. Tomorrow, Hilary decided, she would explain to him how she liked to be touched, and she would ask him his preferences. The newness of their union provided the necessary excitement to raise her to orgasm now, but familiarity would dull that edge. He was a little too quick to grab her, a little too rough in his handling before she reached a level where his touch was pleasurable, not painful. And, she reminded herself firmly, she might not be doing what he wanted, though she had asked and he had merely groaned. Either he was incredibly easy to please, she decided as she lay beside him, or he didn't want to talk about it.

"Are you awake, Hilary?"

"I think so."

"Could you make a living from just writing magazine articles? I mean, if you didn't work for the newspaper, you'd have more time. You'd have a chance to explore more issues in depth."

"I'm not the world's best self-starter," she murmured sleepily. "The newspaper job gets me up and out of the house. It gets my adrenaline flowing; it gives me daily deadlines. I'd have to write several articles a month to make the same kind of income. Right now I do only three or four a year."

"Yes, but think of the freedom you'd have without a nine-to-five job." He nudged her to make sure she hadn't fallen asleep. "There are innumerable benefits to being your own boss."

"And loads of headaches. Like where your next meal is coming from."

"I don't think you'd have to worry about that," he said persuasively. "If you can come up with an idea for a column five days a week, you can come up with a couple of ideas for articles each month. You ought to think about it."

Hilary pulled herself up on her elbows. "I like my job on the newspaper, George. The contact with other people is stimulating. Damn, now I'm wide awake. I might as well go home."

But he convinced her not to.

Sunday was emotionally draining for her. Hilary had been to the hospital twice since she'd arrived, on two of Janet's "better days," when the doctors had thought her sister could handle it. But Janet at home, at her parents' home, was exhausting. It was painful to see her attempt to lift above her depression, to see the way in which she clung to her "babies," to see Jason's confusion and Lisa's shyness, to see the pain in her parents' eyes. Everyone tried to keep the situation casual, but when a silence developed, the efforts to fill it were so obvious as to make Hilary cringe. Janet was effusive in her thanks to Hilary for taking care of the children but carefully avoided any questions about her husband and how he was managing with them now.

"It was as though he were a forbidden topic," Hilary told George later. "Even when Jason spoke of him, Janet sort of withdrew. Poor Jason. He's not old enough to understand why his mother's in the hospital. She looks all right to him, and he can't see why she doesn't come home. And Lisa . . ." Hilary bit her lip. "George, I'm not sure she even recognized her mother."

They were sitting in his living room, and he put a protective arm about her shoulders. "She's little. Things will sort themselves out in a while, when Janet's better."

"Maybe." Hilary didn't sound at all sure. "I just ached for all of them. And when I took the kids back to Bill, he didn't even ask about her. I told him anyway."

"He probably wanted to know but couldn't bring himself to ask."

Hilary regarded him speculatively. "Is that how you'd feel?"

He gave a minimal shrug. "Who can say? It would depend on the circumstances. Look, Hilary, he's made it quite clear to you and your parents that he doesn't want to have anything to do with her. He can't very well start bombarding you with questions. It would give the wrong impression."

"That he still cared about her?" Hilary looked disgusted. "He's married to her, for God's sake. I don't expect him to declare his undying love, but I do expect him to show some interest, some curiosity, if nothing more, about the woman he's been married to for five years. Surely that's not asking too much."

"Maybe it is, of Bill." He took a sip of wine and set his glass on the coffee table. "A lot of bitterness can grow up between two people over five years, a lot of hurts. You seem to think that the longer the relationship, the more attached the couple. It doesn't always work that way."

His voice had changed subtly, and she stared at him. "You sound as though you've had experience."

"I have."

"But you said you'd never been married."

He gave her a brief smile. "You don't have to be married to live with someone, Hilary. I'm sure you know that."

"I do. But in a town the size of Klamath Falls . . .".

"It was a little difficult at first. I told you I'm not all that conservative."

"Still, it surprises me."

"Well, it wasn't what I wanted. Not after a while anyway." George ran a hand through his hair before picking up his wineglass. "She was already married."

"My word! Now you've shocked me." She tried to keep her tone light and teasing, but she really was almost astonished. "Did her husband live here?"

"Oh, no. She'd run away from him. Somewhere back East, I think, though she was never specific. After a year of living together I urged her to get a divorce, but she wouldn't. She said it wasn't necessary for us to get married. By that time people had come to accept us, so in some ways she was right."

"But didn't her husband divorce her?"

"Probably. I begged her to check, through a lawyer or anything, but she said she wasn't interested in finding out."

"She sounds a little . . . flaky. I'm sorry if that sounds nasty."

"She was different. Unique in her way." He sighed and moved his hand to massage her neck under her hair, as though it were she who was suffering the stress of relating a painful story. "Her marriage had been a bad mistake, she said, and she didn't intend to marry again, so it didn't matter if she was still married or divorced. I know I pestered her about it, but I really wanted it settled. I wanted to marry her and have a family. When we'd been together for three years, she accidentally got pregnant. Then I really put the pressure on. I thought everything was going to work out perfectly."

"Did you engineer the pregnancy?"

He met her eyes and nodded. "It seemed the best way to bring the situation into focus. If she realized it, she never said. But she went to California and had an abortion. She never came back."

Hilary could feel the hairs on the back of her neck bristle where he touched them, but she forced herself not to move away. "Do you realize how ugly that story is to me?"

A flush rose from his neck to his face. "Damn it, Hilary, women have babies all the time! What's so awful about it? I would have taken care of her and the baby. I wanted to marry her. I loved her."

"You, you, you," she snapped. "If you loved her so much,

how could you possibly take the decision on how to use her body away from her? It's having babies that keeps women in subjection, George. Having control over when and if they will have children is essential to their gaining some sort of equality in this country. You *knew* she didn't want to have a baby, yet in your superior male wisdom, you decided that she should. That's disgusting." Hilary managed to keep her voice from rising, but just barely. Her hands, clenched in her lap, felt suddenly cold.

"I know." He let out a long breath, as though he'd been holding it throughout her diatribe. "But I didn't know then. I swear I thought of almost nothing else for months afterward. I was just madder than hell, at first at her and then gradually at myself. By my own stupidity I had forced her into doing exactly what I didn't want her to do. But hell, Hilary, there are so many women who want to have families. And even if they're not too thrilled about the idea when they get pregnant, as soon as the baby arrives they dote on it. I've seen it happen again and again."

"Yes." Her hands unclenched slightly in her lap, but she couldn't reach out to touch him. "I'm still not sure you understand, George. I mean, from my point of view. You understand that what you did drove her away from you, and you regret that. Maybe men won't ever understand, because they can't get pregnant. They see the fruits of the pregnancy, these adorable little babies their mothers dote on. And they see the little kids romping around the playgrounds and saying cute things. They may even see teenagers on television receiving awards for something or doing well at sports. It seems to them, too, that they do their share in the child rearing: provide the money, play with the kids for a few minutes when they get home from work, take the family on excursions on the weekend. But very few of them take the ultimate responsibility for the kids. Bill's an extreme example, I know, but he almost rejected his own children completely. To him they were Janet's responsibility. And to a lesser extent that's the way it's been for a long time with fathers. Things are changing; I've seen it with some of my friends and their husbands. But in the crunch, it's Mom nine times out of ten who, if she doesn't *have* the responsibility, *feels* she does, and it's a heavy one."

"But most women accept that, just as most men accept the responsibility for supporting their families," George protested, his hand unmoving now on her neck.

"And just as men sometimes get tired of the continued necessity of going to work each day, so women get tired of wiping noses and changing diapers. The initial excitement wears off. But that's only half of it. In today's economy more and more women are forced to go out of the home to work because one salary won't support the family. And even if they go out only for the intellectual stimulation, they find themselves with the double burden of children and job. Your liberated husband may, out of the goodness of his heart, help with the dishes."

"I think you take too negative a view, Hilary. As you said, things are changing. More couples are working on the problems together. You're especially concerned about the difficulties right now because you've just had the experience of being a single parent, suddenly, and it was rough." His wineglass was empty, and he motioned toward hers. "Would you like more?"

"No, thanks." She watched as he walked to the kitchen, his tall frame moving with muscular economy. His energy was boundless—on the tennis court, on a hiking trail, in bed. And he faced problems pragmatically, with a not unrealistic approach to life. It wasn't precisely her approach to life, but what the hell! Hilary was a little tired of worrying about the problems of women in general just now. She didn't want to quarrel with him; she wanted to hold him and be held by him. Let the rest of the world take care of itself for the next week. Her vacation would end soon enough. He'd had a rough time when his married woman left him, and she wasn't making him feel any better about it by harping on his conduct. When he returned and sat down beside her, she reached out to cover his hand with hers.

"How long ago did your friend leave?"

"About two years ago." He eyed her intently. "I didn't bring it up for your sympathy—or for your censure, for that matter. It happened, and it's over with. I think I learned something from it, but I'm not still hung up on her. I don't want you to think that's why I told you."

"Okay," she agreed, smiling, "I won't think that."

"Do you want to take the kids to see the fish hatchery tomorrow?"

"If you can spare the time. I just have another few pages to type, and I'll be able to put the article in the mail. Jason would love it, and I think even Lisa would be fascinated."

George reached over to stroke her hair. "Sometimes you sound like their mother, you know. Just think how much stronger your attachment would be if they were your kids."

Hilary didn't answer him. Instead, she snuggled closer, allowing only the sensuous sensations to penetrate as his hands wandered down her body, his mouth closing on hers. He tasted of wine and smelled of a subtle after-shave lotion. Her arms went around him, feeling the texture of his plaid flannel shirt and the solidness of his flesh beneath. His hands at her breasts were insistent, and she whispered, "Gently." For a moment he paused and then carefully unbuttoned her blouse, sliding his hand in to cup her, softly, his thumb stroking gently. Hilary murmured her appreciation and pleasure, and his kisses deepened. "Let's go upstairs," he said gruffly.

Every day during the week George managed to spend at least a few hours with her, in addition to the evenings. Sometimes they took the children on an excursion; sometimes they merely had a long lunch together. Hilary warily parried any comments and questions that suggested a deeper entanglement, trying desperately to keep their relationship a short fling, a mutually satisfactory vacation affair. But she could see he was making every effort to prove to her that he would be a good husband and a good father. George was solicitous of her welfare, interested in her career, eager to please her. She found herself actually being courted, something that had seldom happened before. Having arrived in Oregon exhausted, discouraged, she found his attention flattering, his admiration soothing and seductive. She didn't have to prove herself; in his eyes she was already proved.

At times she scolded herself for her abdication of her principles. She had never been able to bring herself to tell him exactly what she liked sexually. She allowed him to pay for her meals and her entertainment, though she often offered. She let carelessly spoken derogatory comments on women slide by, telling herself that they represented not his attitude but unthinking and changeable habit. Was he not a supporter of equal rights for women? Hilary was determined not to nitpick about the casual use of phrases he had grown up with, which her own family might have used. On the bottom line was his declaration of support, and she refused to question his commitment to it.

Because there were so many wonderful things about him: his sense of humor, his charm, his enthusiasm. Even the casual pace of his life. He was a businessman and obviously very successful, yet he wasn't compulsive or so dedicated that everything else was forgotten in the shuffle. George made the time to enjoy himself. His refusal to be absorbed by his business intrigued Hilary, if perhaps his enthusiasm for outdoor sports was not matched by her own. She reminded herself that she liked hiking and boating, though she was bored by fishing and turned off by hunting. The excitement with which George talked of snowmobiling made her want to try it. (But was it ecologically suspect?) Dogsled racing she had her doubts about, but sledding and ice skating and skiing she had always enjoyed.

When she realized the direction of her thoughts, she put a halt to them. Yes, she might come back for a visit in the wintertime, perhaps at Christmas, but she was thinking of a more prolonged stay than she would have time for. Once she had even caught herself musing that the rocking chair in one of the bedrooms would be ideal placed in the turret room of the unfurnished third floor, along with a desk and chair for a working space. Hilary had pictured herself taking a break from an article she would be working on, rocking in the chair, looking out onto a clear autumn day. Absurd.

But on Thursday evening it didn't seem quite so absurd when they were lying in bed after making love. George was holding her possessively and whispered in her ear, "Stay with me."

Purposely misunderstanding him, she said, "I shouldn't. Bill isn't usually awake when I get in, but he always finds me there in the morning, and he doesn't say anything."

"No, Hilary," he said, stroking her bare shoulder. "I mean, don't go back to San Jose. Stay here with me, always."

Her attempt at a laugh went astray. "George, we haven't even known each other for two weeks."

"We know enough." His eyes were steady on hers; his face was serious. "I know I'm proud of you. I know I want to take care of you. I know I want you to have my children."

Hilary allowed her fingers to play over his lips. "You can't know all that in so short a time, George. You only know me as I am here, in Klamath Falls. There's another side to me you haven't ever seen. On the newspaper I'm driven. Everyone but Marsh and Harry is intimidated by my feminism. No, it's true," she insisted at his lifted brow. "I take my work seriously, perhaps too seriously. If you were to read a month's worth of my columns, you wouldn't be so skeptical."

"Okay, let's assume you're right." He rolled over on his back and stared at the ceiling for a few minutes, thinking. "Even if it's true, I don't see how it affects us. Hilary, when you arrived here, you were completely worn-down. You don't need that kind of annoyance. If you lived here with me—and I mean, married me, Hilary—you could make a career of just writing articles. You wouldn't have the pressures you've been under. And you wouldn't have to make as much. Actually," he said, turning to face her, "you wouldn't have to make anything, but I assume you'd want to. I realize you want your independence, and what I'm saying is that you don't have to lose it."

"But I like the newspaper work," she said uncertainly. "The strain recently has been having both the children and the job. I'm not usually the wreck I was when I arrived here."

"Probably not," he conceded, "but the kinds of demands your job makes are self-defeating. Look, don't you think you'd enjoy the kind of life we've been having? Don't you think your ideas would be fresher if you didn't have to come up with them five times a week? In the articles you can explore a subject more fully, more persuasively. And there would be time to have fun, too. To go boating and skiing and swimming without necessarily feeling guilty about shirking your work. And when we have kids, you'll still be able to do it. That's what's so great about being able to work at home."

"You've thought it all out." Hilary didn't know whether to be pleased or annoyed. She was used to planning her own life, but she realized that he was simply putting forth arguments to convince her because he cared about her. And how did she feel about him? There was the sexual attraction, and certainly a compelling fondness, but what of the "love" that everyone talked about? Was this all it was?

His voice interrupted her thoughts. "You don't have to think you'd be stuck here in Klamath Falls all the time either. I make at least two trips a month to one city or another, and I'd take you with me. You could drink in all the culture you wanted or just shop and see movies that hadn't come here yet. You could even visit your friends. It wouldn't be a matter of being stuck in the sticks."

The best of both worlds—that's what he was offering her. Possibly. Hilary felt panicked at the thought of a decision. "George, it's too soon. I couldn't even think of accepting you without getting to know you better. And especially without your getting to know me better. I'm not at all sure you'd like me, the way I am in San Jose on the newspaper."

"But you wouldn't be in San Jose on the newspaper," he explained patiently.

"No, I wouldn't." The thought made her slightly breathless. Not to see Harry again or to work with Marsh.

They would think she had lost her mind. "Still, that's how I've been, and I don't think I would change all that radically. I haven't quite been myself these last few days."

His lips sought hers. "No, and you've been happy, haven't you? Not driving yourself and still accomplishing the work you meant to. You've been able to relax. That counts for more than you seem to realize, Hilary. Life is meant to give us some pleasures; otherwise, it's not worth living."

But she got pleasures from her work. True, they had been a little scarce recently, but that would change when she returned without the children. Hilary wasn't sure, when his lips sought her breast, which pleasures were more important, and he wasn't giving her a chance to think about it. "I don't want to talk about it anymore tonight," she said firmly.

"Fine," he agreed in his husky, captivated voice.

As if she hadn't had enough on her mind, her brother-in-law called from his office the next morning to drop a small bomb on her.

"Hilary, you know I was prepared to keep the kids," he began. *Was* sounded threatening to her, but she said only, "Yes."

"And I would have, except that this fantastic opportunity has come up. You know I told you they were sending Ralph Ross to Chicago for a training program?"

They had had to have something to talk about during the hours, no matter how few, that they spent together in the house. Searching her mind for the proper context, she remembered that Bill had expressed some envy of his friend for the chance at promotion. "Yes, I remember."

"Well, he was in a car accident yesterday. Nothing serious! But he ended up with a broken arm and leg and will be out of commission for some time. So, what they've decided here is that I can go in his place since they don't want to lose their spot at the training program. It's offered only once a year, and if we miss this one, it will be that long before someone can go." His voice practically shook with excitement. "I've never been out of the West, Hilary. This would give me a real chance to step up in the company."

"I see."

"It's only for a month."

Hilary's heart sank. Only a month.

"If Janet isn't home by then, I'll take the kids. I promise you. But this is important." He was pleading now.

"Yes, I can see that it is." Hilary had unconsciously begun to twine the telephone cord around her fingers. Could she manage this time? After such a thorough rest she was inclined to believe that she could, yet . . . "Can I call you back in an hour or so?"

"They want to know right now, or they'll give it to someone else. I'd have to leave Sunday morning."

She tried desperately to fight down the chagrin she felt. Doing a favor for her brother-in-law seemed entirely inappropriate after the way he'd behaved. On the other hand, it was only a month, and important to his career. It might even be important to Janet, in the long run, because of his increased ability to support his family. The likelihood of Janet's recovering enough in the near future to help support herself and their children didn't seem great. Hilary cleared her throat.

"Would you take the time to explain it to Jason? Would you call him and Lisa and send postcards and generally act as though you were their father and missed them?"

"I promise, Hilary."

"All right." She had to force herself to say it. "I'll take them back with me."

"Thanks, Hilary. I'll never forget you for this."

She didn't need him never to forget her. She wished she'd never heard his name or seen his face. Suddenly she was right back where she'd started, in charge of a baby and a little boy. For her own sanity, she reminded herself that, really, she was doing it not for her brother-in-law but for her sister. That she was doing it because her father couldn't live with the kids, no matter how much he wanted to. That her mother had just given her two weeks of relief from child care obligations by staying with them almost daily in their own home. But what she really had on her mind was Marsh's reaction. He wasn't going to believe that she was returning with them, after giving her two weeks to set up alternative arrangements. She wouldn't be able to make him understand how she had gotten trapped again. Well, she decided stoically, what the hell? She didn't care if he understood.

George didn't understand either, when she told him over lunch. "You've got to be crazy!" he said, groaning.

"What was I supposed to do?" she asked.

"Tell him he couldn't go to the damned training program. Tell him to stay home with his kids where he belongs. You're not his keeper."

"I'm not doing it for him." Hilary felt defensive. "I'm doing it for my sister and for the kids and for my parents. Sure, he could stay home with them and miss his big opportunity. And he'd just be resentful. What kind of father would he be to them if he blamed them for standing in the way of his big chance? He's only just coming around to seeing his duties clearly and to feeling something fatherly for them. I don't want to see that spoiled, George."

"Are you forgetting the condition you arrived here in, Hilary? You were a wreck from taking care of them."

"Yes, but that was because the baby was sick." Hilary shrugged. "I admit it's been difficult for me, George, but this time it will only be for a month. I already have their day care set up. We'll fall back into the pattern very easily."

"Couldn't your mother take them, just for the month?"

Hilary slowly shook her head. "Dad's much worse when they're around. He loves them, George, but the tremors get worse from any kind of emotional upset. It's enough that Janet's in the hospital. His speech starts to slur when he's with the kids for more than an hour or two. And if mother lived at their house, who would take care of Dad? There's no choice, George. I have to take them with me. Really, I don't mind so much now. You've given me back my sense of humor, I think."

He shook his head in exasperation mixed with admiration. "You're going to make a hell of a mother, but I think you're dissipating your energies on Janet's kids. Let's have some of our own right away. Don't go back to San Jose at all. Call your boss and tell him you're quitting. You can stay with the kids in their own house, and when Bill gets back, we'll get married and you'll move in with me."

Despite his half-teasing tone, Hilary knew he meant what he said. Not that she would give it serious consideration, of course. You didn't just throw up your job and get married because you had your doubts about whether you could manage your job and your sister's kids for a few weeks. But maybe you did it if it was what you wanted, a part of her said. Maybe being out on your own, frequently lonely, often nerve-rackingly pressed, was not all it was cracked up to be. She needn't become dependent on George. She could maintain her identity in spite of his strong desire to possess her. But he would expect her to have children, and soon. Hilary wasn't ready to decide that issue.

"Please don't press me, George. We need time, both of us."

"Then stay another week." When she turned startled eyes to him, he continued. "You could do what you did when you first came up to get the kids or something like it. Write your columns here and call them in. I'll have to go down to San Francisco in another week or so, and I can fly down with you. If you feel you have to give them some notice, you can stay for a few weeks." At her gesture of protest he said, "Even if you haven't decided by then, it would be nice to have someone fly down with you and the kids, wouldn't it?"

"Yes," she admitted. Her plate of spaghetti had barely been touched, and she offered him a hesitant smile. "I could have Harry send along a batch of my columns for you to read."

"Great idea. And I can meet the financial wizard when I come down with you."

His flippancy was meant to amuse, but Hilary wasn't in the mood. She merely nodded and attempted a bite of the spaghetti, wondering what Marsh's reaction would be.

Chapter Thirteen

HILARY WAITED until two-thirty to make the call, person to person, so Marsh would be back from lunch. When his secretary, Susan, came on the line, she could feel her palms begin to sweat. Though Susan said he was on another line and asked the operator to hold for a moment, he was almost instantly on the line, verifying his identity to the apparently skeptical operator.

"Hilary? I didn't expect you to call."

"I hadn't planned to, but something has come up." When he made no response, she hastened on. "My brother-in-law was going to keep the children, but he's been given the opportunity to take a training program in Chicago. He just heard today, and he leaves on Sunday."

"So?"

His voice, she decided, must have frozen the lines from San Jose to Klamath Falls. She moistened her lips. "Well, it means I'll be bringing the children back with me—just for a month. Then he'll take them, or Janet will if she's well enough." He still didn't say anything. "The reason I called . . . I thought, if it was all right with you, that I could write my column for a week from here."

"Nonsense. Why would you do that?"

Momentarily she couldn't remember. "Um, because I'd like to stay for another week. The following weekend a friend could fly down with me and help with the children. It would just make things a lot easier for me."

"No."

"I beg your pardon?"

"You heard me. I said no. I want you at your desk Monday morning, preferably on time. Listen to me, Hilary. You have a job here—and a job which you need to take firmly in hand. Lois Greer has done a fine job with the column. She's milder than you are. A lot of readers find that appealing. You don't want to lose your audience, do you?"

"Of course not," she snapped. An icy feeling was invading her insides. "Mr. Marsh, would you prefer to have Lois continue the column?"

A mild expletive slipped over the phone. "Certainly not! At your best you can run circles around the woman. Her stuff is thoughtful but hardly thought-provoking. She hasn't your bite, Hilary. But you haven't been giving me much bite recently. Are you tired of the column?"

Hilary swallowed the lump in her throat. "No, I'm not tired of it. Sometimes it's a little draining, but basically I still find it exciting. I thought I might become a little broader in my scope."

"Such as?" He sounded interested.

"I'll discuss it with you when I return. Monday. I'll be on time."

"Excellent. And is our arrangement for attending functions still intact?"

"I suppose so."

"Then plan on Thursday evening, if you will. I'll arrange with Mrs. Rainer to sit with the children."

"Thank you. Good-bye, Mr. Marsh."

George was disappointed but not completely discouraged when Hilary told him that evening. Instead of trying to change her mind about leaving on Sunday, he emphasized his coming trip. "Then I'll see you in your habitat, Hilary, and you won't be able to say I don't know you anymore. I'll meet your friends at work and take you for lunch while you're under the pressure of a deadline. What do you think I'll find? That you snap at me? That your columns offend me?"

"Possibly. They offend a lot of people in San Jose." But she smiled as his arm tightened around her shoulders.

They walked slowly from the restaurant to his car, enjoying the brisk autumn night, peering in store windows, nodding to acquaintances. The town was familiar and comforting, even if it did close down rather early in the evenings. In San Jose Hilary was thoroughly on her own, could walk for hours without running into anyone she'd ever seen before, stood a much greater chance of being mugged or raped. She shivered slightly.

"Are you cold?" George asked, surprised.

"No, I was just thinking about San Jose. It's not the best place for the kids to be, but my neighborhood's all right."

"*Your* kids are going to be reared in a much nicer neighborhood." he insisted.

Hilary didn't reply.

Her parents had silently watched the progress of the relationship between Hilary and George, hopeful perhaps but never pushing. Hilary felt sure they'd be delighted to have her back in Klamath Falls, knew they liked George, yet she thought she sensed some hesitation in their attitude. She reminded herself that they might not approve of the sex, which they could surmise from the long hours the two spent together and from the fact that she had remained at George's house Saturday evening when they left.

It had been George's suggestion to have them to dinner; Hilary had laughed and said, "You just want to see if I'm a decent cook." But she had done her best to make it a special meal, even while she mocked herself for the domestic nature of the endeavor. She had done as much for Jack and tried to consider it only a challenge to do well anything that she undertook.

Though she was about to return to San Jose, she chose not to speak with her parents about George, even when they had an hour together alone the next morning. George was driving her to the airport along with the children —and with Bill. It seemed senseless for him to make a separate trip when their planes left so close together. It also gave the children a chance to see him off on his flight, making very real to them his explanation of why they were going back to San Jose with Hilary. After Bill had left and when Hilary was about to board with the children, George delighted Jason by telling him he would be coming to visit the next week. Gratefully Hilary hugged George, clinging to the security of his warmth.

"Be sure to line up some evening sitters," he said as he kissed her good-bye.

"I will," she promised. With Lisa tucked in one arm and Jason clinging to the other hand, she led her little procession off to the plane.

Even though Hilary had hoped Bill would take the children, she had also learned to plan ahead for contingencies. Before she'd left San Jose, she had checked with her friend Mary Lou and found that she would be coming in from a flight about the same time as Hilary. Now they joined forces at the airport, and Mary Lou drove them all to San Jose, remarking that Hilary looked well rested from her vacation.

"It was an especially enjoyable vacation," Hilary admitted.

Mary Lou glanced over at her, not the least perturbed by the chaotic traffic on the Bayshore. "Sounds intriguing. Ten to one, a man."

"Yes. A very nice man."

"Is it serious?"

Hilary was playing pat-a-cake with the baby in her lap. "I don't know."

"You wouldn't really consider living up in Oregon again, would you?" Mary Lou looked absolutely shocked.

"I'd consider it. Whether I'd decide to do it or not, I'm not sure. He owns a sporting goods store, actually a couple of them. My parents know him. He's an outdoors type —hunting, fishing, boating."

Mary Lou actually laughed. "You can't be for real, Hilary. What would you do with a man like that? No, don't answer me. There are children in the car."

"George isn't a red-neck or a hillbilly, Mary Lou. And he's not a macho type. There are a lot of outdoor things I enjoy, and he's impressed with what I do."

"Has he read any of your columns?"

"None of the columns, but several of my articles. He's reasonably attuned to women's rights."

Mary Lou snorted. "Reasonably! I can just see it. He'll brag about how you're so clever you can write articles for national magazines and then keep you in the kitchen surrounded by babies."

Her analysis, though glib, was a little too close to the possible truth for Hilary to respond directly. "He's amusing and intelligent. Mary Lou, I sometimes get tired of being on my own. Having a supportive man might be just the thing I need to keep my strength up. You know I'm not likely to go all domestic and dependent."

"Aren't you?" Mary Lou glanced over at her again. "You have no idea how seductive a trip it can be, Hilary. Someone to take care of you, to lift the burdens from your poor tired body and mind. That's why I take mine in doses," she confessed. "Otherwise, you get caught in the trap. A few babies, not enough money to support yourself, too many obligations to the family to expand beyond it, and snap! you're caged. Like one of those doesn't-kill-'em traps where the poor mouse runs around and around. It'd probably prefer to be wiped out immediately."

"You don't have to lose your independence in marriage," Hilary said stubbornly.

"To someone like your George, you do. Okay, okay, I don't know him, but you have to admit the setting is ripe for it. Small town, small businessman. I'll bet he wants kids unless he already has them."

"He wants kids. He's never been married."

Mary Lou's brows rose.

"He's not gay either, Mary Lou. I promise you."

Her friend grinned. "I'll take your word for it. Look, Hilary, I don't mean to sound so negative. All I want you to do is think very carefully about it. Don't rush into anything just because you've had a difficult time recently. Why don't you put off any decision until the kids are back with their parents and you have a chance to remember what it's like being just you on your own?"

"Sometimes you surprise me, Mary Lou." Hilary sighed. "I thought you'd think the situation was ideal: a good-looking, well-to-do man who travels a fair amount and would take me with him. Someone who's tickled with my career and wants me to continue writing articles. A man who isn't so obsessed with his job that he can't take time off whenever he wants to do something sporting."

"Sounds okay on paper. But you aren't mentioning those kids, or staying at home, or being in your old home-town with your folks and your sister. Then there are the times he pushes off on a hunting trip when the kids have the measles and the times when you're too pregnant to take off on a trip with him. Once you have the kids, in fact, the trips stop, pretty much, for you. Oh, Mom would be happy to stay with them once in a while, but you'll feel guilty about leaving them, or he will, especially when they're little. You'll be too tired to write articles, and you'll get the itch to be out at the newspaper office again, having lunch with all those stimulating people instead of spooning Pablum in some kid's mouth."

"I've *enjoyed* having Jason and Lisa with me," Hilary insisted, turning to smile at the little boy in the back seat, who was paying no attention to their conversation.

"Sure you have. They're adorable. And they've made it impossible for you to concentrate on your job."

"But I've been in a single-parent situation. That wouldn't be true with George."

"Your sister didn't think it would be either."

Hilary stared thoughtfully out the window. "I don't think that would be a problem with George. Some of the other things you've said . . . Well, maybe. It would be up to me to keep some perspective."

"So what's the bottom line? Do you love him?"

There was a moment's silence in the car, as if even the children were waiting to hear her answer, though Hilary knew Lisa couldn't follow their discussion, and Jason wasn't listening. "I like him; I'm attracted to him. Is that love? I've been mildly infatuated half a dozen times, Mary Lou, but I wouldn't describe it as love. He wants to marry me. That's very impressive. Not many men have, as you know, and none of them has had George's qualifications. It's stupid, I suppose, but I have this feeling that he's been searching for someone like me—someone independent, capable, different from the women he knows."

"Just because he's been looking for someone like you doesn't mean he'd be a good husband for you."

"I know." Hilary gave an impatient flip of her hand. "Tell me what's been happening with you."

The sight of the newspaper building on Monday morning made Hilary's heart leap slightly. She wasn't sure whether it was the challenge that lay ahead in her column or the possibility that soon she would not climb these steps five days a week. The greetings she received made her feel welcomed back into the fold, gave her reassurance that she had friends here and admirers of her column. Harry was already in the office when she entered and glanced up to growl at her, "It's about time you came back. I thought that woman was going to smother us in niceness."

Hilary laughed. "Marsh said she did a fine job with the column."

"Sure, if you like that sort of thing. Well-reasoned, unstimulating pap, I consider it."

"Marsh said he got a lot of favorable comment."

Harry waved a hairy hand. "Each to his own. It put me to sleep over my breakfast."

"I'll have to read them." She set her briefcase on the chair and wandered over to the window. "How are Carol and the kids?"

"Everyone's fine. You look as if you really had a vacation. I haven't seen you so healthy-looking in months."

"It was a perfect break, but I did bring the kids back with me. Their father was going to keep them, but he got a chance to attend a training program in Chicago. I'll have them for only another month."

There was a knock at the door, and they both called "Come in," at the same time. Hilary's eyes widened as the door swung open and Marsh strode into the office. To her recollection he had never been there before.

"Checking to see if I made it?" she said, keeping her tone light.

"Something like that," he retorted. "Hello, Harry. How's Carol?"

"Couldn't be better." Harry glanced from Marsh to Hilary and said, "I think I'll go get a cup of coffee."

Hilary, still standing by the window, watched him march out of the office and smiled hesitantly at Marsh. "Does he know something I don't?"

"No, he's just being tactful, I think." He looked around the office briefly and indicated the chair onto which she'd tossed her briefcase. "May I?"

"Sure." She hastened to take the briefcase from him and set it next to her desk before seating herself. "What can I do for you?"

Ignoring the question, he studied her face, his own a polite mask. "You look rested, Hilary. That's what I wanted, though you may think my tactics were a little rough. Believe me, I insisted on the vacation only because you needed it—for your own good as well as the paper's. I hope you won't harbor any resentment."

The intensity of his gaze made her feel vaguely uneasy. Well, not uneasy exactly. Flustered, perhaps, would better describe her emotions, though that was not precise either. She began, more and more, to feel the way she had the night of the dinner-dance and mentally scolded herself for the comparison. That had been a momentary attraction, a fleeting physical desire. They were sitting now in her office at the newspaper, having a professional discussion. Such thoughts, let alone the tension throughout her body, had no place here.

After adjusting the position of a pen on her desk, she said, "No, of course not. But I think you should be perfectly honest with me about my position. On the phone you pooh-poohed the idea that you wanted Lois to continue the column. Of course, I was delighted to hear that because it was my idea and my execution that has built it to—whatever it is. You were dissatisfied with my work before I left, and I admit that my personal problems were interfering with my concentration. I don't think that will happen again, though I can't be positive. Let's assume I start writing the way I used to, doing the job you expect of me. Will that be enough? What I'm asking, I guess, is whether you'd rather abandon the column altogether."

A puzzled frown creased his brow, and he shifted to cross one leg over the other. "That's a rather strange question. I don't believe I've said or done anything that would lead you to believe I wanted to do away with your column."

"But do you? I know I have a contract that comes up for renewal in another month or so. It would be just as well for you to tell me now if you're considering a change. Or if, for instance, it would make it easier for you if I resigned."

"Resigned?" He uttered the word as though he weren't quite sure of its definition. "Are you considering resigning, Hilary?"

Deciding there was no reason to give any more information than necessary, she said, "What I asked was whether you would be just as pleased if I did."

"Just as pleased as what? As I am when my car breaks down?" He ran a hand through his hair, looking slightly disgruntled. "Your column is good for the paper. It's a drawing card. And I think it makes an impression, helps shape the kinds of attitudes you're looking for. That's why you don't want it to get careless or shoddy. You *stand* for something."

"And I can't let down my side by being human." Hilary gave an unamused laugh. "Actually I know that's true, and sometimes it requires a little more of me than I have to give."

"That's because you've had the children recently."

"I still have them."

"But you won't for too long, and barring crises, you weren't doing all that badly."

"I like doing things *well*."

"I know." He grinned at her. "There's only so much you can do well all at the same time."

"Some people do it."

"Your circumstances were special. Come on, Hilary. What's really bothering you?"

"Nothing. I just want to know where I stand."

Unsatisfied, he looked for a moment as though he would press the issue, but Harry returned then with his cup of coffee. When he made as if to back out again, Marsh waved him in, saying to Hilary, "You stand just where you did two months ago and two years ago. You write a good column, and it's helping the paper's circulation as much as it ever did. Read the columns Lois wrote while you were away. You'll see the difference. They're competent but unexciting. I wouldn't be tempted to carry a column like that more than once a week, if that. But you'll also see why they appealed to a certain segment of our readers. Don't despise that segment, Hilary. They're good, honest, hard-working people who sometimes want a little pat on the back for encouragement, and they deserve it. They're trying to do things right, even when it isn't easy, and there's not always someone there to appreciate their efforts."

Hilary merely nodded. Since she showed no sign of wishing to speak with him further, he rose and touched her shoulder lightly. "I'm glad you're back and looking so well. When you bring up your column this afternoon, come in and tell me what you meant about becoming broader in your scope."

"All right."

When he left, Hilary found Harry regarding her speculatively. "What's the matter?" she demanded, laughing. "He's always that way. A little praise, a little criticism. Sometimes it's difficult to tell the difference between the two."

"Did you press him to know where you stood?"

"Yes. It seemed possible to me that he'd rather do without the column."

Harry raised bushy brows incredulously. "Did you leave your self-confidence in Oregon?"

"It's not a matter of self-confidence, Harry. If Marsh wasn't enthusiastic about the column anymore, I . . . would make other plans. I could do free-lance work."

Harry snorted. "Sure you could. You'd just love that, sitting in your house all day with no one around to sound your ideas on, or to inspire them for that matter."

She lifted her shoulders in a nonchalant shrug. "I write articles fairly regularly. With a little shift in my mental processes, I could make it a career."

"But why would you want to? Even if Marsh didn't want your column, he'd give you a job as a reporter. Or you could find a position on any one of half a dozen papers in the area."

"Perhaps." Hilary opened her briefcase and took out the legal pad on which she'd jotted down several ideas while she was away. "I'd better get to work if I want today's column to live up to expectation. He didn't force me to take a two-week vacation so I'd mess up the first day back."

"Are you annoyed with him for doing that?"

"Not anymore. I did need the change; I just didn't have the two weeks left."

"So you'll miss a week's pay?"

"Yes, but it doesn't matter all that much. I got the article in while I was away."

"Is that what made you think about free-lancing full time?"

Hilary turned briefly to meet his eyes, which were alive with curiosity. "Maybe."

"You'd miss the paper." He cleared his throat. "And we'd miss you."

Refusing to satisfy his interest further, she said firmly, "Thank you, Harry. Now I *must* get to work on this."

It was a good column, and she knew it. Hilary had chosen one of the many incidents that had sparked her feminism while she was in Klamath Falls. Unable to give the proper vent to it then, she took the opportunity now, even going so far as to mock herself for her prudence in restraining comment at the time. But this, too, she turned to advantage by relating it to the people Marsh had spoken of earlier, who would understand her reluctance and would identify with her in the situation.

"He wanted to see me with the column today," Hilary told Susan. "It's a package deal."

"You look great, Hilary," Susan said as she pressed a button. "Must have had a good time."

Hilary was beginning to wonder just what she'd looked like before she left. They all made her feel as though she'd gone off to Oregon looking hagridden and bleary-eyed. "It was a nice, relaxing vacation."

"I'm glad. You can go on in."

The office was exactly as she remembered it, but somehow it seemed a long time since she'd been there. It was completely different from the space George called his office at the store, which was as littered with papers and catalogues as his study at home. George's decor was warehouse-casual, in fact, was no decor at all. Which was only reasonable, Hilary reminded herself, even though it had been necessary for her to remove a backpack from the only other chair when she'd visited him there. It was a working office, not a place for impressing business associates and advertisers on a city newspaper.

Marsh smiled as she entered and took the pages she held out to him. "Please sit down, Hilary. May I have Susan bring you a cup of coffee?"

Since he'd never offered her one before, she regarded him suspiciously. "No; thanks."

He made a gesture of acceptance and seated himself, not behind his desk but in a chair beside hers. Hilary patiently waited for him to finish reading the column, studying his face as he did so. The wide forehead and stubborn, square chin were what made him look so forbidding, she decided. And the way he narrowed his eyes when he was concentrating. If you didn't notice his lips, you would probably take him for a hard man, driven to succeed, oblivious to those around him. But you did notice his lips, and they made all the difference. They added the touch of sensitivity to his face that would otherwise have been lacking.

Though the lips were thin, it was a generous mouth, wide and delicately bowed.

"Excellent," he said, looking up to find her eyes on him. "You've got your old sting, yet you've included your reader in a subtle conspiracy. That's the way I like to see you write, Hilary."

"Thank you." She had trouble forcing herself to keep eye contact with him because she found his gaze disturbing when there was a hint of approval in it. Often he'd sat in the position of critic, the deeply etched frown on his face. Not that praise was entirely missing from their interchanges, but it was usually milder, more reserved. Had he ever told her a column was "excellent" before? Usually it was "good" or "fine" and quickly dismissed. Today's comment might have been purely relevant, though, to the poor ones she'd been doing before she left.

"Now tell me what you have in mind for broadening the column," he urged, sitting back comfortably, the interest in his eyes wholly apparent.

"Two things, really. I want to go a little further in depth on some matters." She found herself looking slightly to the left of him and returned her gaze to his face. "You know I write magazine articles."

"Yes, I've seen some of them."

That surprised her since he wouldn't come in contact with them in the course of his work, but she said only, "Yes, well, I enjoy writing them because they cover a topic more fully. They require more research and can't be glib, but they're also more persuasive because they can handle more facets of a topic. I'd like to do more series types of columns, and what they would be, actually, would be serializations of longer articles. New ones, of course. Nothing that I'd published before."

"Still on feminist topics?"

"Yes, but with an orientation to the family as well. Discussions of crisis points in family life with the emphasis on the woman's role—in causing them, solving them, enduring them. In other words, step beyond personal opinion to a more sociological level, not all the time, but occasionally. I minored in sociology and could probably dig out the sources I'd need without any trouble."

"I like the idea," he admitted, frowning, "but it would be more work for you."

"I wouldn't do them regularly, perhaps once a month for a week. And it wouldn't be any more difficult than what I do for the magazine articles. In fact, it would be very similar."

Marsh nodded, but his thick brows were bunched, making him look especially endearing. "Do you realize that because the column is generally personal opinion, people reading the studies will take them less seriously than they might if they were published in a magazine?"

"Yes, but I think it will work both ways." Hilary grinned at him, her eyes alight. "After reading a few of the studies, they may take my personal opinion more seriously."

He laughed. "Crafty woman. You may be right. What's the other idea?"

"That's a little trickier because it involves travel. Let me think about it some more before I discuss it with you," she suggested, offering the bait.

"Travel? You mean, your traveling somewhere and the newspaper's paying for it?"

His incredulous expression didn't appear to daunt her. "Something like that. Look what my trip to Klamath Falls did. I don't mean the vacation itself. I looked at my hometown through my columnist's eyes, and it was fascinating. I'd like to be able to do that with a lot of places. Remember, we're different on the West Coast, especially in California. I'd like to see what it's like for women in Kansas, and Maine, and South Carolina."

"Hilary," he said seriously, "the paper can't run to that kind of expense for a columnist. You're talking airfare, a couple of weeks' lodging, meals, incidental expenses. We don't even send reporters very far to cover events; we rely on the wire services."

"I know." She laughed, a delicious peal of golden notes. "I was teasing you, Mr. Marsh. Everyone was so tickled with how much good this vacation did me I was sure you'd want to do it regularly. And you all were so sure I'd resent your forcing me to go. Everyone is walking on eggshells, telling me how good I look and how important I am around here. You all must think that I've lost my sense of humor or that I never had one. I was going to suggest that you send me to Europe, but I thought that was pushing it too far."

In her amusement at really having fooled him, at the way his concerned expression became ludicrously bemused, Hilary didn't notice immediately when he moved in his chair. She couldn't fail to notice, though, when his hands gripped her upper arms and lifted her effortlessly to her feet. When he had her standing there facing him, he didn't know quite what to do with her, she supposed, because he hesitated even as his arms started to go around her. Instead, he dropped them to his sides, placed a chaste kiss on her cheek, and then pointed to the door. "Out, young woman. I'm a busy man who hasn't time for columnists who poke fun at me." His dark eyes, half-amused, half-tempted, searched her face for something, but she was so stunned by the suddenness of his response that she regarded him with bewilderment. Shaken, Hilary backed a step from him.

"I—I'm going," she whispered.

"I didn't mean to startle you," he said levelly. "I meant only to hug you but realized that was inappropriate. If you were my sister, I would have, for so thoroughly pulling the wool over my eyes. She's always trying, but she rarely succeeds."

"Your sister . . . yes," Hilary murmured. "Did you initial the column?"

He looked about him and found the papers on the floor beside the chair. He rapidly wrote his bold initials in the upper corner. As he handed it to her, he asked, "Was there a real second idea for the column?"

"No, not yet. The rest of what I have will fit into the daily effort." Since he ordinarily opened the door for her and he hadn't moved, she started walking slowly toward it. He overtook her and stood with his hand on the knob, looking down at her.

"If it weren't so expensive, it wouldn't be a bad idea, you know. Living here, we start to think the rest of the country shares our way of looking at life, and it's not particularly true. Have you traveled around the country much?"

"No, I've been only to New York and Boston really. A number of the people I know have moved here from the Midwest, though, and I've watched them survive the culture shock and adapt to California living more or less."

"You must have found somewhat the same thing when you first came from Oregon."

"It's so long ago I hardly remember," she admitted, moving slightly closer to the door.

Marsh opened it then, and she could feel his eyes on her as she waved to Susan and marched toward the elevator. While she waited, she didn't turn around, for fear he was still standing there because she hadn't heard the door close. Her relief when the elevator arrived was profound.

Chapter Fourteen

Hilary found that she slipped more easily into the routine with the children the second time. They, too, had some familiarity now with their surroundings. Jason returned from play group each day in good humor, and Lisa was beginning to wriggle about the floor like a fat worm. Hilary considered the years of grit in the worn carpet and rented a machine from the supermarket to give it a good cleaning.

With the magazine assignment finished, she had the early evenings to spend with the children, and the later to recuperate. Even though she knew their father would take them in a month, she refused two assignments that were offered her, determined this time not to extend herself unnecessarily. She scoured the neighborhood for baby-sitters and came up with two.

This organization of her life did not lead her to any conclusions on George. Except for Mary Lou, she didn't tell anyone about him. He called the evening she got home, and two days later, and then on the evening she was to go out with Marsh. She was talking with him when the doorbell rang.

"I've got to go now, George. I'm going out for the evening."

There was a moment's pause, and then his voice, very tight, came over the line: "You have a *date*? With a *man*?"

"Hold on a moment." She set the receiver down and went to answer the door. She excused herself to finish the phone call. Unfortunately the only phone she'd bothered to have connected was in the living room, where everyone could hear what she said. She turned her back to Marsh as the children gathered around Mrs. Rainer. "George? Yes, it's newspaper business. Remember I told you I went to civic functions with my editor? It's part of my job."

"Is this man married?"

"No."

"How old is he?"

Hilary had no intention of answering a question which could so easily be interpreted by Marsh. "I have to go now. I'll talk to you soon."

"Call me tomorrow."

A spark of anger flared at the commanding tone of voice, but she said pleasantly enough, "Okay. Talk to you then." Without waiting for him to answer, she hung up. She didn't want to hear him say he loved her at a time like that. Did he know what love was any better than she did? It seemed on a par with his loving his store, or his hunting trips, or his house—something he possessed or enjoyed or admired.

Afraid that he might call back immediately, she grabbed her coat, kissed the children, said good-bye to Mrs. Rainer, and fairly flew to the door. Marsh regarded her with undisguised amusement. "That eager to get out of here?" he asked as they walked to his car.

"Things are running smoothly so far. I have my fingers crossed."

"Tell me about Klamath Falls," he suggested. "How's your sister doing?"

"She's better. In two weeks she'll probably get out and live with my parents for a while. When she's ready, she'll move into her own house and see if she can cope. Her husband will be back in a month, so whoever is ready first will take Jason and Lisa."

"Did you spend all your time in Oregon caring for them?"

"Oh, no. My mother watched them most days, and their father in the evenings and on weekends."

"What did you do?"

Hilary glanced over at him, but his attention was on the

road. "Lots of things. Hiking at Crater Lake, boating on Upper Klamath Lake, visits to various parks, tennis. I met some old friends and made some new ones."

"Your columns this week have been delightful. I gather you got most of your material there. How did you happen to hear so much country music?"

The column Hilary had written the day before had expressed her exasperation with the antifeminist lyrics of so many of the country songs she'd heard on George's car radio. "A friend had the radio on a lot while we were driving. I rather liked the music; most of it has a good strong beat. But, my Lord, they're living in the nineteenth century with their attitudes! A few of them were okay, and some of them were downright funny, but none of them is going to win the feminist award of the year. I did like the one where the woman put up with a lot of guff from her husband for years without saying anything until the children were grown and then just walked out."

"That's an old one," he told her. "I listen to country music when I'm puttering in my workshop."

"What do you do there?"

"In the workshop? Build furniture, mostly. Simple things. I don't get much opportunity to work with my hands, but I find it soothing." He returned the conversation to her. "Did you tell your friend how you felt about the music?"

"No, why should I?"

He shrugged. "It's the sort of thing you can talk about with friends. If there are too many things you limit yourself to discussing with someone, as you seemed to indicate in your column Monday, then it's not a very close friendship."

"You can't just go into Klamath Falls and ride roughshod over people's opinions. You have to use a little discretion."

"True. I'm not disputing that. On the other hand," he said meditatively, "you don't get very close to people you have to mind your tongue with, do you?"

Hilary had turned to stare out the window. "It depends.

You can get close in other ways." She realized, as soon as she said it, that she shouldn't have. If he knew they were discussing a man, and presumably he did, then . . . "Like my parents," she hastened to add. "We don't agree on a lot of things, and I wouldn't think of forcing a discussion of the ones we don't, but we're still very close."

"You'd find the differences more apparent and the silence harder to sustain at constant close range. If you still lived with them, for instance."

"Possibly," she said, annoyed that he made her feel defensive about George when they weren't even talking about him. Or maybe they were.

"I didn't marry until I was twenty-six," he said, as though it were relevant.

"Fascinating."

He chuckled. "I assure you I was going to say something fascinating if you hadn't interrupted me." They were stopped for a red light not far from their destination.

"Don't let me stop you," she grumbled.

"When I married Alice, she was twenty-eight. I told you about her children. Well, she was a beautiful woman, sophisticated, intelligent, from a socially prominent family who'd lived on the peninsula for ages. My own family was more middle-class, maybe upper-middle-class, and that seemed close enough. But the differences mattered in insidious ways. She thought working for a living was a bit déclassé and thought I should be able to take off when and where I pleased, with her. If the Bloomingdales were having a cocktail party at deadline time, I was expected to traipse off to shake hands and exchange inanities with her friends instead of doing my job. I was city editor then. Even a difference in attitude that seems as small as that can put a huge strain on a marriage."

"I'm sure it can. Was that the fascinating part?"

"It was the object lesson," he muttered, glaring at her as he parked the car.

"Did you want me to write a column about it? 'The Perils of Interclass Marriages' would make a good headline. You don't suppose your former wife reads my column, do you? I'm very conscientious about not embarrassing people by writing up their stories so they recognize themselves."

Marsh studied her face's mock seriousness and gave a doleful shake of his head. "Your vacation seems to have restored your humor, Hilary, but not to my advantage. I had no intention of boring you with the details of my private life."

Contrite, Hilary reached over and placed a hand on his arm. "I didn't mean to mock your confessions, Mr. Marsh. And your advice is sound, I'm sure. It's just . . . I have to make my own decisions, weigh a number of factors, judge what's most important to me."

His face wore a slightly stunned look. "You really are thinking of marrying someone up in Oregon, aren't you? Someone you've known for only two weeks."

"Two weeks of time spent largely with one person is enough to get to know him fairly well. And I'm not going to get to know him any better living here. How long did you know your wife before you married her?"

As she started to remove her hand from his arm, he grasped it between both of his. "Six months," he said virtuously.

"Hmmm. And did you date her all that time, or had you just known who she was part of the time?"

He gave her a crooked smile. "I dated her for only a month before I asked her to marry me, but I knew who she was all that time. I met her shortly after her divorce. I don't want you to think I precipitated it."

"It wouldn't matter if I did, would it?" Hilary asked, gently withdrawing her hand.

"You went to Oregon a wreck, Hilary. At low ebb. As susceptible to a romance as you would have been to a germ. You were run-down from trying to cope with a difficult situation, and anyone who looked competent would have appealed to you. No," he said when she tried to speak, "I want you to think about that. Maybe he is the right man, but you're going to have to separate out your own emotions from the situation. Take an objective look at him, at the kind of life you'd have there. You thrive on the newspaper work. The Klamath Falls newspaper isn't going to offer a column like yours."

"I could free-lance magazine articles. The change wouldn't mean giving up my career entirely."

"I realize that." He opened his door, stepped out, and came around the car to open hers. As he looked down at her, he made a gesture of impotence. "I know you don't want anyone, especially me, interfering in your personal life, Hilary. But you don't want to make a mistake, so please think about what I've said. Now I promise I won't say another word on the subject."

And he didn't. Not that evening or on any subsequent meeting. Hilary didn't know what to make of his speaking out or of his shutting up. It seemed to her that he had said either too much or too little, that he should have clarified on what basis he was giving her advice. Was it as a friend or as an employer? After a time she came to see that it didn't matter, that it was probably a combination of the two, producing a not completely disinterested third party.

The times she talked to George on the phone were not the relaxed occasions being with him had been. She could feel the pressure he appl'ed and braced herself against it. He was rushing her, part of her mind insisted, asking for too many decisions at once. Or perhaps he wasn't asking her to make them at all. He was trying to make them for her, ready to sweep her along on his own wave of enthusiasm.

Hilary couldn't blame him for that. It was precisely his certainty of his affection for her that was so compelling. The mental image of herself in the garret of his house working on her articles was dimming slightly, pushed aside by his urgent desire to have a family. But still, she thought, if she had children, she wouldn't be alone with them, as she was here. George would be there to share her burdens, to give her the support she had enjoyed with Jack. Sometimes she wondered if she confused him in her mind with Jack, giving George some of her previous friend's more endearing qualities. Other times she told herself that was a lot of nonsense.

George had to delay his trip by a few days at the last minute, only to arrive on a day when Hilary was supposed to attend a function with Marsh. And even then George didn't call her until he was already in San Francisco, forcing her to make a change in her arrangements. She called Marsh immediately after she had hung up.

"Mr. Marsh, my friend from Oregon just arrived in town, and I told him about this evening. He offered to escort me, and I accepted. I don't like to muddle things for you, but he'll be in town only two days. Is that all right?"

With a long-suffering sigh Marsh said, "I don't have much choice, do I? What about Mrs. Rainer?"

"Well, I thought, if it was okay, that George could pick her up and take her home. He's rented a car."

"It's out of his way. I'll drop her off and take her home."

Hilary considered the logistics of that. It would mean she and George had to go home immediately after the charity cocktail party, and she had said they could go on to dinner together. "That wouldn't work, Mr. Marsh. I'll have George do it. We're going to dinner afterward."

"I'll bring her. George isn't familiar with the area. He can take her home. It's not out of my way, Hilary."

Hearing George's name on his tongue sounded strange to her. "Thank you." What else could she say? George might appreciate the convenience, or he might resent the familiarity of the gesture. That was his problem, she decided. It didn't bother her in the least.

When George arrived, he swooped Hilary up in a bear hug, while Jason danced around them, waiting for his share of the attention. Not to be outdone, Lisa pounded on the top of her playpen with a chubby fist, gurgling happily. George surveyed the scene with satisfaction. "You're going to make a terrific mother, Hilary," he commented, not for the first time, as he released her.

Instead of responding to the leading suggestion, she

said, "Pour yourself a glass of wine while I change Lisa. Mr. Marsh will be here with the sitter any minute."

"Why's he bringing the sitter?" he asked, frowning.

"Because she lives near him and he always brings her. You'll have to take her home, though, since we'll be out later." Before he could say anything further, she whisked the baby off to the bedroom, to emerge only when the doorbell rang.

The introductions felt a little awkward to her with the two men patently attempting to size each other up, George suspicious, Marsh urbane. "Would you like a glass of wine, Mr. Marsh?" Hilary asked.

"No, thanks. I have someone in the car." He turned to go, ruffling Jason's hair and smiling at Lisa. "I'm sure I'll see you both shortly at the hotel."

Hilary nodded, and George watched him closely as he shut the door. "We don't have to leave right away," she said. "You can finish your wine and tell the kids what's happened in Klamath Falls since they left."

But George wanted to be alone with her, and she found herself in his rented car within minutes. "He's a good-looking man," he said.

"Yes."

"How long have you worked with him?"

"Eight years, though not very closely until I started doing the column a few years ago. I've clipped a bunch of the columns, by the way. I'll give them to you later." She settled back against the seat, determined not to let his ill-concealed jealousy disturb her. "Have you seen my parents since I left?"

"I took them to lunch Saturday. Your mother said Janet will come to stay with them next week." He couldn't let the subject drop. "And you go out with this Marsh every week to some society do?"

"He got tired of answering questions about my column. At first he wanted me to provide myself with an escort, but that would have been a little hectic when I had the kids, so we just go together. It costs the newspaper less."

He grunted. "I'll bet. Have you ever slept with him, Hilary?"

She could feel her body stiffen while he studiously concentrated on the traffic in front of them. "That's none of your business, George."

"Of course it is!" he exclaimed, his hands clenching the wheel. "I'm going to marry you, and I don't want you left down here in San Jose alone at the mercy of some shark. Remember, you don't have to keep your job that way. You're going to be leaving in a few weeks anyhow."

"Back up a minute, George," she said coldly. "I want to make sure I understand what you just said. You think I would sleep with Marsh to keep my job?"

His face flushed. "I didn't mean to put it that way. I'm sorry. Women do, Hilary. Sometimes. Especially when their bosses are handsome single men. It's not just for the job then, I suppose. People who work together can become interested in each other sexually."

"I wouldn't for the world deny that some women sleep with their bosses for advantage, any more than I would deny that men sexually harass their female employees. But if you think for one minute, one second, that I would be willing to prostitute myself for any job in the world, you don't know the first thing about me, George. No job, no amount of money are worth that degradation. You would never assume that a man would do such a thing. Why a woman? And why me?"

While he made the left turn she indicated, he said nothing, but as soon as he could, he pulled the car off to the side of the road to inspect her frozen face. "Look, Hilary, I didn't mean you. I didn't mean to say what I did. If you slept with him, it was because you wanted to, not for any gain. Honestly I believe that. You have very high principles."

"No higher than the majority of my sisters," she retorted. "*That's* what you don't believe, George, and that's what I can't accept from you. You're willing to put me on a pedestal, to believe that I'm some shining example of womanhood rather than representative of all of us and what we're striving for. But what you want to do is put me in a glass cage and show me off to your friends. You want to domesticate me, load me down with children and housework, train me to play the role of your wife. And when you do, I'm not going to be any different from all those women you passed up in Klamath Falls, George."

"That's not true! You *are* different. You won't ever be the way they are: dependent, bored, boring." He ran a hand distractedly through his hair. "That's why I fell in love with you: because you're special."

Hilary reached over to touch his cheek. "I know you believe that, and it flatters the hell out of me. But what you can't see is that those women you pass over so glibly have every ounce of potential I have, and more. They've fitted themselves into the mold they were supposed to. Their husbands expect it of them, and their parents, and the community. They're wives and mothers, doing the kinds of things their husbands wouldn't dream of doing, and doing them well. They're running the PTAs and doing the charity work and cleaning the houses and caring for the children. Right now you want me to stand out in that domestic wilderness, you want me to be the Christmas tree. But soon you'll want me to be the best mother, the best cook, the best housekeeper because those are the standards of the community. After a year or so you'd come home from the store to find me writing in the garret with the house a shambles and the baby crying. Which do you think would be more important then, George?"

"It wouldn't be like that," he insisted, catching her hand. "You'd be proud of the house and the kids, and even me maybe. There would be time for everything when you weren't going out to an office every day. You could write when the children took their naps or when they were playing quietly in their rooms. Or you could have a sitter come in for a few hours a day while you shut yourself off in the attic."

Hilary squeezed his hand. "I've had friends who tried that. Usually their husbands couldn't understand the necessity, expecially if they didn't earn any money for their endeavors. Pretty soon the wife got to feeling guilty about the extra expense and did away with the sitter, which meant she did away with her projects because you simply can't do them both really well."

"But you'd make money. You could handle both without the least effort."

"Such faith." She sighed. "I'm not Superwoman, George. If it could be done without effort, millions of women would be doing it. What happens is that they beat their heads against a wall of frustrations. Granted, a lot of them are of their own making. They want to prove they can do everything well. Few men try to prove that. Not only don't they want to do housework well, but they don't want to do it at all. Hell, I don't blame them. It's not much fun. Can you picture yourself doing the dishes and vacuuming the floor and dusting the furniture?"

"No," he said flatly. "I have a housekeeper come in to do it."

"And you'd expect me to become your housekeeper." When he opened his mouth to protest, she hurriedly continued. "I'd expect it of myself. God knows why. I don't think we were granted any special equipment for being the ones to get shackled with it. Physically I'm sure men could do just as good a job."

"So what are you saying? That you don't want to do housework? That you don't want children to mess up your life?" A tinge of anger clung to his words.

"Can you blame me? If getting married meant those things to you, would you leap right in?"

He shook his head in disbelief. "Hilary, you're nutty. You're doing housework now and caring for kids. Despite the hardships, you're managing to work at a full-time job."

"And it exhausts me. I don't have time for the other things—for going out to movies and for playing tennis. I feel guilty if I enjoy myself at the expense of the kids. They deserve my attention, too. If I have them, I have to care for them."

"So you'd rather not," he said scornfully. "My God, Hilary, it's the one special function a woman has, having kids.

But you'd rather play tennis. That's incredibly selfish."

"I don't know if I want to have children, George. But I do know it's a decision I don't take lightly. Selfish? Possibly. I could make a good case for people having children as being the selfish ones. Why do they have them, George? Do you think it's some great altruism? To populate the world with replicas of themselves?" She shrugged off the subject. "We're going to be late. Let's discuss this later."

"It sounds as though we don't have much to discuss," he said as he started the car again and pulled it out into the stream of traffic. "You had led me to believe that you'd marry me."

"No, George. I told you I'd think about it. I have been thinking about it. Strenuously. We had a wonderful time those two weeks in Klamath Falls, and I like you, a lot. But the reason you want to get married is so you can have a family, and I'm not sure I'm ready for one. You don't give me any choice. If I marry you, I'm expected to have a baby right off."

"Neither of us is twenty years old anymore, Hilary. And it's not just that I want a family. I want you. And *your* children. They'll be special children, the way you're a special woman."

"It doesn't necessarily work that way, George."

"I talked to the editor at the paper. He's a friend of mine. You could probably get a job there, with your experience."

"And your influence." Hilary bit her lip to repress any further sarcastic statement. "Oh, George. You don't understand at all, do you?"

"Yes, I understand. I understand that you think you'd be restless there. You think you'd be tied down with housework and babies, that you'd go batty without your job. So I checked to see if you could find something there, and that just makes you angry."

"I used to work there, George," she said gently. "And if I ever worked there again, I'd expect to get the job on my own, not depend on my husband's influence. I know you thought you were doing something for me, and I appreciate the thought. The parking's on the left up ahead."

While he parked the car, he didn't say anything. After Hilary had stepped out of the car to stand beside him, he put his arms around her, pressed her close to him. "But, Hilary, I love you. Doesn't that count for anything?"

Her throat had begun to ache, and her arms tightened around him. "Yes," she whispered. "It counts for a lot. But it doesn't count for everything, George. It won't make us right for each other. I've tried to believe that we were, and I've just been deluding myself. We'd be miserable after the first infatuation wore off. Read my columns. I think you'll understand. My feminism would begin to tear at you. As much as you think you like the differences in me, you'd find they were precisely the things that you wanted to change, so I'd be more like the other wives and mothers. And if I did change them, there'd be nothing left of me for myself."

"I don't want you to change."

"You already do," she said sadly. "You want me to want to be a mother right now. You're caught in a bind, George. The women in Klamath Falls seem too tame to you, too conventional. But you want your wife to lead a basically conventional life. I'm very much afraid you don't have much respect for women as a whole, especially the ones you see every day. A woman has to be out of the ordinary to appeal to you, and then you want to force her into a pretty rigid form. Like the woman who lived with you for those years."

"I should never have told you about her."

"It's a good thing you did. It's probably saved us both from making a dreadful mistake."

"It wouldn't *be* a mistake, Hilary."

Hilary met his eyes with a sorrowful, steady gaze. "Tell me that after you've read the columns, George."

The evening itself proved eye-opening for him, Hilary could tell. Her answers to the questions people asked her made him uncomfortable, though the attention she received didn't bother him, so long as it didn't come from Marsh. Hilary had never met Marsh's "date," who turned out to be his aunt, a bouncy white-haired woman of about seventy who appeared to know everyone in the room. Her name was Evelyn Phillips, and she took Hilary aside to tell her how much she enjoyed her column.

"I'd like to see a little more on older folks, mind you," she admonished. "May I send you some information?"

"I'd be delighted. Mr. Marsh has given me permission to do some articles in depth, a five-day series once a month, and I've had some vague thoughts on senior women. I really haven't written enough about them. Please send the information. I'll probably use it."

Marsh took the opportunity, while they were talking, to speak with George. Hilary watched them from the corner of her eye and was relieved to see that George had dropped his stiff, suspicious attitude and was conversing at ease. As she and Mrs. Phillips joined them, the two men were laughing.

"Can you go now?" George asked quietly. "I'm starved."

Hilary glanced at Marsh, who nodded. Her appetite had pretty well deserted her, but she found George at dinner to be his most charming. He said nothing about the two of them, concentrating on the various catastrophes which had befallen him on business trips. His stories made her laugh, and his attention made her want to cry. Their rapport was just slightly off center, not quite where it had been in Klamath Falls, but not disastrous either. Hilary could see that he was obliquely trying to point out to her that they would travel, that she would have the opportunity to be more open in the cosmopolitan centers than she was in the small town. And she could see that he was trying to absorb what he had heard earlier in the evening.

"Does this fellow Marsh agree with the things you write in your columns?" he asked abruptly when they were drinking coffee.

"Some of them. He won't stop me from saying what I want so long as the writing is adequate. Or if I don't libel someone and get the newspaper in trouble. That's basically why he reads the column each day." She sipped at her coffee, looking over the rim at him. "My friend Jack, who moved out awhile back, agreed with almost everything I said about women's rights. He'd read my columns and say, 'You've hit it just right, Hilary.' But he left me because the people at his office made fun of him for being under my thumb. He wasn't, but their thinking he was almost lost him a promotion he'd expected. What I'm trying to say, George, is that I'm not an easy woman to match up with. And I don't really want to change in any significant way. Maybe it would be better to say that I don't think I *can* change."

"We got along fine for two weeks."

"Yes, but they were special weeks. I was particularly vulnerable; I was tired; I was ready to have someone take care of me for a while. That isn't my usual situation. Ordinarily I like to take care of myself."

"Hilary, everyone needs to be taken care of sometimes. People need each other."

"I know, but what they need from each other is emotional support. And you can't keep on giving that kind of support when you disapprove of what the other person stands for." She watched him make a dismissive gesture with his hand. "You were uncomfortable with things I said tonight at the cocktail party. You'll be uncomfortable when you read my columns."

"You wouldn't be writing columns like that in Oregon."

"Ah, but I'd be wanting to write them. And I'd be biting my tongue every time we were out with other people, wanting to shake up the chauvinists and instigate a little rebellion among the subjugated wives."

"Is that how you felt when you were there?"

"Yes." He didn't look as though he believed her, and she said gently, "I'll let my columns speak for themselves."

"You wrote about us?" he asked, incredulous.

"Sort of. I had to let it out, George, just as I'd have to let it out eventually if I lived there."

They were silent on the drive to her house. As they walked to the door, he asked, "You don't want me to spend the night, do you?"

"No. I'm sorry, George."

As he left to take Mrs. Rainer home, she slipped a file

folder in his hand. "My columns. Will you call me tomorrow after you read them?"

He held her eyes for a long moment before nodding. Then he bent to kiss her, a short, unsatisfactory kiss because of Mrs. Rainer's presence. "I'll still feel the way I do," he insisted.

Hilary smiled sadly and stood in the doorway until he drove out of sight.

Chapter Fifteen

A BRIGHT autumn sun was shining through the office window as Hilary entered and set down her briefcase. Harry mumbled a greeting but was engrossed in the financial report he was underlining with a yellow marking pen. Almost immediately her phone buzzed.

"Hilary Campbell speaking."

"It's George, Hilary." There was a brief pause. "I read every one of the columns."

"And?"

"They're different from your articles."

"Yes."

"I don't agree with a lot of things you say."

"I didn't think you would."

He cleared his throat. "They make you sound hard and hostile."

"Sometimes I am. But you have to remember that the column is supposed to be controversial. It wouldn't go over very well if I said things everyone agreed with." She pushed back the hair which had fallen forward on her face and held it against her head with her free hand.

"I understand that. And I can see that you'd feel trapped in Klamath Falls . . . with me. I'm afraid I'd smother you or resent you. Neither would do you or me the least good."

"No." Hilary clutched the phone tightly. "George? You're a wonderful man, and it was a wonderful two weeks. I won't forget them . . . or you."

"I won't either." He sounded tired. "I wanted it to be more."

"I wish it could have been."

"I'll tell your parents I saw you. Will you be bringing the kids up when Bill gets back?"

"He's talking about coming to get them here on his way back from Chicago."

"Well, I'll probably see you the next time you're in Klamath Falls."

"I hope so."

"Good-bye, Hilary. Take care of yourself."

"You, too. Good-bye, George."

As she sat staring at the receiver, she felt a hand on her shoulder.

Harry asked sympathetically, "Another one bit the dust?"

"Um-hm. You know, I meet some very nice men, Harry. And I don't really think I'm such a bad person myself. But it never works out. I'm a little too strident; they're a little too . . . something." She let out a long breath and smiled sardonically. "Maybe Carol's brother would be just right for me."

"Don't waste your time. Who needs a man anyhow?"

"You don't want me to lose my sweet feminine attitude, do you?"

"Tell you what. I'll buy you lunch today."

"It's about time," she muttered. "I've bought the last three times."

"Carol keeps me on a tight budget," he informed her virtuously as he returned to his desk.

Though she had written a column to which Marsh could have no objection, and she sent Susan in with it, Marsh came to the door of his office and waved her in.

"I liked your friend George," he said.

"Thank you. He seemed to like you, too."

"Would you sit down for a minute, Hilary? I want to ask you something."

While she seated herself, he walked to his desk and stood reading the column. Without even glancing at her, he took his pen from his pocket and initialed the copy. "Now. I don't want you to feel I'm prying, but you must realize it makes a difference to the paper whether you decide to stay on or go to Oregon. Have you come to any decision?"

She met his curious gaze frankly. "I'm staying."

"Permanently?"

"Yes, permanently. Or at least as permanently as I can imagine right now."

He nodded. "Good. That is, it's good for the paper. If you've sustained a personal upset, I'm sorry."

Hilary didn't answer, though she didn't doubt his sincerity. There was just no reasonable remark she felt like making. "Was that all, Mr. Marsh?"

"Well, no." He looked slightly uneasy and paced over to the window so his back was to her. "My stepdaughter has taken a weekend job at Great America. You know, the amusement park. She's assisting at one of the children's rides. It's her first job, and I wanted to . . . sort of welcome her to it." He shrugged and turned back to her. "But I'm afraid it would only embarrass her if I showed up there alone with no other reason to be there than to say hello. I thought, if you'd be interested, I could take you and the children there this weekend. Jason's old enough to enjoy the rides, and even Lisa would probably love going about in a stroller and seeing all the people."

Hilary felt torn. She was sure the children would enjoy the outing, and she was willing to do a favor for Marsh, but it would also, in a certain sense, set a precedent she wasn't sure she wished to establish. It wouldn't fall into the category of newspaper business. On the other hand, it wasn't exactly a date either. She wouldn't be alone with him. And for heaven's sake, she was alone with him each time they went to some charity or civic gathering. Hilary realized she'd been staring at him and abruptly lowered her eyes.

"That would be fun for the kids. Thank you."

"Saturday?"

"Sure." Hilary rose. "What time?"

"I'll pick you up about ten."

* * *

It was a perfect autumn day, but Hilary was frowning when she opened the door to him. "I think we'd better take my car," she said without preamble. "The car seat is already in it, and they're bound to have sticky hands when we come back. I don't want to have to worry about your upholstery."

"Whatever is easiest."

Hilary had never seen him in jeans before. He wore a crew-neck sweater under a shirt, and comfortable walking shoes. Just before he arrived, she'd wondered if maybe she wasn't a little casual herself. But she'd wanted to look completely different from the way she did at the office or on their evening excursions. So she'd put on jeans and a navy blue sweat shirt from the University of Oregon and tied her hair in two low ponytails at her neck. If he found anything objectionable in her appearance, he didn't say so. He smiled and took Lisa, who was holding her arms out to him, making her usual happy burbling sounds. Jason danced excitedly at his feet.

"We're going to a 'musement park! Hilary says there's a merry-go-round and lots of other stuff. And cotton candy!"

"All that and more," Marsh agreed, releasing Lisa's fingers from his hair. "Let's help Hilary get the stroller in the car."

Marsh offered to drive, but Hilary only laughed. "You've probably forgotten what it's like to have kids in the car. They squeal and squirm so you're a nervous wreck if you're not used to it."

Actually, considering their level of excitement, Jason and Lisa behaved extraordinarily well. Marsh had no difficulty in talking over them and frequently to them. He told Hilary more about his stepchildren—where they lived, what grades they were in, what their ambitions were. "Jennifer thinks she'd like to be a doctor, but she could change her mind half a dozen times before she has to decide finally. So far she's gone through interior decorating, acting, being a travel agent, a caterer, and a princess —that I know of. Did you always want to be a journalist?"

"For almost as long as I can remember," Hilary admitted. "I either started or worked on a paper in every school I attended. Ferreting out changes in school policy was my greatest thrill. I hated to be upstaged by an assembly announcing them."

"You were a good reporter, but you're an even better columnist. And you don't have to be upstaged by the evening news."

Hilary laughed. "That's why I like it."

"George seemed a little surprised at your answers to some of the questions the other night. Hadn't he read any of your columns?"

"Only my articles. I gave him a bunch of columns to read that night."

"Couldn't he handle it?"

"No." She glanced at him as she turned into the Great America parking area. "I've never met anyone who could, Mr. Marsh. I don't blame him. Down deep I always knew he wouldn't be able to. It doesn't make him a bad person. Very few people are comfortable with fanatics."

"You're not a fanatic, Hilary. And stop calling me Mr. Marsh."

With Marsh pushing the stroller and Jason holding tight to Hilary's hand, they started wending their way through the various sections of the park. On the double-decker carousel they could take both children, with Lisa squealing joyfully and Jason bouncing up and down on his mythical beast. In Hometown Square Jason took turns going on Lady Bugs and Red Barons, finding another little boy eager to run as fast as his little legs would carry him between the two rides.

"I'd never thought of bringing him here," Hilary told Marsh. "I suppose I didn't think he was old enough, and I'm not very familiar with amusement parks myself. Oregon wasn't crawling with them, and I was too old by the time I came to San Jose to enjoy them."

"Too old! Nonsense. My aunt Evelyn comes here now and again." He cocked his head to look at her. "You don't get sick on rides, do you?"

"I never have, but it's been a long time since I was on one. The ones that keep you upside down a lot make me nervous." She picked up Lisa and pointed to where Jason was winging along in his Red Baron. "There he is! Wave to him, Lisa."

"There's one ride I want to take you on," Marsh said. "It's my favorite."

"Do you come here often?"

He laughed at her astonished question. "No, but I've brought the kids several times. Jason can keep an eye on Lisa for one ride, or we'll find someone to watch both of them for a few minutes."

Since he didn't tell her which ride, she surveyed each as they passed by, rather relieved that it wasn't Willard's Wizzer or the Demon, two terrifying-looking roller coasters. Marsh took Jason on the auto ride, and they all went on the antique carousel. Then Jason discovered Fort Fun, where he could dive into colorful balls and wander through dark tunnels, climb on nets and navigate a wobbly suspension bridge. Hilary thought he'd decided to stay there for the day, but he eventually emerged to announce that he was hungry.

After eating as much as they could hold, the children were content to pet the animals at the miniature zoo and watch the Wilderness Theater's dolphin and exotic bird show. Hilary passed the water flume rides, and the Tidal Wave, with some relief. She had begun to think that Marsh was teasing her about taking her on a ride, especially when they finally came to the Buzzy Bee, where he announced, "Here we are."

It was a children's ride with bright yellow and black bugs for cars. Jason immediately headed for it, and Hilary followed him, looking questioningly at Marsh. A long-legged, curly-haired teenager exclaimed, "Jon! What are you doing here?"

"Hi, Jennifer," he said, giving her a quick hug. "I've brought my friend Hilary and her niece and nephew. How's the job?"

"Terrific! I wish they stayed open past the end of the

month, but I can work here again next year. Mom thinks I'm crazy." That didn't seem to disturb her, for she smiled broadly at him.

Marsh introduced Hilary, who was subjected to a frankly curious stare by the girl as they shook hands.

"We won't keep you from your work," Marsh hastened to assure her. "Jason's going on the ride."

Jason went three times, and Marsh spoke with his stepdaughter briefly when she was close to them. "Are any of your friends around?" he asked.

"Sandy's over by the Lobster."

"Perfect." Marsh grinned at Hilary. "That's the ride we're going on."

At most amusement parks the ride was called the octopus, because it ordinarily had black (rather than red) cars at the ends of tentaclelike poles. Hilary watched skeptically as the cars swung up and down, while also whipping around and around. "That's your favorite ride?" she asked.

"Definitely. I like it better than the roller coasters, but if you'd prefer . . ."

"No, no! I'm sure it will be a lot of . . . fun."

Marsh laughed at her uncertain expression and immediately drew her and the children toward the ride. Lisa was asleep, and Jennifer's friend Sandy was more than willing to keep an eye on them while Marsh took Hilary on the ride. They had to wait in line for a while and Hilary could feel a bit of trepidation building in her, which only made her talk rather breathlessly.

When they finally climbed into a car and the bottom was snapped up to lock her in, she felt a moment's panic. Marsh's arm went around her shoulders protectively. "There's not a thing to be alarmed about, Hilary. I knew a woman once who adored amusement parks because she could scream all she wanted to at them. She called it Primal Therapy. Where else can you yell your lungs out without anyone's thinking a thing of it?"

"I have no intention of yelling," she said repressively. And, as the huge machine began to move: "Oh, God."

The Lobster is a ride which, because of centrifugal force or something, tends to throw its occupants against each other in determined contact. As it swings around in a circle, it is also swooping perilously close to the ground, or being flung up as though at any moment the car would come unhooked from its anchor and soar off into space. But those are only two of its attractions. The car itself, at the end of its tentacle, is also able to rotate in its own little orbit, creating a dizzying, if exhilarating, motion. Whether Hilary squealed because of that motion or because of her embarrassment at being continually pressed so closely against Marsh, she never afterward explained. But she found herself laughing and protesting and groaning along with the rest of the riders. Throughout the ride his arm remained firmly about her shoulder, and as often as not she found herself practically sitting in his lap, feeling his strong length against her. When they descended from the car at last, her legs felt slightly weak, but her eyes were sparkling, and she grinned at him. "I loved it!"

"I thought you would. Want to go again?"

"Oh, no!" Since she seemed to have called him by his first name several times during the ride, she added, "We have to pick up the kids, Jon."

"Another time," he agreed matter-of-factly.

Jason demanded to know when he would be old enough to go on the Lobster, and Lisa woke in need of a fresh diaper. While Jon took Jason to play a remote-controlled boat game, Hilary found a changing room for Lisa. Gazing at herself in the mirror, she couldn't shake the sensation that the four of them were a temporary family group. Her cheeks were flushed with excitement, and her eyes bright with happiness. For an instant a part of her insisted she clamp down on her exuberance and act her age and position. But she dismissed the practical thought. Why shouldn't she enjoy herself? She had just decided that she didn't want a permanent family life with George, that probably she would never fit quite into the role of wife and mother. It didn't mean she shouldn't enjoy the times like today when she formed part of a short-term extended-family unit. Hilary smiled at Lisa and whispered, "Today is fun, for all of us, because who knows what tomorrow will bring?"

And it was fun. Although Hilary suggested once or twice that perhaps Jon wanted to leave, he only laughed and said, "Not until Jason is exhausted." And Jason's boundless energy didn't give out until a few rides after dinner. Jon had to carry the little boy most of the way back to the car, but he didn't seem to mind. Lisa had fallen asleep again in the stroller and didn't awaken when put in the car seat. Both slept during the entire ride back to Willow Glen, while Jon and Hilary talked quietly in the front seat, mostly about Janet's condition and whether she'd be able to cope with the children in the near future.

"My mother will help her, of course," Hilary explained. "She'd have taken the kids herself if it weren't for Dad's illness. But Janet's not going to be able to go out and get a job to support herself either. At least not right away. For a while she'll have her hands full just coping with the house and the kids and trying to adjust to Bill's leaving her. There may be times in the future when I'll have the kids again, to give her a break. And now that I've got the hang of it, the same problems won't seem so earth-shattering."

"What's the hardest part of having them?"

"The guilt." She hazarded a rueful smile in his direction. "Thinking you should be spending more time with them, but not having the time or even the energy. Trying to balance your needs and theirs. They've been through a rough time."

Hilary pulled the car into the driveway. "Did I ever thank you for having the house painted? The neighbors were ecstatic. Three of them stopped me in the street and told me it improved the area so much they weren't ashamed to live near me anymore."

"It wasn't that bad," he protested.

"I know, but people like to say things like that. They think it will keep you on your toes."

"You unlock the door. I'll carry the kids in."

He took them straight to their room. He handed Lisa to

her and laid Jason on his bed. "It seems a pity to wake him. Shall I just cover him?"

"Sure. It won't hurt for one night." Hilary followed him out of the room, switching off the light as she went. Ordinarily she would have offered him a glass of wine, but she was tired, and his presence was suddenly unnerving, as though the platonic relationship of the day had abruptly shifted when night fell. "It was a delightful day, Jon. I've never seen the kids have more fun, and I . . . well, I enjoyed every minute of it, too. Your stepdaughter's charming, and I'm glad you got a chance to see her on her job."

"So am I." He hesitated for a moment before giving her hair a playful tug. "Thanks for coming, Hilary."

"Thanks for asking me."

In the weeks that followed he asked her to do other things: go to dinner, play tennis, go to the movies. But she wouldn't accept, saying she was busy. Even when he included the children in an invitation, she refused. He never pressed her, in fact, always asked in an offhand manner, when he was reviewing one of her columns or out with her at an evening gathering for the paper. The more Hilary wanted to go, and she did want to go, the more she drew back from him, the firmer she was in her refusals. Eventually, perhaps afraid she would regard his persistence as harassment, he stopped asking her.

When her month of taking care of the children was over, her brother-in-law came for them, as promised. They were delighted to see him but clung to her as well, making the little house seem frightfully empty after they left. For a week she moped, and then she started to do some decorating that she'd always intended to get around to but had never found the time for. She shortened the draperies she'd brought from the apartment so they fitted the house windows and she bought more material for the children's room, now a study. Her typewriter was installed again on the desk where it belonged, and she sent off several query letters to magazines about articles. And she called Kitty for a tennis game.

"We're very evenly matched," Kitty announced as they finished, "only you have more stamina. You probably got that from taking care of the kids. How are they doing?"

"Just fine. My sister's taking care of them, with Mother assisting. They all called me last night. Even the baby cooed over the phone." Hilary wiped her brow with the sleeve of her shirt. "I miss them."

Kitty laughed. "You miss having someone to talk to. Why haven't you started seeing someone?"

Hilary set aside her racket and slumped back on the bench. "I've decided it's useless. Think about it. There was Jack, a warm, loving man, and he couldn't handle it. And then there was George, an amusing, self-confident type, but he couldn't handle it either. I'm tired of getting emotionally involved only to find the rug pulled out from under me. It's not their fault. It's me. I could have made it easier for Jack, and I could have agreed to have babies for George. There were a lot of things I liked about having the kids with me. Maybe someday I'd want to have kids, but I'm not ready yet. I like other people's kids. They aren't a permanent responsibility, a permanent guilt."

"You need to find someone who's divorced and his wife has the kids," Kitty said teasingly. "Then you could lavish your stray maternal leanings on them on weekends. That's what I do."

Hilary was in the process of rolling down her shirt sleeves and stopped abruptly to stare at her. "With whom?" she asked a little sharply.

"You haven't met him. His name's Steve, and he has an auto dealership in San Jose." Kitty ducked her head, ostensibly to look in her purse as she said, "I'm very fond of him."

"Good God! Why didn't you tell me? And you've let me ramble on about George and Jack and my niece and nephew. Aren't you seeing Jon Marsh anymore?"

"Oh, no, that was just an occasional thing, though he was the one who introduced me to Steve." Kitty had straightened up from her purse and noted Hilary's wide-eyed gaze. "What's so astonishing about that?"

"I—I just assumed you were still seeing Marsh. He didn't say you weren't."

"I'm sure he didn't say I was either," Kitty said dryly. "He probably thought you knew. I haven't seen him in—oh—probably two months. I met Steve shortly after you came out for that game of tennis we never played. That was a great series of columns, by the way." She giggled. "You should have heard the women discuss them the next time we met."

"Did they recognize themselves?"

"Hell, no. Maybe, though, after we talked for a while, they were beginning to see a vague similarity to some of their problems. It was uncanny how each one would look at someone and think it applied to her friend, but not herself. I wouldn't be surprised if they came to some conclusions later, but none of them said."

Hilary nodded. "Look, I'll buy you lunch, and you tell me about Steve."

Chapter Sixteen

STILL, THAT WAS only one of the problems, Hilary constantly told herself during the next two weeks. If Marsh wasn't seeing Kitty any longer, she didn't have to concern herself with her loyalties in that direction, but it didn't solve the problem of having an affair within the office, with her boss. Because it would be an affair. There was no way, if she started to see him other than for the business occasions, that she wasn't going to go to bed with him—unless he didn't want to, and she thought that highly unlikely. There was that current between them, unacknowledged but always alive.

Without the buffer of Mrs. Rainer now, Hilary had been finding it more and more difficult not to invite him in when he took her home. He often touched her cheek or kissed the top of her head, striving desperately for some nonerotic signal of friendship. But Hilary herself had been unable to keep from touching him in the course of an evening—his hands, his arms, even his knee or thigh—when they sat in the car and she wished to make some point, to draw his attention. They acted, she sometimes thought, as though they were already secret lovers, carefully controlling themselves in public because theirs was a guilty love. But the urge to touch, and to be touched, was there, barely restrainable between them.

And he must see it as clearly in me as I do in him, Hilary mused, and think me an idiot. No, he would be as aware as she was of the difficulties posed by their positions at the paper. The affair itself would be only half the problem. Even if they both could maintain their professional detachment in their work while it progressed, what would happen when it would end, as it surely would? Hadn't all her affairs ended? Hilary realized that this was what she not only feared but expected. She had already, almost imperceptibly allowed herself to get close to him. If the physical element was added to their relationship, she very much suspected she would not come out of this affair with a whole heart. And that didn't make for a good working situation.

So she hesitated, considered her options, maintained her distance as best she could. Another two weeks passed in which, knowing she had no obligation to Kitty, to anyone for that matter, Hilary weighed the benefits and the risks, the pleasures and the possible heartache. On the Tuesday after a lonely Thanksgiving, when she was slated to attend a function with Marsh that Thursday, she finished her column early. With her address book propped up in front of her she typed four letters to friends on newspapers across the country and addressed large manila envelopes to them. Then she proceeded to photocopy some of her favorite columns and two of her articles, which she inserted along with her letters. Before taking her column up to Marsh's office, she left the building briefly, to deposit the envelopes in a nearby mailbox.

"I'd like to see him today if I can," she told Susan.

After he had read her column, he raised a brow quizzically, smiling at her. "It's fine, Hilary. But not the least objectionable. You don't usually come in unless there may be a problem."

"Well, actually I wanted to ask you something. There's a movie I wanted to see, Jon, and I thought, if you weren't busy tonight, you might like to join me." It wasn't the first time she had instigated a date, but it suddenly occurred to her that he would already have plans, that perhaps, because of her refusals, he had started to see someone else seriously. Nonetheless, she sat calmly, her nervousness illustrated only by the solitary finger that rubbed slowly back and forth on the arm of her chair.

His eyes narrowed momentarily, and then he moved

closer to her. "I'm having dinner with my parents. Join us, and we can go to the movie afterward."

A dozen protests rose to her lips and were resolutely forced down. His mother would have enough food. They wouldn't mind if he brought her; they'd probably be interested in meeting one of his colleagues. If he hadn't wanted to go to the movie, all he had to say was that he couldn't. She would grant him the same respect for knowing his own mind as she would expect from him, had expected from him and gotten. "All right. What time?"

"I'll pick you up at six-thirty."

Hilary nodded as she rose. He hastily scribbled his initials on the column copy and walked her to the door. "It's just family. You don't have to wear anything special. What you have on is fine."

After turning in her column, Hilary left for the day. She wanted to make sure the house was reasonably clean, that there was a bottle of wine in the refrigerator, and that she had time for a good, long bubble bath.

Jon arrived precisely on time, bearing a bottle of champagne. "I thought we could put it in the refrigerator for later," he suggested hopefully, giving her a light kiss on the lips.

She met his eyes without hesitation. "Fine. Would you like a glass of wine before we go?"

"Better not. We have to drive to Woodside. Where's the movie you wanted to see?"

"Here in town."

"Would you mind if we saw it tomorrow night? My folks won't mind if we eat and run, but I'd like them to have a chance to get to know you." He put his arm around her shoulders and hugged her. "My mother's always wanted to meet the 'fiery lady' who writes the feminist column."

"You've told them you're bringing me?"

"Of course. Did you think I was going to spring you on them?" He ran a hand over her hair, twisting a lock of it around his finger. "I've wanted to take you before, but it seemed pointless to ask. I'm glad you changed your mind."

"It was a difficult decision," she said softly.

"I know." He drew her close to him, holding her gently with one arm about her waist. "I gave a lot of thought to it, too, Hilary, and I'm convinced we can keep our personal and professional lives separate. You must have come to a similar decision."

She grinned. "Either that or I just decided to be self-indulgent."

"I like the thought of being an indulgence." He bent to kiss her slightly parted lips. His kiss was as tender, if not as short, as the previous one had been, gently exploring her lips and her reaction. "I'll put the champagne in the refrigerator while you get your coat."

The evening was pleasant. His parents, Hilary found, were charming people, his father an attorney and his mother active in volunteer work. The meal was delicious, and the conversation after dinner ranged over a variety of interesting topics. Mrs. Marsh was fascinated by Hilary's column, though Hilary suspected she was slightly scandalized by it as well. Mr. Marsh was more interested in the fact that her father was an attorney and sympathized when she related that he had had to retire on account of Parkinson's disease.

"Your poor mother," Mrs. Marsh murmured. "With your father suffering and your sister being hospitalized, she must think there's no end to the disasters."

Hilary cast a startled look at Jon; she hadn't mentioned her sister at all.

"I told Mother how you came to have your niece and nephew staying with you," he said smoothly, "but I hadn't mentioned that your sister was home again. Is she still managing well with the children?"

While Hilary answered the question, her mind was frantically searching for some reason that he would have mentioned her to his parents. There was her position as a columnist on the paper, of course, but it would hardly necessitate his bringing her sister into the conversation—unless he had explained how having her niece and nephew had played havoc with her work for a while. And she wasn't sure she liked to think of his discussing that with his parents. Hilary and Jon were sitting on a couch together, and she found her hand firmly enclosed in his as he slightly altered the direction of the conversation. He continued to hold her hand until they rose to leave.

In the car she asked, "Why have you discussed me with your parents?"

"There wasn't anyone else I could talk to about you."

It wasn't the answer she'd expected, but she knew exactly what he meant. There were times when she'd found herself wanting just to say his name to someone, just to make a comment on him, to hear her voice speak out loud for the relief it would give her constant thoughts of him. She had found, during the last few weeks the children were with her, that she brought up the trip to Great America now and then just so she could say his name and hear Jason say it. Hilary couldn't very well discuss him with Harry at work, or with Kitty, who had just stopped seeing him, or with Mary Lou, who thought he had sensuous lips and would jump to conclusions Hilary didn't want her to make.

When she didn't say anything, he asked, "Can you understand that?"

"Yes. I talked to the children. Very rewarding," she said with a laugh. "Lisa would gurgle and smile, and Jason would remember that you bought him cotton candy."

"I wish you'd have let me take you more places with the children. On outings with them you know I wouldn't have pressed you, wouldn't have made any assumptions."

"It was too hazardous for me," Hilary admitted, laying a hand on his thigh. "I wasn't ready."

He covered her hand with his, rubbing the soft flesh between her thumb and forefinger. "I was beginning to think I'd deluded myself, that you didn't share my interest after all. And then again, I wanted to tell you that it wouldn't make any difference at the office, but if you weren't interested, that was almost a form of harassment. It's the very devil developing a fondness for someone you work with."

"For someone you employ," she corrected, "or for your employer. I'm in a particularly vulnerable position for having fingers pointed at me, Jon."

"I realize that, and I won't do anything to jeopardize you."

"It's going to be awkward no matter how you look at it." Hilary sighed. When he glanced over at her, she smiled. "I wouldn't have asked you out if I hadn't thought the pros outweighed the cons."

"My sentiments exactly."

They finished the drive in silence, her hand remaining in his. She had forgotten to leave a light on in the house, as she usually had when they'd gone out on newspaper business. On those occasions he'd seen her to her door, waited until she let herself in with her key, and said good night. Now he followed her into the dark house and stood close behind her as she switched on a lamp in the living room. After she had dropped her purse on the table, she turned and walked into his open arms. It seemed the most natural thing in the world to do, yet she had resisted the desire for months. Already there was no turning back, and she felt a profound relief.

His lips on hers were gentle, were urgent, his arms holding her firmly to him. That generous mouth bestowed fluttering kisses on her eyelids and her cheeks, her forehead, and her chin, as though he wished no spot to be untouched. Hilary could understand the impulse, as her own lips brushed across his rough chin and sought the place that was almost, not quite, a dimple when he smiled. With her fingers tucked in his hair she experienced the total contact with him from head to toe that made her breathless. She drew back gently.

"The champagne," she suggested. And then, grinning: "I'll slip into something more comfortable."

"Do you have something more comfortable for me?" he asked, loosening his tie. His eyes were softly amused.

Hilary cocked her head to take in the whole of him. "I'll see what I can find, if you'll pour the champagne."

It was a cotton madras caftan Hilary had in mind for

herself. For him she dug out an old beach robe she'd never bothered to throw away. Though it was miles too big for her, she wasn't sure it would be all that "comfortable" for him and certainly not particularly modest. Not that she thought he was likely to be modest. She'd met very few men who were.

"What do you think?" she asked, holding it up for him in the doorway of the kitchen.

"I'll probably catch pneumonia," he said mournfully, handing her a glass of champagne as he took the robe.

"Well, try it on. If it doesn't fit, you can sit around naked. I won't mind." He had already removed his tie and sports coat, which were draped over a chair.

"I'll bet. And you'll be sitting there in your granny gown ogling me."

"It's a caftan."

"It comes all the way down to your ankles," he protested. "You call that comfortable?"

"Sure. I wear one most evenings when I'm snuggled up with a book."

"I can think of better outfits for snuggling up with a man." But he was smiling as he carried his glass of champagne and the robe toward the bathroom. "You don't have to tell me where anything is. I used to live here."

"Yes," she said, "I often think of that."

Hilary carried the bottle of champagne and her glass into the living room, where she curled up on the sofa to await his return. When he came, it was in the robe, which looked ludicrous on him, falling far short of his knees.

"You look adorable," she told him. "Who would have thought you had the figure to carry it off? And I had decided, most definitely, that I liked you best in jeans."

"You're jealous of my knobby knees and hairy legs," he retorted. "If you'd agreed to play tennis with me, you'd already have seen them, and there would have been none of this shilly-shallying around. Once a woman has seen my knees, she hasn't the power to resist me."

Hilary chuckled and patted the sofa beside her. "Prove it."

First he added some champagne to their glasses and made a toast. "To us, alone together at last." He seated himself carefully beside her, pulling the robe closely about himself, muttering, "Too much all at once you wouldn't be able to handle," and put an arm about her shoulders. "You know, Hilary, I like what you've done to this room in the last few weeks. I take it you don't plan to move out now the kids are back in Oregon."

"No, I've gotten to like the place. And if the need should arise to take the kids again, I wouldn't have to scramble around for the right place." She also liked the way his fingers were stroking the side of her neck, and she leaned closer to him. "It doesn't matter to you if I stay here, does it?"

"I hope you will. I can find my way here blindfolded."

He lifted her glass from her hand and set it with his on the coffee table. Hilary turned in his arms to meet his questing lips with her own. Just being close to him had made her breathe more quickly, and she could feel her heart fluttering mildly in her chest as his tongue traced the lines of her lips. Slowly his hands, which had been at her waist, moved upward to stroke the sides of her breasts. How incredibly gentle he was! And how slowly he progressed to cupping her breasts in his hands. He had shifted to a slightly reclining position where she could lie beside him, her hands around his back unconsciously giving him the signals he interpreted with such ease.

"You have the most glorious hair," he whispered into it, "and the most wonderfully responsive lips. Has anyone ever told you how soft your lips are?"

"Yes." She looked up at him, her eyes laughing. "But don't let that stop you from telling me again."

"Everything about you is amazingly soft!" One hand slipped inside the neck of her caftan to touch the silky skin of her breast, to find the tautened nipple. "Well, not everything."

"No, not everything." She sighed, her own hands sliding inside his robe.

"Would you mind if I took this granny thing off?"

"It's a caftan."

"Whatever."

Hilary moved to sit up. "Let's go to the bedroom. I have to put in my diaphragm."

"You won't need it," he said, watching her carefully. "I've had a vasectomy."

She nodded slowly. It had never occurred to her. He had no children of his own. "When?"

"Shortly after I married Alice. She didn't want any more children."

They were standing beside the sofa now, and she reached up to kiss him. "You're the most incredible man," she said softly.

Momentarily he looked stunned by her reaction. Then he enfolded her in his arms. "And you're the most astonishing woman."

Hilary had left the lamp on in the bedroom, to cast a soft glow over the simple furniture, the profusion of plants, and the scattering of books. It was a cozy room, intimate rather than elegant, the quiet spot to which she retreated when she had had enough of the sophisticated life she led. Here she felt comfortable reading for pleasure in the big easy chair or stretched out on the bed, staring at the ceiling, when she had personal problems. Though most of the furnishings she had brought from the apartment, the room itself felt different to her in the house, special, her home base. No man had yet been invited to cross its threshold.

His glance swept over the room and came to rest on her. "The vulnerable Hilary lives here," he said softly, his arm tightening about her waist.

"Yes. But it's not an unhappy place. I think of it as warm and friendly, not as an escape but as a retreat. This is where I recharge my batteries." She picked up a book lying on the bedside table. "Have you read this? It's about women and depression, a very interesting and important work. I got it because of Janet, but I think I'll mention it in my column. That wouldn't be infringing on the book reviewer, would it?"

"No, it would be very much in keeping with your work."

He took it from her, noted the title and author, and then set it down again. When he turned to her, he found that she was slipping the caftan over her head and he untied the terry-cloth belt of the beach robe and shrugged the garment onto the floor.

Hilary studied him as openly as he studied her, then drifted into his waiting arms. "It's not your knees," she murmured.

His hands ran along the side of her back down to her buttocks. "I've been here before," he retorted, easing her back toward the bed.

"The sunglasses. I never offered to replace them."

"I should hope not. It was my carelessness that nearly scarred your dear derriere permanently. I don't feel any lingering reminders."

"Not a scratch. I checked in the mirror later."

"I'd have been happy to do it for you," he said as he climbed onto the bed beside her.

"Even then? That was ages ago."

"Long before that, Hilary." His lips found hers as her arms went around him.

The play of his hands over her body was gentle, evocative, and she knew there would be no need to caution him to give her time to respond properly. There was a languorous sensuousness about the way he stroked her shoulders, her breasts, her hips. Hilary was accustomed to touching her partners to give them pleasure, but she found, with him, that her hands were almost greedy in their desire to explore every inch of him. And she followed her hands with her lips, tasting the hollow of his neck, the tangle of hair on his chest, as he tasted her. The feedback, that burgeoning, bursting desire that was rising in her, came not only from his touch on her but from her delight in touching him. It was unique in her experience, and a little frightening.

Her hands stilled on him.

He looked in her eyes and smiled. "Yes, it's different," he agreed aloud. "But it's better, Hilary." He began to stroke her hair, running his fingers along her scalp and down through the soft tresses. "Every nerve ending is alive to a double sensation, touching and being touched. Surely that's the way it's supposed to be when it's right."

Unable to speak, she nodded, taking his hands in hers and pressing them between her chin and shoulder, a curiously affectionate gesture. "Perhaps it's the champagne," she whispered.

"Perhaps." But he didn't sound convinced. "Would you like a glass now?"

"No, thank you." The turmoil in her body, in her mind, had barely diminished. She could feel the urgency of him against her, yet he allowed his hands to stay quietly within hers, stroking her fingers, his lips pressing soft kisses on her face, undemanding. She released his hands to run her fingers over his face, smoothing his eyebrows, touching the soft flicker of his eyelashes, tracing the lines from his nose to the corner of his mouth. Still, the desire raged unabated in her body, unsoothed. "I'm not going to have any control," she said, her voice a whisper.

"You don't need any, Hilary. Please don't fight it." His lips covered hers, his tongue gently probing. At first she resisted, trying to tame the almost unbearable need, trying to keep it at a level that was comprehensible, familiar. But that proved impossible. She gave her mouth to him, took his tongue, searched frantically with her own.

Aware that she wasn't going to last much longer, he spread her thighs and entered her, holding her tightly while he murmured soft endearments. Her body moved with his, desperately, primitively, giving everything, taking everything. Her moans of pleasure escaped into his mouth, absorbed into his own groan of satisfaction. She found herself clinging to him, laughing while tears oozed onto her cheeks, unnoticed. She felt giddy with release, with relief, shaken to her very core. She had never flown that high, never experienced such a volcanic orgasm . . . and she had survived. "Oh, my God." She sighed.

"Control isn't what it's cracked up to be, is it?" he demanded as he kissed away the tears.

"You should talk," she grumbled, avoiding his eyes. "You were in perfect control."

"I won't always be." He turned her face so she had to look at him. "You needed me to be tonight, Hilary. And I can be anytime you need that. But you won't always need it, and you won't always want it."

"No," she admitted, "probably not. But, Jon, I couldn't have gotten control if I'd wanted to."

"Well, you could have, but only by walking away." He regarded her questioningly. "Why was it so important to have control?"

She shrugged, embarrassed. "I don't know. Would you like some champagne now?"

They finished the bottle while they sat on her bed, pillows plumped up behind them, talking. It was late when he said, "I'd better leave now. Or did you want me to stay?"

"No, not tonight."

"We'll go to the movie tomorrow, and I'd like you to come home with me. You've never seen my house. Okay?"

Hilary was watching him gather the beach robe from the floor and hang it carefully over a chair. "I'd like to see your house, but let's save the movie for another time. We're going to be together Thursday evening anyhow."

He turned to face her, standing comfortably naked across the room. "You don't want this to get too intense?"

"Jon, you have a lot of obligations. I have a few myself. We don't need to see each other every night." She smiled at the slight frown that creased his brow. "That's the surest way to take the edge off an affair, isn't it?"

"We'll see each other almost every day at work anyhow."

"But at work," she reminded him, "we are professional newspaper people, nothing more."

He approached the bed and touched her cheek softly with his forefinger. "I'm not going to forget that, Hilary, but I'd still like to see you tomorrow night."

His hand had come to cup her cheek, and she turned to place a kiss on the palm. "Thursday . . . please."

"By Thursday I'll probably ravish you at the charity bazaar," he muttered.

"I'll look forward to it."

When he was gone, she brushed her teeth and took a quick shower before nestling back into the rumpled bed. She had made the right decision, she thought with satisfaction. It was going to be worth every moment of pain, even the necessary career change—afterward. Her body still radiated euphoria, and not from the champagne. She had never felt so in tune with any man—sexually or otherwise. Determinedly she pushed from her mind any calculation of how long it would last. She knew only that it would last longer if it didn't become a daily routine, and she was intent on savoring every drop of pleasure their relationship had to offer before it had to end.

Chapter Seventeen

HIS HOUSE in Los Gatos was a Spanish-style bungalow tastefully decorated with Mexican artifacts. Somehow Hilary had expected the place to be larger, more opulent. Instead, it was medium-sized and comfortably homey.

"When we were divorced, Alice kept the house, and I got the other property. I didn't want to be out of the neighborhood, so I bought this place. The kids walk by here on their way to school. Sometimes they even stop in for breakfast if they're up early enough." He waved her to a chair and carried her overnight case down the hall to the bedroom.

Hilary wandered over to a table on which there were framed photographs of two teenagers, one of whom was Jennifer. The other was a freckle-faced boy several years younger, who, despite his lack of resemblance to Jon, nevertheless reminded her of him.

"That's Jeffrey," he said, coming up behind her. "He's just turned fourteen, but that's a year old. I've asked the kids for pictures of themselves for Christmas."

"What are you getting them?"

"I haven't decided yet. Maybe you'll help me think of something. Alice always says they don't need anything."

"Don't you ask them?"

"Sure, but the things they know they want, Alice gets them. I have to think of something they don't even know they want. Would you like a glass of wine?"

"Please." Hilary turned to follow him into the kitchen, but he hadn't moved. "Are you going to give me a tour of the house?"

He was standing with his hands at his sides, staring at her or perhaps past her at the pictures. She couldn't be sure, since his eyes were thoughtful, rather than observant, almost preoccupied. "Jon?"

"I was thinking about Christmas," he said apologetically. "Will you be here? Or are you going to Oregon?"

"I have reservations to fly up on the Thursday evening and come back Sunday."

"Too bad. It would have been nice to have you here when the kids come on Christmas Eve. Do you always spend the holiday with your family?"

"Usually."

"Hilary, how are we going to handle the round of Christmas parties?" The thoughtful look had come back again.

"I—I don't know. It's still a few weeks away." Hilary had no intention of considering the matter. A few weeks was a very long time as far as she was concerned. She turned toward where she assumed the kitchen was. "Shall I get the wine?"

He laid a restraining hand on her arm. "It's something we have to decide. I'll want to take you wherever I'm invited, but some of those are going to be the homes of people from the paper. And you're not going to want to make our relationship public."

"I'll be invited to some of them, too. For those we can come separately; for the others . . ." She shrugged. "I don't want to think about it now, Jon."

His lips tightened slightly, but he said only, "I'll get the wine."

When he returned, however, to find her curled rather unhappily in the corner of his sofa, he stroked her hair. "I'm sorry. I don't want to press you, Hilary. It's just that for a moment there I had the feeling you were implying we might not even *be* a couple by Christmastime."

Her wide hazel eyes met his briefly. "It's possible." She accepted the glass of wine with a steady hand.

"*How* is it possible?" he demanded. "Christmas is less than a month away." When she didn't answer, he walked stiffly to the stereo and chose an album. His movements were carefully controlled as he slipped the record from its cover, set it on the turntable, and carefully adjusted the volume very low. He stood for a moment by the cabinet, tapping a finger restlessly against the wood as he stared across the room at her averted face. "Why, Hilary? Because of our work situation? Because you think I have only a sexual interest in you and it will quickly die? Or because you have only a sexual interest in me and you *know* it will quickly die?"

Her throat felt painfully constricted. "They're all possibilities, aren't they?"

"No, Hilary. Only two of them are possibilities." He crossed the hardwood floor, his shoes slapping angrily against the wood until he came to the rug in front of the sofa, where he stopped to tower over her. "I want you to understand something. If you were the most desirable woman on earth (and I'm not saying you aren't, my dear), I wouldn't have an affair with you if you were an employee of mine—unless there were some far more significant factor involved. I'm not going to tell you I love you, Hilary, because I've long since lost track of what the word means. I thought I loved Alice. I suppose I *did* love Alice, and I certainly can't hate her even after what she did."

"What did she do?"

He waved a hand, as though it weren't relevant. Then he sighed and sat down beside her. "She found someone else while we were married. More than that actually. He was the publisher of the *Reporter* and owned a batch of smaller papers. *My* boss, Hilary. During the divorce he sold the paper to a small group of investors who don't wish to have any involvement other than the financial arrangement. In many ways, of course, professionally, it was to my advantage."

Anger flared in her eyes. "Don't say anything so absurd, Jon! It was a cruel, heartless thing to do to you."

He grimaced. "I don't think she did it to hurt me. In fact, I don't think she's ever even realized what a double blow it was. He did, certainly. Otherwise, he wouldn't have sold the paper. I had planned to change jobs, was even negotiating with another paper when he announced his intention. Everything was done very quietly, very circumspectly. Alice has always called it an amicable divorce!"

Hilary cast her eyes heavenward. "Amicable! You lose your wife, your children, your home, and get a kick in your professional respect. Very convenient for her to think of it as amicable."

"For her it was. She got what she wanted. He's older, but he's from the same sort of social world she is. A distinguished man, with plenty of old money. His wife had died shortly before this happened. I used to have nightmares, afterward, that Alice had poisoned her." He grinned at Hilary's startled expression. "She died in a car accident."

"I'm very sorry, about the whole mess," she said sadly.

"It's long over with now. I only tell you so you'll know the background. We were discussing something entirely different." He lifted her free hand, toying with her fingers. "I want to know why you think our relationship could be as short as a few weeks, Hilary. Do you tire of men that quickly?"

She set down her wineglass and sat back, leaning her head against his shoulder. The position had the merit of bringing them close together, while she didn't have to meet his eyes. "Usually it takes only a few weeks to find out whether one or the other of us can't handle it. Either I find myself being forced into a role I can't accept, or he finds he doesn't really relate to all of me. What I mean is, he can accept me as a woman, but not as a feminist columnist. Even the most liberated men I've met eventually find that difficult to swallow. They start out thinking it's fascinating and end up finding it threatening . . . or something. Maybe that's not it at all; maybe it's just me personally, but the arguments generally hinge on my feminism."

For a while he didn't speak, and the music was the only sound in the room. His arm was about her shoulder, his hand gently stroking her arm. "What is it you want from a man, Hilary?"

"Ideally? I want him to accept me for exactly what I am.

To respect the column and my views, whether he agrees with them or not. I want a lot of affection and support, because I'm willing to give them, too. I want an equal share in decisions, conversations, sex, and housework. I don't want to be made to feel guilty, or inferior, or even superior." She twisted in his arm to look up at him. "And I don't want to spend all my time fighting for that equal partnership or having to cajole or persuade to get it."

Since she'd set down her wineglass and he couldn't reach it without disturbing their position, he offered her a sip of his. Hilary took it eagerly, her throat feeling dry and constricted.

His eyes stayed on her face. "And you haven't been able to find a man who fits your requirements? Haven't had any long-term relationships?"

"Oh, I have, a few. But sometimes I've had to work my tail off to maintain them, and that defeats the purpose. I don't want to go through life exhausting myself keeping a relationship going. And generally what it means is that I'm constantly compromising."

"People do compromise, Hilary. It's part of every long-term association."

"Not when it's always on one side."

"You probably only thought that. He was probably making as many compromises as you were."

"Possibly. It never felt like it." Hilary leaned forward to reach her wineglass and, when she sat back, did not put her head against his shoulder. "I think basically what happens is that the man thinks of himself as making a great sacrifice just taking me on, with all my feminist baggage, and that's enough of a compromise. From then on I'm the one who's supposed to do the giving in. He's already made the supreme gesture."

"They all can't have done that," he protested, his hand now massaging the back of her neck.

"Jack didn't. He's the only one I can think of, though. He . . ." But it seemed senseless to try to explain Jack, and she fell silent.

"He what?"

"Nothing." She shrugged and rose. "Would you show me around the house?"

"After you've told me about Jack."

Hilary refused to sit down again beside him. Instead, she walked nervously around the room, pausing now and then to look at a painting on the wall or lift an object or book that was resting on a polished surface. She decided he must have someone come in to take care of the housework; everything was clean, waxed, shining. Impossible to picture Jonathan Marsh, executive editor of the *South Bay Reporter,* pushing a vacuum cleaner or wielding a can of furniture polish.

"Jack was different," she said finally. "He believed in women's rights, in equality of the sexes, quite as thoroughly as I did. But the clods at his office teased him about me, and he began to feel that his promotion wouldn't come through simply because of me. They thought he was under my thumb, I guess. Their jokes bothered him, and it upset him that they bothered him. He was a gentle man and very sure of himself until all that happened. The whole situation degenerated into making him feel torn and insecure. He didn't tell me until he was ready to walk out. I don't suppose there was anything I could have done about it if I'd known, but still . . ."

"Didn't you have to make compromises with him?" Jon asked from the sofa.

"Yes, but he made compromises, too. When he left," she said with a half-smile, "he told me how much he hated housework. But the reason he left, according to him, was that he couldn't handle the situation: me, the column, his co-workers' scorn. No one can, for long."

Hilary stood uncertainly by the stereo, looking back at him across the room. "It's even more difficult for us, Jon. You're my employer. Sure, we'll both try to keep the two facets of our lives separate, but it won't be easy, and it probably won't be successful. They'll start talking at the office: Did you know Hilary is having an affair with the

Monk? Some of them will accept it casually, but others will read dire meanings into it."

"The Monk? Is that me?" he asked, amused.

"Yes, a little nickname you've acquired since your divorce, presumably."

"If you let the talk at the office bother you, you'll be doing to yourself exactly what Jack did." Jon rose and came to put his arms around her. "It doesn't matter what they say, Hilary. It's none of their business. We're adults. You already have an established position on the paper. No one can question that."

"There's the matter of the raise I got when I started going to civic functions with you," she reminded him. "For all I know, they thought I was sleeping with you right from the start of that."

"That didn't bother you when we weren't. Don't let it bother you now. Forget the paper," he advised, lowering his head to kiss her. "Let me show you the house."

Hilary kissed him back with an urgency she couldn't conceal. "Just the bedroom will do for now, thanks."

It was a large room with a fireplace in one wall and a patio off to the backyard. The king-size bed was covered with a down comforter, and her overnight bag had been placed beside a rolltop desk. Hilary hadn't bothered to pack a nightgown, but her outfit for the next day was in the bag, so she could spend the night without hurrying home to change in the morning.

Jon unfastened the buttons at the back of her cowl-neck wool jersey dress and slid it off with gently wandering hands. "Would you like a fire in the fireplace? I just have to set a match to it."

She nodded her agreement as she helped him out of his jacket. Already she could feel warmth spreading through her body, but the smell and sound and sight of a fire were appealing. She watched as he got it started, then stood back to make sure it had caught. But that was as long as she was willing to wait. She wanted to feel his hands touching her bare skin, wanted to learn whether their first encounter had been an aberration or whether touching him was as exciting as she had remembered. Her impatience grew as he bent to shift the logs a bit, to poke around at the grate.

"Jon."

"Hmm?" he said absently.

"I don't really care if you get *that* fire started," she complained as she divested herself of her bra and panties.

He laughed and swooped her up into his arms, crushing her naked body against himself. "I was going to get around to you, Hilary." He set her down on the sheepskin rug in front of the fireplace while he removed his clothes, carelessly tossing them on a chair. "Firelight becomes you," he whispered as he lay down beside her and pulled her over onto him. "Since you're so eager, you can do the work tonight. It'll burn off some of your excess energy."

The firelight played on the rugged contours of his face, making the dark eyes gleam. She couldn't be sure whether he was teasing her, but it didn't matter when his hands stroked the curves of her breasts, circling in toward the already hard nipples. Being astride was not a position in which she had often found physical gratification, but she had always liked the concept. It made her feel that she was more a part of the process of making love, that she was more active and therefore more giving. But tonight there was never any question of her gratification. Every movement she made heightened her pleasure almost unbearably. She watched the bemused expression on his face, felt his hands direct her rhythm, heard the rapid intake of breath as he reached climax with her, tasted his lips as she lay spent against his chest.

"You are the most remarkable woman." He sighed, stroking back her hair to kiss her eyes and nose. The warmth of the fire made him edge slightly away from it even as he held her tightly to him. "I just bought this rug yesterday. Somehow I felt sure you'd like a good place in front of the fire."

"It's lovely and soft, and sheep aren't an endangered

species. Now if it had been some poor animal tottering on the brink of extinction . . .''

"I wouldn't have bought it," he replied promptly. "Are you warm enough?"

"I'm fine, but I think I'd like to go to bed now. It's been an exhausting day."

She separated from him with a sigh and rose to make her way to the bathroom. Jon continued to lie on the floor, watching her movements as she returned to retrieve her toilet kit from the overnight bag. His expression was puzzled, his brow slightly furrowed in a frown. Hilary cocked her head at him when she climbed into the bed. "Aren't you going to join me?"

With his head propped in his hands, elbows firmly planted on the floor, he asked, "Hilary, is it just a sexual interest on your part? You never really answered me."

The fire was beginning to burn down, and there was very little light in the room. Nevertheless, she turned to plump up the pillow behind her before answering him. "No, it's not just that. I like you; I like being with you."

When that was all she said, he nodded, dissatisfied but accepting. "I'll be right with you."

Hilary woke twice in the night to find his arm around her and his body pressed close against her back. In the morning she drifted straight from sleep into a sensual haze that culminated in their making love again. They took a shower together, lathering each other's bodies teasingly because they knew they didn't have the time or the energy to make love a third time. "Tonight," he suggested.

"I'm having dinner with a friend," she murmured as she stepped out of the shower and handed him a towel. At his grimace she said, "It's been planned for a long time, Jon. This is a woman friend."

"Would you come here afterward?"

"I don't think so. There are some things I have to do around the house in the morning."

"How about tennis Saturday afternoon and then dinner out?"

Vigorously toweling her hair, she struggled for the right answer. Right now she wanted to spend every minute with him, and she knew that was the worst possible thing she could do. He would tire of her. She would become dependent on his attention and drop all her usual activities to be with him. It was a familiar pattern with women, she told herself in disgust. They overdosed every time they felt an infatuation. Rolled themselves out like carpets to be walked on, used, and left behind. They didn't act like normal, rational human beings. They sighed and spent their time daydreaming, waiting for phone calls, acting like lovesick teenagers.

"Hilary?"

She wrapped her hair in the towel before saying, "I have some research to do at the library, Jon, but I'd love to go out for dinner."

Their two naked bodies were reflected in the full-length mirror on the bathroom door. She saw his frown in the mirror as he bent to dry his feet. "Okay. About seven?"

"Fine. I'll have you to dinner next week before we go to the city program if you'd like."

"That's Wednesday." He sounded incredulous.

"Yes, that's Wednesday," she agreed.

He straightened to face her. "And I suppose, Sunday morning, after you've spent the night, you'll tell me you have to run off to gather daisies with some kids from an orphanage."

"That's Sunday afternoon," she said with a laugh. "In the morning I thought we might play tennis."

"I'll make breakfast," he said abruptly, and left the bathroom.

By the time she joined him in the kitchen he had bacon frying and toast in the toaster. He wore an apron to protect the striped oxford cloth shirt he wore. "How do you like your eggs?"

"Fried hard as a rock. Nothing the least bit runny."

"Do you like eggs, Hilary?"

"Not particularly. Especially not for breakfast, but I got used to them last year, when I went to England for a few weeks and did the bed-and-breakfast routine. They had the most peculiar-tasting sausages, and breakfast often came with a broiled tomato. It was enough to make your stomach turn over." She was trying to get a smile from him, but he continued passively lifting the bacon from the frying pan, spreading it out on paper toweling to drain. "Jon, I've obviously annoyed you. Tell me how, and we'll straighten it out."

"I don't understand you, Hilary." He cracked an egg against the side of the frying pan with so much vigor that it seeped onto the stove. "You told me last night that you like being with me, yet you're doing everything in your power *not* to be with me any more than absolutely necessary. You're making me feel as though you'd entered this situation under duress. I've told you this has nothing to do with work. This is a personal matter between the two of us which cannot affect your employment in any way, for better or worse. So why are you acting so skittish?"

"Because I want to savor it," she said honestly, sitting down at the table where a place had been set for her. "I told you the other day, I don't want to take the edge off. And we will, Jon, if we see each other every night, all night. Pretty soon we'd be like an old married couple, cherishing the familiarity rather than the excitement."

"There's nothing wrong with familiarity," he grumbled. "I'd like to be familiar with you."

Hilary moved her fork so he could set down the plate of bacon, eggs, and toast. When he sat down opposite her, glaring, she laughed. "You'd like the excitement, too, the newness. The familiarity will come soon enough, whether you want it or not. I've taken on two magazine article assignments, Jon, and I have to put some time in on them. I'm sure you have projects of your own."

"Nothing that couldn't include you." He took a bite of toast but continued to stare at her. "You're still convinced that this is wholly sexual, aren't you?"

"Not wholly. But it's bound to be largely sexual, isn't it? We like each other . . . and we want to go to bed together. Jon, that doesn't bother me. If it bothers you *for* me, I'm

225

sorry. I'm trying to be realistic. There's no reason for me to
expect any more from this relationship than from any
other I've been involved in. Which doesn't mean that I
don't enjoy the casual familiarity, the long-term support
and affection of an ongoing partnership. I do. But we work
together, Jon, which pretty well precludes that sort of arrangement. We're professional people, and in the long run
we'll act professionally. The pressures will grow until it's
easier to discontinue seeing each other than it is to continue." Hilary took a sip from the mug of coffee sitting at
her place. "I'm not going to like that when it happens, but
I'm going to accept it."

Although he obviously paid close attention to her while
she spoke, Jon made no attempt to interrupt, in fact, continued eating his breakfast. "How do you know you're not
going to like it when it ends?" he asked, his eyes intent on
her.

Why hadn't she been more careful in what she said? Hilary thought with annoyance. The two cooling eggs stared
up at her, making her stomach rebel. She ate a bite of
bacon before replying, "Because I've become very fond of
you over these last few months, Jon."

He grinned at her. "Excellent! Now we're getting somewhere, my dear. I told you, or tried to tell you, last night
that I've become very fond of you, too. So let's not waste
the short time you're so convinced we have by not seeing
each other more than two or three times a week. That's
senseless, Hilary. We're not teenagers out for a sexual
joyride. We're adults who need stimulating companionship, and we've found it in each other. So let's enjoy it. If
the sex becomes less than earthshaking, I think we'll both
be able to handle that."

Her toast was cold now, too, but she ate some of it anyhow. He was probably right, and she was just playing
games in trying to slow down the inevitable denouement.
But she feared the intensity of the type of relationship he
was suggesting. The likelihood of being deeply hurt was
even greater because she knew she wasn't going to be able

to exercise the control that some distance and a large body of time to herself would give her. She negotiated.

"I'll have to have at least two evenings a week to myself. My obligations on the magazine articles . . ."

Jon threw up a hand in exasperation. "I'm not going to engulf and devour you, Hilary. You can bring your work here, or I can bring mine there. We aren't going to be perpetually on the run. I won't distract you. We don't even have to be in the same room, but in the same house would be nice."

"We might as well live together," she said with some asperity.

He smiled. "I'd suggest it if I thought there was the slightest chance of your agreeing."

"There isn't."

"No, I didn't think so. Are you finished?" He glanced at the two eggs lying untouched on her plate but made no comment.

"Yes. You'll drop me off at home, won't you? I have to get my car because I'm going directly from work to my friend's."

"And coming here afterward?" he asked hopefully.

"Yes"—she sighed—"I'll come here afterward."

Chapter Eighteen

F OR TWO WEEKS no whisper of their changed relationship
seemed to make its way into the newspaper offices. But
then the Christmas parties began. Hilary struggled for the
best resolution in handling them. The first two were parties to which they could go separately, but the third was
given by the paper's attorney, and only Marsh was invited,
along with the executive-level employees. Everything was
going so well, she lamented to herself. They fitted very easily into each other's lives. She liked having him around
her house, reading a book while she researched an article
or fixing some minor problem of the house's innards. It
was, after all, his house, she reminded herself. At his
house in Los Gatos she felt at home, so much so that she
used a leftover piece of material from her curtains to cover
two pillows. He was easygoing in his habits, without patterns that required adaptation. When she steadfastly
maintained her own schedule, he worked around it with
astonishing flexibility. Nothing she did, including falling
asleep one night while he was still getting ready for bed,
seemed to irritate him.

The invitation for the Larsons' party sat on his desk and
was marked on his calendar, but they didn't discuss it. Hilary realized this was a mistake; it showed her fears. She
knew he expected her to go with him, and if she didn't, she
wasn't giving him an opportunity to make other arrangements. Presumably he could go alone. There was no rule
inscribed in stone that he had to take someone with him,
she fumed. But they both knew it was her own confusion
that made the problem. Was she willing for everyone at

the party to know they were having an affair? Her liberation was in question somehow. If she were as independent,
as self-contained as she proclaimed, the possible censure of
others shouldn't affect her.

The morning of the party he finally brought up the subject while they were still in bed. His dark eyes flickered
open to catch her observing him. He blinked a few times
and smiled, his hand coming up to stroke her face. "Are
you going to want to dress at home for the party?"

Hilary could feel the muscles in her throat constrict. As
far as she was concerned, this was the beginning of the
end. Once they were placed as a couple, their time together
was limited, had to be limited. There would be so many
subtle opposing forces. But she had prepared herself for
that, hadn't she?

"Yes, I don't have anything here good enough to wear."
She drew away from his caressing hand to climb out of bed.
"We can have dinner at my place before we go."

What made Hilary most nervous as she later dressed
for the party was knowing that Harry would be there with
his wife. The Stevenses were personal friends of the Larsons, as much through Carol's work as Harry's. The zipper on her dress stuck when she tried to pull it up with
fingers made clumsy by nervousness. "Damn! Have I
ruined it, Jon?" she asked, turning to find him watching
her.

He crossed the room to her, a slightly quizzical expression on his face. "No, I don't think so. Let me work it back
down."

Made impatient by her nervousness, she could hardly
stand still while he eased the zipper back by fractions of an
inch. She toyed with the chain bracelet at her wrist until
it, too, fell to the floor, broken. "Oh, never mind," she
snapped. "I'll wear something else."

Jon turned her around to face him. "Relax, Hilary. I've
already told Harry I'm bringing you. He'll have had several hours to get used to the notion, and Carol, too. For
God's sake, they're good friends of yours. I don't see why it
upsets you so badly that they'll know about us."

"How do you know it does?" she demanded, bending to pick up the bracelet.

"Because you've mentioned them half a dozen times today, including breakfast this morning. Harry didn't seem so astonished when I told him I was bringing you, Hilary. In fact, he grunted something like 'It's about time,' before wandering off to his car. I wasn't sure whether he thought I'd been treating you shabbily by not taking you to the other parties or whether he thought it was time the two of us got together. Either way, it didn't sound as though he disapproved."

"Well, you're his boss. He's not going to let you know." She felt remarkably stubborn.

"He's also a friend of mine, Hilary, and no less likely to stand up to me than you are. Turn around." Surprisingly she did, and he completed his work on the zipper. "There. It's fine. Would you rather not come tonight?"

"How can I not come after you've told him you're bringing me?" she demanded indignantly.

He laughed and patted her bottom. "Easily. You've done exactly what you pleased so far. I see no reason for you to change now."

"You don't have to be patient with me," she muttered as she worked her feet into a pair of shoes. "And you're not going to make me feel guilty."

"I wouldn't dream of trying. But I'll tell you something, Hilary. If you were to decide to bend a little in my direction, I wouldn't think any the less of you. I wouldn't see any concessions as a weakening of your independence but as a strengthening of your affection."

"Precisely," she said stiffly. She was changing her earrings to dramatic gold hoops and caught his wistful expression in the mirror. Without turning, she talked to his reflection. "Jon, I know you've made concessions. And I know I'm not making concessions with a good grace, but I have made them. We're practically living together. I'm going with you tonight. That may not seem like much to you, but it is to me."

His face disappeared from the mirror and appeared beside her in person. "So you would say," he asked judiciously, "that your attachment to me has grown?"

Hilary made a face, then laughed. "Yes, I guess I would say that if you forced me to."

"Forcing you is the only way I'm going to get you to say it. Do you understand why I want you to go tonight, Hilary? Because I want to be there with you. I can't envision myself having the least fun if you're not there. God, I *want* people to know we're a couple. You're the most incredible thing that's happened to me in years!"

"Well," she said, feeling suddenly shy, "I'm glad, Jon. You're . . . important to me, too."

He kissed her gently on the forehead. "Thank you, my dear. Are you ready?"

It was just a party after all. In some ways, it went a great deal better than Hilary had foreseen. In others, it fulfilled her expectations. The older executives eyed her speculatively when she came in with Marsh and tended to ignore her when she was in a group with them, but then they ignored most of the women. Carol and Harry Stevens were decidedly an exception in appearing to view the two of them as nothing out of the ordinary, but Carol's eyes were lively with curiosity, and she got Hilary aside as soon as possible.

"How long has this been going on?" she demanded, smiling.

"A few weeks," Hilary admitted. "I know it's crazy, Carol, but it was what we both wanted. It can't last long, of course, but it's worth it."

"Why can't it last long?"

Hilary made a small gesture toward the congregated executives. "They won't like it, and they'll put pressure on Jon, maybe even on me. It's not a feasible situation when we work together. I haven't overlooked that."

Carol snorted. "You should. It's none of their business."

"You know that won't make any difference. Think about your own office, Carol. If the situation arose there, all hell would break loose. It's unfortunate, but a fact of life."

Without contradicting her, Carol gave the impression of being unconvinced. "What does Jon say?"

"That it's none of their business." Hilary laughed. "We're all agreed on that, at least. But he's an intelligent man and particularly observant. By tomorrow our private lives will be common knowledge at the paper. These solid pillars of our community wouldn't think of gossiping, but somehow the word will spread. And there will be a subtle, or maybe not so subtle, difference in everyone's attitude toward us. Despite everything I've tried to do in the column, there will be people who see me as trying to get advancement or see Jon as taking advantage of me. It's human nature."

"You're too pessimistic," Carol objected, but her eyes were doleful. "Can the two of you come for brunch Sunday? I don't want to pass up this opportunity." Though she attempted to say it wryly, the effect was more fatalistic.

"I think so. I'll check with Jon and let you know."

Having Harry's support was important to her, as the relationship (or what people guessed of it) became common knowledge at the paper. Very few people said anything directly to her, but she could read in their eyes their various reactions. Hilary knew Harry was running interference, and she could see that Jon was determined to play down any problems. He was, after all, almost totally in charge of the paper, and the highest level of executives had to answer to him. That would not, she knew, prevent them from speaking if they considered the matter detrimental to the paper, or morale, or whatever self-righteous opinion they might have.

Ultimately it was a matter of propriety, and to those who had lived their lives according to a longtime set of social and business rules, Hilary and Jon were making a glaring mistake. Hilary could fully understand their attitude, had, in fact, anticipated it, but she further had to consider whether the friction was damaging to her work, taking the authority from her column. There had been an item in a rival morning paper gossip column about her appearance with Jon at the Larson party. Had she put herself in a position where her readers would not take what she said seriously?

"Not in the long run," Jon assured her when she hesitantly put forward the subject. "For a while they may scoff or be disappointed in you, but when they see that nothing has changed in your attitude, the memory will fade. Are you getting rotten mail?"

"A little more than usual, not too much." She was in his office and, being unable to sit still, rose to pace about the room. "I don't want to undo any good I may have done, Jon. The column is important to me. It makes me sick to think of people gloating and pointing a finger, saying, 'See what she's really like!' Because if they're saying that, then they aren't paying attention to the content."

"You're lucky it's Christmastime, Hilary. People are too busy getting ready for the holidays to give the whole matter a lot of thought. Or have you developed so great an ego that you think the whole South Bay is talking about you?" he said, teasing her.

She tried to match his tone. "Sometimes I picture myself as the sole topic of conversation over every breakfast table. He says, 'Pass the toast,' and she is weeping quietly into her coffee cup, betrayed by her only staunch supporter. He says, 'This toast is burned,' and instead of telling him if he doesn't like it, he's perfectly capable of toasting a piece for himself, she meekly gets up to do it. He says, 'Look at this, Ethel. That Campbell woman is having an affair with her boss. What do you think of that? Didn't I tell you she was nothing but a tramp and a troublemaker?' And she just stands there, crying, while the toast burns again."

"You have a vivid imagination, my dear," he retorted, not moving from his chair. When they were in his office at the paper, they maintained as businesslike a stance as possible. At home he would have come to put his arms around her; here he comforted with his words alone. "More likely *he* is saying, 'Why, that lucky SOB,' and *she* is saying, 'By

God, I hope she's having fun after all the effort she's put into making my situation better.' It all will blow over, Hilary."

She turned to face him. "You're getting flak from your executives and advertisers, aren't you, Jon?"

His face was impassive. "Some. It doesn't worry me, Hilary. As far as the newspaper is concerned, nothing has changed. Your column is exactly what it's always been —stimulating and well written. No one can deny that, so no one really has any argument. Our personal lives simply don't enter in."

"I wish it were true." She offered a sad smile and picked up her initialed column. "Promise me you won't jeopardize the paper or your career in any way, Jon. I don't want to be responsible for that."

"What about your own career?" he asked angrily.

"I can take care of myself. This isn't the only paper in the country."

The lines of his frown deepened into alarm. "You aren't thinking of changing jobs just because of a little temporary turmoil, are you, Hilary? There's probably no more receptive area for your kind of column. If you went somewhere else, even with your track record, you might not have the freedom you have here. You'd end up being a reporter or doing a column on less interesting issues."

Hilary forced herself to laugh. "Yes, I don't think Peoria or even Bakersfield is ready for me. I dropped my car to have a tune-up, so I may be a little late getting home. Let yourself in."

If he intended to make a comment, he was prevented by his phone ringing. While he was saying, "I'll be right with him," Hilary went directly to the door, waggled her fingers at him, and stepped out into the reception area, where she was subjected to a hard stare by the waiting executive. She had the distinct impression he was inspecting her for signs of dishevelment, and she tossed her head crossly just as Jon appeared at the door. Susan smiled her sympathy, and Jon's eyes turned coldly on the newcomer, but Hilary merely walked to the elevator without looking back.

* * *

Sometimes the strain of such incidents depressed her and made her question the wisdom of following her inclination. But it was holiday time, and Hilary was too busy, for the most part, to give the matter much consideration. And her emotional dependence on Jon was growing deeper and deeper, almost to the point where it frightened her. The physical excitement had settled into a wholly satisfying sexual relationship, perhaps more potent than any she could remember, but she allowed for some illusion on her part, some fogging of memory, because when she was with him, there was more than the physical desire happening. And it was this other component that disoriented and alarmed her. With Jack she had achieved a companionable routine that required little emotional energy from either of them because they were similar in their interests and outlook on life. With George there had not been time to establish much of a partnership, and she realized now that she had, in her exhaustion, simply absorbed his energy and his admiration. But with Jon . . .

There was something unique in their relationship, something she hadn't experienced before. The force of his personality had at first made her wary, cautious of becoming his shadow or muted in the shade he cast. She had consciously struggled to maintain her independence . . . until she realized there was no need for her to struggle. Her own personality was just as strong as, if softer than, his. She didn't understand, until she had spent a considerable amount of time with him, that she had never before given full rein to herself in a one-on-one association. It wasn't her feminism; that had almost always been allowed to stand out. And it was more than her femininity, which she experienced naturally.

Jon presented her with an intellectual and emotional challenge that called forth more of her than she had ever known existed. He discussed issues she hadn't considered, insisted on an emotional integrity she wouldn't have dreamed of suggesting. His intensity was not of the painful soul-searching variety, but of a fascination with living, an intention to savor life, that intrigued Hilary. When she remembered what Kitty had said of his being uncommunicative about himself, she was in awe of the amount he was willing to share with her, never self-pitying or self-congratulatory, simply *giving*. He expected a great deal in return—her trust, her affection, her thoughts and feelings—all of which, if she'd thought about it, sounded exhausting, but it was exhilarating. She had never felt so closely bound to another human being; she had never felt so deeply in love, so completely loving. Though the extent of her involvement frightened her, she treasured it as well.

Jon welcomed her participation in any activities with his stepchildren and regretted that she wouldn't be there Christmas Eve to share their festivities. He drove her to the airport and presented her with an autographed copy of her favorite novel as a Christmas present.

"Yours is in your study, Jon. It was a little awkward to bring with me." She had found a strange little sculpture of a printing press and placed it on his rolltop desk with a red ribbon around it. "I'll miss you."

"Good."

On the plane, away from him, she tried to sort out her emotions, but the exercise was too fatiguing. There was no sense in analyzing what she felt and no use in looking ahead to the time when things would change. Her family —her parents, her sister, her niece and nephew—met her at the airport, full of the excitement of the season. If Christmas Eve hadn't been a traditional celebration for Jon and his stepchildren, she would have invited him to come; she wanted him to meet her family, to have them meet him.

Janet was holding up well under the stress of her first Christmas without her husband, and the children were infected with the suspense of waiting for their presents. The baby didn't understand what she was waiting for, but her high spirits were witness to her anticipation of some pleasurable activity. They reminded Hilary of the day spent at the amusement park.

Christmas morning was spent in the leisurely opening

of packages, after the Campbells had slept in late, since the children were at their own house. Hilary found herself telling her parents about Jon, a little surprised at their rapt attention but pleased. No one asked her if this was "serious"; no one mentioned George. At noon her sister came with the children, and the house once again became chaotic with activity, which diminished only as the adults began the preparation of Christmas dinner. The house was filled with the children's laughter and the aroma of turkey and baking rolls when the doorbell rang.

"You get it," Mrs. Campbell suggested to Hilary. "I have my hands full."

Neighbors frequently dropped in to say "Merry Christmas," and Hilary thought nothing of the interruption until she opened the door. Jon stood there, grinning, his arms filled with packages. She was too dumbfounded for a moment to say or do anything but stare at him.

"Your parents are expecting me," he said. "Merry Christmas, Hilary."

"Oh, Jon! Did you drive?" she asked inanely.

"Yes, and I'm hoping you'll drive back with me on Sunday. May I come in?"

Before she even had a chance to kiss him, her niece and nephew had discovered and recognized the visitor. Hilary relieved him of his coat and the packages while she made introductions to her family. "Are you staying with us?" she asked.

"If you want me to. Your mother invited me when I called last week, but I checked with a hotel to make sure it had some rooms."

"Of course, I want you to stay. I've never been so surprised and delighted in my life." Hilary absolutely beamed at him, heedless of how transparent her love was. No one had ever managed to surprise her with a party or a visit in all her thirty-two years, and it thrilled her that he had made such an effort, just for her. "I'll show you your room."

He had to retrieve his suitcase from the car, but when they stood alone in her sister's old room, she wrapped her arms around him and nestled her head against his shoulder. "Thank you, Jon. That's the nicest Christmas present you could have given me."

"It was for me, too," he reminded her. "I love the sculpture of the printing press. I'm going to keep it right where you left it, but maybe without the ribbon."

"Definitely without the ribbon." She looked around the room with its single bed and soft feminine trappings. "You won't mind our not being able to sleep together, will you? I wouldn't want to make my parents uncomfortable."

"Of course not. That's not why I came, Hilary." He ran his long, gentle fingers through her hair. "I just wanted to be with you on Christmas."

She smiled at him. "Did the kids like their gifts? Did they give you pictures of themselves?"

"Yes—to both. We had a good time; my parents came over, too. Hilary, there's something I should confess."

Her eyes widened slightly as she asked softly, "What's that?"

"One of the reasons I wanted to come . . ." He paused, obviously embarrassed. "Well, I wanted to be with you, and I wanted to meet your family, but I have to admit that I couldn't get it out of my head that George is here." He sighed, toying with a lock of her hair. "It's not that I doubt your feelings for me, but you're so hung up on the problem of our working together that George might start to look like a reasonable alternative to the hassles."

"But, Jon, he's not going to look like a reasonable alternative to *you!*"

"I don't know, Hilary. He's a nice enough man, from what I've seen. And I can't shake the idea that you're preparing an escape hatch, that you have right from the start."

Hilary could feel a flush creep into her cheeks, and she turned her head away from him, reaching out to smooth the coverlet on the bed. "That has nothing to do with George."

"What does it have to do with?"

"A job."

"Are you actively looking for another job?"

"Not exactly actively." She faced him now, serious. "Before I started to see you, I sent out a résumé and some columns and articles to a few of my friends who work for newspapers. It wasn't a good time of year, of course, and several of them have written that they'll pursue it for me in the new year since I'm not in a hurry."

"Why did you do it?"

Hilary sat down on the bed but met his eyes. "Because when we stop seeing each other, I don't think I'm going to want to work for the *Reporter*. It's as simple as that, Jon."

His expression was mild. "Okay, I guess I can understand that. Your parents probably think we've gotten lost—or worse. We should probably go down."

She nodded and led the way.

Chapter Nineteen

HILARY AND JON didn't discuss the issue again over
Christmas or during the subsequent weeks, for that
matter. New Year's passed, and a fairly untroubled Janu-
ary. People at the paper gradually came to accept their relationship, and if Jon was receiving any pressure, Hilary
wasn't aware of it. The first sign of trouble appeared during the second week of February, and it had to do with her
column.

When she arrived at her office on Tuesday morning,
Harry greeted her with a message that Marsh wanted to
see her in his office. It was an unusual summons, considering they had spent the night together at her house, and she
felt a certain amount of dread as she took the elevator to
the top floor.

"He wanted to see me, Susan. Is he free?" she asked,
glancing briefly at the closed door.

"He's on the phone, but he said you could go straight in
when you got here."

Hilary slipped through the door and took her usual seat
opposite him. He made a slight motion with his hand to acknowledge her presence but continued his phone call, the
intimidating frown deeply etched on his face. At first Hilary made some effort not to listen, but when she realized
from his side of the conversation that he was discussing
her, she gave up any pretense of finding her hands fascinating.

"None of her columns go in without my approval," he
said bluntly into the phone, not even glancing at her. "It

was a valid opinion, Roger, and very much in keeping with
her usual observations. . . Yes, I know, but I think you're
overestimating her influence. Just because she was sarcastic about women who make shopping a sport, I don't think
you'll find that your sales go down. . . That has nothing to
do with her column or its content, Roger, and I'm not willing to discuss the matter." Here he did look at Hilary as he
unconsciously loosened the knot of his tie. "It's my policy
to censor the column only for possible libel or poor writing.
This one posed no problem on either score. . . Yes, I realize
she's promised another column to follow on the same subject. Apparently it's of absorbing interest to her."

As she watched, Hilary saw his lips tighten, but he said
nothing while he waited impatiently for his caller to exor-
cise himself on the topic. Jon leaned back in his chair, his
fingers toying carelessly with a pen on his desk, his eyes
focused on a far corner of the office. "By all means, put
your complaint in writing to the owners if you wish. I
think you're making a mountain out of a molehill, but
you're entitled to your opinion. Her column is one of the
features that attract readers to our paper rather than to
the opposition's. If her views are occasionally offensive to
one group or another, it's only to be expected. People enjoy
that kind of diverse criticism. I'll be surprised if you
find any diminution in your sales, Roger. . . Fine. Good-
bye."

He hung up the phone, tight-lipped, and buzzed Susan
immediately. "Take messages for a few minutes, please.
I'll get back to them as soon as I can." And then he turned
to Hilary. "When I got in, I found five messages, with
much the same complaint. Our advertisers are irate at this
morning's column, as I'm sure you've gathered."

"Yes." Hilary tried to sort out the various impressions
she'd been receiving from the way he handled the phone
call. Obviously there was a point at which he'd been called
to task for his relationship with her and had refused to respond to it. He had defended her column—but as editor or
lover? Was this the point at which their personal affairs

collided with their professional ones? She tried to keep her voice steady as she asked, "What do you want me to do about it, Jon?"

"Nothing. I merely want you to be aware of the situation because you aren't likely to receive any of the complaints through your usual mail."

She saw him run his hand over his chin and remembered watching him shave only an hour or so earlier. "I didn't give the thought I should have to the column," she said carefully. "Yesterday, when I was out to lunch, I heard two women talking while they ate, and the idea grew on me by the time I got back to the office. I seemed to have a lot more to say about it than the column I'd planned, so I scrapped my original idea and zipped this one off. If I'd given any thought to the advertisers and to you, I wouldn't have done it. I'm sorry."

His thoughtful regard rested on her for some time before he spoke. "You aren't supposed to think about the advertisers, Hilary, or about me. I don't want your apology. I was perfectly aware of the consequences."

"You never said."

"Why should I? You wrote a good column; that's all the newspaper requires of you. Your reasoning, your examples were excellent and persuasive. The advertisers are making far too much of the matter."

"But you knew they would." Hilary drew in a deep breath. "I won't write a second one."

"You've promised a second one, and I expect you to deliver it. And not toned down, Hilary. All that would tell the readers is that the advertisers had gotten to you or to the paper, and they'd feel cheated. They love the underdog. They'll be waiting to see if someone tries to muzzle you. The *Reporter* will look better if you continue than if you stop."

"But you're going to get even more complaints," she protested, uneasily twisting a bracelet on her wrist.

"I can handle it," he said, and smiled. "It's my job, Hilary."

"I've made it harder for you."

"You've written the kind of column I expect of you. If we weren't involved, you wouldn't give a second thought to this rumpus." He rose in dismissal. "I have a lot of calls to return. I just wanted to make sure you understood that I want the second column on schedule."

Hilary wrote the column, and she wrote it exactly as she had planned, but she found Jon preoccupied when she brought it up to show him.

"I won't be able to come straight home tonight," he said absently as he initialed it. "In fact, I'm likely to be rather late. Shall I come to your house when I'm finished?"

There had been many occasions on which his business or family affairs had made this sort of arrangement necessary, but each time he had explained precisely where he was going and why. He offered no information now, and though she could guess that it had something to do with the advertisers, his decision to leave her uninformed was unnerving.

"Why don't we take a break from each other tonight?" she suggested with a forced smile. "You'll be tired, and I have a batch of mundane things to do around the house."

He eyed her sharply as he handed her the copy. "If that's what you want, Hilary. I'm never too tired to see you."

"We'll see each other tomorrow." Before he could reply, she turned and headed for the door, and he followed to open it for her in silence.

All evening she half expected him to appear. She left the bathroom door open while she showered so she could hear the phone if he called. More of their time was spent at his house than at hers, and she had neglected the housework, but she found herself too edgy to do more than tidy the place perfunctorily. If she used the vacuum, she might not hear the phone. Even in bed she still half thought he would come, that he would stand by the bed loosening his tie, telling her how his evening had gone. But he didn't come, and for the first time in weeks she lay alone in bed, unable to fall asleep. She was awakened from an unrefreshing sleep by the phone. It seemed totally unlikely that it could be anyone but Jon, and she was relieved rather than annoyed to be awakened so abruptly.

But it wasn't Jon. It was a friend calling from Boston.

"Hi, Hilary, it's Janice Cook. I've shown your packet to my editor, and he'd like to talk with you."

The next fifteen minutes presented Hilary with the best job offer she'd ever received. She explored in detail what freedom she would be allowed, the salary offered, the terms of a contract. "When do I have to give you an answer?" she asked finally.

"As soon as possible. Definitely by Friday."

When she hung up, she stared at the phone for several minutes. So this was the way it would end, she thought unhappily. With a splendid career opportunity and without the man she loved. With a salary better than she could hope to reach in five years in San Jose, and without the companionship and support she had come to trust. But it was a good time to go, when they both had been made aware of the difficulties their obligations imposed on them. If only the job offer had been one where she wasn't so far away, where she could have seen him from time to time . . .

Hilary dressed with special care, choosing a gray linen suit and a burgundy blouse with a stock tie. Her closet was sadly depleted since she had continually left outfits at Jon's house. He had cleared a closet for her sole use, insisting that there was room enough in the place for him to put away everything he owned twice over. Hilary tried to relish the solitary use of her own bathroom, not having to take turns at the sink, waiting for him to finish shaving or brushing his teeth, but all she could feel was a sense of loss that he wasn't there. Having breakfast alone was depressing, and leaving for work without kissing him good-bye made her feel incomplete.

At the office Harry teased her about her column. "Carol says you'll have all the advertisers up in arms. They depend on women who shop out of boredom."

"They are up in arms." Hilary sighed. "Lord, if I

thought I had that much influence, I'd tell everyone exactly what to do to improve the economy. Think of it: Hilary Campbell solves the inflationary spiral! San Jose newswoman enlightens the world! I can just see the headlines. I probably didn't make one woman think twice about going out to buy her fiftieth pair of shoes."

"Advertisers are very sensitive," Harry said as he removed the cover from his ancient typewriter. "But Marsh isn't likely to let them bother him."

Hilary frowned at the back of his head. "Do you think he should have stopped me from doing that column?"

"Stopped you?" Harry swung around, incredulous. "You must be kidding. That's what you're paid to do, Hilary: write columns that interest readers. Hell, the *Reporter* gets points from printing something like that. Otherwise, we look like a mouthpiece for the advertisers."

"Maybe," she murmured as she seated herself. "I should have thought about it before I wrote it."

Harry fixed her with a baleful eye. "Hogwash. Marsh can look out for himself and the paper, my dear woman. What you have to do is remember that, on the paper, your obligation is to your readers. If you start trying to protect Marsh, you'll just become mealymouthed in the column, Hilary. And I promise you he won't appreciate it."

Since she hadn't considered it in that light, Hilary simply stared at him for a minute. "You're probably right, Harry."

"Of course I'm right," he said indignantly, and turned to bang away at his typewriter.

During the morning Hilary had a call from Mary Lou Meyer, the flight attendant from the apartment building where she'd previously lived. They weren't in touch very often nowadays, but Mary Lou knew of her affair with Marsh.

"How's your editor?" she asked right off.

Hilary was cautious. "Fine, but I think it may be time to end it."

"Why?"

"It complicates our professional lives."

"Who gives a blinking damn? A little complication adds spice to life."

Hilary could easily envision Mary Lou's entering a room holding two or three men who were former lovers without her blinking an eye. "I don't thrive on complication. Besides, I've been offered a better job."

"Where?"

"In Boston."

"So you're going to put your career ahead of your personal life?" Mary Lou sounded astonished.

"Not exactly." Hilary turned her chair so she was facing the window. The day was overcast. "This is bound to end sooner or later, and it looks like sooner right now. I'd be a fool to give up an opportunity like the Boston one."

"So be a fool, Hilary. There will be other jobs."

"Is this the Mary Lou Meyer I know?" Hilary demanded. "Haven't you always resisted every effort to lure you away from your airline job?"

"Yes, but we're different. I like variety; you like stability. Which is why I'm transferring to Denver, by the way. I need a change of scene."

The conversation never worked its way back to Marsh or to Hilary's job offer, but she thought about Mary Lou's assessment long after they'd hung up. In many ways Hilary acknowledged that she *did* like a secure base from which to operate. The challenge of her column, of her career was enough stimulation for her. Behind her she liked a calm home life. Not necessarily placid, but full of continuous affection and warmth. She needed to share herself with someone essential to her, and that someone was Jon. He was the only one she'd ever known who complemented her so thoroughly, who had captured her heart so completely that it ached at the mere thought of being apart from him.

But their attachment was temporary, on his side. He had been too deeply disillusioned by his first wife to allow himself a second permanent arrangement. Hilary didn't doubt that he cared for her, but she was realistic enough to see that he didn't want a new commitment. He had accepted without comment her admission at Christmas about looking for another job. He had understood that they would eventually part and that she would naturally use the occasion to advance her career if she could.

Shortly before lunchtime her phone rang. This time it was Jon, asking, "Have we taken a long enough break from each other? Will you have lunch with me?"

His tone was teasing, yet it was an unusual request. Hilary had steadfastly maintained the separation of work and home, even to the point of considering the lunch hour as part of the working day. But she wanted to see him, to be near him, and she asked cautiously, "Do you think this is a good time, Jon? I mean, with the advertisers so annoyed about my columns. It would be flaunting our relationship at a rather delicate point, don't you think?"

"No, I don't think. I missed you last night, Hilary. And I've taken care of all the grumbling by making it clear that the integrity of your column is important to the paper. I don't want you to forget that either. How about lunch?"

"I'd like that. Shall I meet you in the lobby or slink off to some dark hole in the wall?"

He chuckled. "In the lobby, my sweet, in five minutes."

The restaurant he chose was a popular one with the newspaper people. It was an Italian restaurant, considerably more expensive than the usual hamburger stand Hilary frequented when in a hurry, but a place where she sometimes met her friends for lunch. There were always people there from work, and today was no exception. As she and Jon were shown to a table, they spoke to half a dozen acquaintances and fellow staff members. Hilary was surprised at the seeming ease with which they accepted her being with Jon. He was almost cross with her. "What did you expect? That they all would snub you? They're probably surprised they haven't seen us at lunch together before this."

"You make it sound as though there were nothing unusual about our association," she said as he held a chair for her.

"There isn't. We're just two adults who have a lot in common and who happen to work for the same paper." He seated himself opposite her, picked up the menu, and said, "The only hurdle was the initial one, Hilary. They've long since accepted us as a twosome."

She felt slightly irritated by his casual attitude. "What about these last two days, Jon? What about your angry advertisers?"

"They'd have been angry about the column whether we were seeing each other or not. Surely you know that as well as I do."

"They wouldn't have thrown the same accusations at you."

His brows rose minutely. "That was the only matter on which they had to be straightened out, Hilary. I won't have anyone tossing my personal life into the fray. The temptation is great, I'm sure, but I won't tolerate it. I'm capable of separating the two, and anyone who thinks otherwise is mistaken."

Hilary gave her order to the waitress and studied Jon as he did likewise, memorizing the thick dark brows and the wavy black hair. His eyes, which she had only a few months ago thought unreadable, now seemed incredibly expressive. She could almost feel the touch of his lips and his hands, and she wondered if the sensation would fade with time and distance.

"I've been offered a job," she said.

A wary, still look entered his eyes. "Where? Doing what?"

"Doing the kind of column I am now, for a Boston paper."

"Boston? My God, Hilary, I didn't realize you were looking so far away. A better salary?"

She nodded. "It's a splendid opportunity, Jon."

"I'm sure it is." His voice had tightened, and one hand lay clenched on the table.

Hilary leaned forward, earnest. "I thought, this morning when they called, that it was probably the best time it could have happened. I don't want to leave you, Jon, but I don't want to cause trouble for you, and that's what will continue to happen if I stay."

He sighed. "You refuse to grasp the idea that I can handle it, don't you, Hilary? I can only assume your obtuseness is intentional, that you have reasons of your own for wanting to leave. I want you to stay, but I'm not going to stand in the way of your career."

For a moment they stared at each other across the table. Hilary wanted to say more, but she couldn't seem to make the words come out. How did you tell a man that though your career was important, being with him was essential to your happiness? That only if you had both were you ever going to feel the sort of satisfaction for which you longed?

Suddenly he started speaking in a low, determined voice. "Obviously it's time we were frank with each other, Hilary. Your career is important. I can accept that because I know what mine means to me. But I also know that it isn't everything. There was little enough reward for me in the newspaper work while my marriage was crumbling. Sure, it kept me busy; without it I'd have been lost. But it wasn't enough, Hilary; it's never enough. You need both sides of your life completed to make your life meaningful. If you sacrifice either side, you're only half-fulfilled."

"I know that, Jon," she whispered.

A pained look crossed his face. "Then it's not being able to have a family, isn't it?"

Her face became puzzled-looking. "A family?"

"The vasectomy," he said impatiently. "You're just at the age when a woman starts having serious thoughts about children if she's devoted her life to her career so far. That's why George held so much appeal for you, I imagine. You could picture yourself surrounded by a few babies, rearing them in pleasant surroundings, still being able to write articles for magazines. I could try to have the vasectomy reversed, Hilary, but the operation isn't always successful."

Hilary had to concentrate on the serious consideration of an operation not to laugh out loud. Her grin spread, and her lips twitched until, in exasperation, he demanded, "What's so funny?"

"One of the reasons I didn't want even to think about

marrying George was that he wanted me to have children right away. I'm not at all sure I want them."

"You could easily change your mind."

"I suppose it's possible." She remained silent as the waitress placed their food on the table and then continued, "I think we'd better be a little specific here, Jon. You seem to be talking about the two of us as a permanent unit. When did this happen?"

"Well, for God's sake, Hilary, I've told you I love you. And you told me you loved me." He was glaring at her.

"In bed, my dear. Making love. I'd hardly expect you to murmur, 'I'm fond of you, Hilary,' at a moment like that. You told me, when we first started sleeping together, that you didn't know what love was anymore."

"And I didn't . . . then. It became quite clear to me shortly afterward." He abruptly changed direction. "Are you trying to tell me that your own declarations of love were pillow talk?"

"No. I do love you, Jon."

"Good." He smiled at her then, his eyes gently probing. "If you love me, and if you don't think you want children, and if you realize that a career leaves a lot to be desired when you don't have a partner, why do you want to go to Boston?"

"I don't." She returned his smile.

"Better. So you are going to stay here with me and let me handle my job while you take care of yours?"

"Yes."

"Are you going to move in with me, preferably marry me, and live happily ever after?"

"I hope so."

He reached across the table to squeeze her hand. "Perfect. You know, Hilary, I don't think I ever *did* know what love was until you came along. Because it was different before—giving and taking, but not really sharing like this. You feel like the other half of me. There's a lot to be said for loving a woman who knows who she is and believes she's valuable in her own right."

Hilary laughed. "I'll write a column about it."

"You do that," he agreed with a rueful grin. "What's your column about today?"

"Women who choose not to have children. Can you handle that?"

His eyes gleamed with amusement. "I can handle it, Hilary."

Dear Reader:

   If you enjoyed this book, and would like information about future books by this author and other Avon authors, we would be delighted to put you on the mailing list for our ROMANCE NEWSLETTER.

   Simply *print* your name and address and send to Avon Books, Room 419, 959 Eighth Ave., N.Y., N.Y. 10019.

   We hope to bring you many hours of pleasurable reading!

Sara Reynolds, Editor
Romance Newsletter

Book orders and checks should *only* be sent to Avon Mail Order Dept., 224 W. 57th St., N.Y., N.Y. 10019. Include 50¢ per copy for postage and handling; allow 6-8 weeks for delivery.

Reader 7-82